A BEATRICE STYLES LINCOLNSHIRE MYSTERY

NEVER LET HER GO

Denise Smith

To Helen and Laura, Enjoy! Denise Smith

Copyright © Denise Smith 2024

All rights reserved

The characters and events portrayed in this book are fictitious. Any similarity to real persons, living or dead, is coincidental and not intended by the author.

No part of this book may be reproduced, or stored in a retrieval system, or transmitted in any form or by any means, electronic, mechanical, photocopying, recording or otherwise, without express permission of the publisher.

ISBN 9798338668856

Cover Design by Bruce Aiken

We stared at the corpse. Sprawled across the floor, unseeing eyes open, he was a leaden bag of meat. A loss to no one. Blood pooled under his head, seeping out onto the rug, the stain spreading. I'd seen other head injuries: sometimes there was no blood at all, other times, the amount could seem endless. The rug would have to go. Would its disappearance be noticed? Much easier to dispose of than the body.

Chapter 1

Monday 18th June

Beatrice's eyes remained fixed on the shadowy figure, as it made its way across the façade of the Golden Goose pub. At the corner, the person disappeared from view. She reached for her phone which was lying on the dashboard. The figure remained out of sight, and Beatrice's heart beat a little faster, certain this building was the arsonist's next target. She glanced down at her mobile and sent a quick text to James: her lodger, boyfriend and occasional employee. *Something happening here 0230. Going to investigate.*

Beatrice slipped the phone into her handbag, then dipped her head through the strap, so it lay across her body, leaving her hands free. She grabbed the handle and pushed the car door open, causing the overhead light to come on. 'Blast,' she muttered, scrambling out of the car and closing the door gently. It caught enough for the internal light to switch off. Her mobile vibrated in her bag: James replying. He was miles away, watching one of the other pubs, so she ignored it. Besides, he was probably telling her to be careful. Recently, he seemed to think he had a right to comment on her choices. Beatrice wasn't sure she liked it.

The sky was cloudless, the quarter moon providing a little illumination. As Beatrice began to approach the substantial stone building, with careful, noiseless footsteps, her eyes adjusted to the dim light. At the corner of the pub, Beatrice stopped and listened. She could hear faint noises: the sound of liquid sloshing, then a metallic scraping sound. They came from behind the hedge, where she knew the ground-level opening to the cellar lay. Should I confront them? What if they rush at me? What was the point of being there if she wasn't going to do something?

Beatrice pulled out her phone. She held it close to her body, shielding its glow, as she selected the camera video app, switching it to record. The light was poor, but it might corroborate the evidence of her eyes. She crept around the corner, stepping carefully on the grass, avoiding the noisy gravel path, the phone held out in front of her as she moved forward.

From her observations in daylight, she knew it was about ten metres to the cellar opening. Drawing closer, she could make out a person hunched down. A can with a long spout was on the floor, along with a misshapen pile of something she couldn't see clearly. The individual was pushing the contents of the pile through an opening in the ground. The stench of petrol was unmistakeable.

The gravel crunched underfoot as Beatrice ran out of grass. It sounded loud in the stillness of the night and the person turned towards her. For a moment they both froze.

'Shit.' There was a brief flare of light, then the other person sprang up, turned and ran.

Cursing herself for being slow to respond, Beatrice chased them. The figure was smaller than her, but faster, and began to pull further ahead. Being tall, she had the advantage of being able to cover a short distance at speed, but despite pushing herself hard, the man - she was sure it was a man, from the build and the way he moved - ducked into the trees ahead, and she lost sight of him. She followed; confident he was making for the lay-by on the other side of the wood. The noise from his heavy breathing, and twigs breaking underfoot as he crushed them in his haste, gave her a route to follow and reassurance he hadn't got away.

When she burst out from the tree line into the lay-by, she heard the roar of an engine and watched as a motorbike raced away. Struggling for breath, she raised her arm, trying to capture something on her phone's video. The bike rode away in the dark, heading back towards Louth. It had no lights on, and was soon lost from sight. It reappeared for a fleeting moment, when it reached a bend in the road, its brake lights illuminating for a few seconds. She was too far away to make out the number plate in the flash of red light before it vanished for the final time.

Once back at The Golden Goose, Beatrice's breathing had recovered from her exertions. At the cellar door, using the torch on her phone to light up the blue metal doors, she saw one of them had been bent out of shape to create an opening. A crowbar and a coil of plastic tubing lay next to a petrol can. Beatrice sniffed the air. Smoke. She hadn't been in time to stop the arsonist. She recalled the brief flame before the man had dashed away.

Beatrice hurried to the front of the building and pressed the bell several times. She couldn't tell if it had rung through the thick wooden door, so banged on it with her fist, pausing to dial 999.

'Emergency services. Which service do you require?'

'I'm at the Golden Goose, outside Louth. There's a fire in the cellar. Send the fire brigade.'

'Are you in the building?'

'No.'

'Is there anyone left inside?'

'Yes.' She thumped her fist against the door. 'I can't get an answer. Hurry, please.'

'Help is on the way.'

Beatrice ended the call and returned to banging on the door. 'Brad! Brad!'

It seemed like she'd been there for hours when the door finally opened and a portly, red-faced, angry man stood in front of her.

'What are you doing here at this time of night?'

'There's a fire in the cellar...'

Brad stepped back, made an abrupt turn and disappeared from view.

Beatrice had wanted to ask him if his family were home, but he'd gone towards the bar, where the interior door to the cellar was. She stepped into the pub. There was a faint smell of smoke. An insistent high-pitched squeal of a smoke alarm began to sound from the bar. Brad must have opened the cellar door.

Rather than go after him, Beatrice, heart racing, turned in the opposite direction and ran up the stairs to the private family accommodation. The blaring of the smoke detector sounded faint up here. She began to hammer on the doors in the corridor. 'Wake up! Fire! Fire!'

A short woman, eyes wide, appeared out of a door at the far end. 'What's going on? What's happening…?' The woman's voice rose as her panic increased.

'Marie, there's a fire.' She grabbed the woman's arm. 'The fire brigade is on the way, but we've got to get out. Where are the children?'

A piercing noise burst into life. An insistent on-off wail. Beatrice looked up at the smoke detector on the landing. A layer of smoke, several inches deep, had collected below the ceiling. She knew it would soon fill the whole space. Her sense of urgency increased.

Marie had shrugged off Beatrice's grip at the mention of her children and moved with haste to a room, throwing the door open.

Peering over her shoulder, Beatrice could see a pair of single beds. Two young girls were crouched on one, clinging to each other with pale faces. She pushed past Marie, moved into the room, and picked up the larger, older girl.

'Hi, Maisie. I'm Beatrice. We're all going to go outside together, OK?'

The girl nodded. Marie reached out for Betsy, whose arms were raised towards her. Beatrice felt Maisie shivering against her body and held her close.

'Anyone else?' She directed the question at Marie, who shook her head. 'Let's go.'

They left the room and hurriedly made their way along the landing and down the stairs. Was she imagining it, or was it more difficult to see than it had been?

Once outside, the muffling of the alarms was a relief, the sound replaced by the gentle sobs of the girls. Beatrice led the way to her car. 'You can wait in here.'

The family climbed onto the back seat, Marie putting her arms protectively around her children. They buried their faces in her neck.

'Brad,' said the woman. 'Where is he?'

'Daddy,' the girls cried out, and began to strain in their mother's arms.

Beatrice glanced back towards the building. There was no sign of the publican. 'Stay here.'

Standing in the doorway, Beatrice shouted. 'Brad! Brad!' She looked back towards the car, thinking of the family. The air in the pub was becoming thick with smoke. She inhaled a deep breath of fresh air, and pulled her T-shirt over her mouth to filter the fumes. Then, very aware of the danger, ran inside, turning the same way Brad had earlier. The smell of burning was strong. Her eyes began to sting and she had to resist the urge to cough.

She found Brad at the top of the cellar steps, ineffectively squirting foam from a fire extinguisher down towards the cellar, punctuated only by coughing caused by the dark smoke coming up the stairway.

Beatrice grabbed his arm. 'Outside,' she shouted. 'Now!'

He was a heavy man, but no match for Beatrice in her roused state, and she pulled him away from the cellar, slamming the door closed. She squinted through the darkening gloom, struggling to see the way out. She dragged Brad along with her, using the bar counter as a guide to the exit. At the foot of the stairs, she had to restrain him, to stop him going up.

'Marie and the girls.' He coughed again.

'They're outside.'

His shoulders relaxed and he nodded his understanding. Together they burst out of the pub. A short distance away they turned and watched as black smoke poured out of the doorway, rolling and billowing up into the night sky.

Chapter 2

Brad bent double, as another coughing fit consumed him. When it subsided, Beatrice could hear him wheezing with each breath. After a minute, he raised his head and looked around. 'Where are they?' His voice rose in pitch and he coughed. 'You said they were out!'

'It's OK. They're in my car.' She pointed.

Maisie burst from the vehicle, running towards them. 'Daddy!'

Brad, hurried to meet her, and scooped her up, wrapping his arms around her.

Beatrice gasped as the sound of breaking bottles began: repeated small explosions, marking the step-by-step destruction. 'The windows could blow out any moment. We need to move, now!' The reports she'd read on the two previous fires had emphasised how, once they'd escaped the confines of the cellars, the flames had spread and become uncontrollable. The arsonist had used petrol-soaked rags to start the blazes, but the large quantities of alcohol acted as an accelerant.

Marie and Betsy got out of the car. 'No!' Brad raised a hand, stopping them in their tracks. 'It's not safe.' He and Beatrice joined the rest of his family and they stood staring at the pub.

The smoke was thicker now, and joined by an orange glow, seen through the windows of the bar. They all flinched as the first window shattered, shards thrown outwards, scattering on the ground. The flames intensified with the influx of oxygen.

They hurried away.

'I'm scared.' Maisie sobbed.

'It's OK, baby.' Brad stroked her back. 'I've got you. You're safe now.'

Betsy began to cry, creating a chorus of sobs. Brad pulled his wife and both daughters into a family hug.

Beatrice watched as the children were soothed by their parents, a dull ache in her chest. Even at her age, there were times she would welcome comfort and support from her parents. But it was no longer possible. Her father was dead, her mother missing. Maybe one day, she would see her mum again, if she could find her.

Beatrice was warm from running around, but saw the girls shivering in their thin cotton pyjamas. 'Let's get you all in the car. I'll turn the heating on.' Another window shattered. 'I'll park further away.' The family piled into the car and she drove it to a spot away down the main road, in the entrance to a field. From inside the vehicle a hedge blocked the view of the pub, so the Staines didn't have to watch as their home was destroyed. She left the engine running, the heating switched on the highest setting. The family were in a state of shock, with both parents trying to calm their distressed children with reassuring words and shushing. The sobs were subsiding to a degree, with the occasional audible sniffle.

Brad was in the front passenger seat, with his eldest daughter. 'I want my bear,' Maisie howled. Her father's arms tightened around her.

'Oh, Brad,' said Marie. 'What are we going to do?'

Turning in his seat, he reached back with his arm, grasping her hand. 'Don't worry, love,' he said, wheezing. 'We'll manage. The important thing is we're alright.'

'But we'll lose everything.'

'Now, then.' He glanced from one girl to the other.

Marie understood his message and squeezed his hand before letting go and putting her arms back around Betsy.

Beatrice felt like an intruder on their privacy. 'I'm going to wait outside,' she said. 'I'll leave the heating on.'

Brad nodded.

Outside, Beatrice scanned the horizon, searching for signs of help. Smoke was still curling upwards from the front door of the pub. If the fire engine didn't arrive soon there would be nothing left. She checked her phone. There was a message from James asking what was happening. Was she safe? Then a couple more messages and a missed call. She texted him back. *0250 Fire started here. He got away. Family out. Fire brigade on way. You'd best go home. See you in the morning.*

Beatrice saw a flicker in her peripheral vision. She turned to stare. There was another brief flash of blue, a pause, then another. As the emergency vehicle followed the twists of the road, it disappeared from view several more times, until, at last, she could see a steady repeating pattern of blue lights.

Beatrice didn't need to direct the fire brigade. The light from the flames and the smoke emanating from the pub were indicator enough. The engine parked in front of the building and officers began piling out. They moved with confidence and precision. An officer with a white helmet watched proceedings and gave the occasional instruction. Hoses were unrolled and some were putting on breathing apparatus. Satisfied everything was under control, the man with the white helmet walked over to Beatrice.

'You the woman who called in the fire?' he asked.

'Yes.'

'I'm Hardwick. Anyone left inside?'

'I don't think so.' said Beatrice. 'The family are in my car.'

'You don't live here?'

'No.'

The fire officer nodded. He took off his helmet, opened the driver's door and bent down to talk to Brad and Marie. Their conversation was brief. Afterwards he approached the firefighters with breathing apparatus, and exchanged a few words, before returning to Beatrice.

'They confirmed there's no-one else inside. We have to make sure.'

'Of course.'

'How did you notice the fire? What were you doing here?'

'I'm a private investigator. I've been hired by the brewery. This is the third arson attack they've suffered. I was here watching the pub.'

'So, it is likely to be arson then?' He nodded.

'I saw a man, he put something in the cellar.' She pointed to the side of the building. 'The other fires were started in the cellars too. Using petrol and rags.'

'I've seen the reports. We wondered if it was another one when we got the call.'

'Will you be able to stop it spreading?'

Hardwick looked back towards the pub. 'I can't tell you. Another engine is on the way, which will help. We'll have to see how it pans out. A fire like this can be unpredictable.' He put his helmet back on. 'I have to get back to the team. The police are on their way. You'll need to wait here for them, and I may need to talk to you again.'

The car pulled up behind Beatrice's VW and its emergency lights were switched off.

Beatrice turned to Brad. 'The police are here. I'll talk to them first, but they'll want to speak to you and Marie too.'

He nodded and stroked Maisie's hair. She'd fallen asleep.

'Do you have anywhere to stay tonight?'

Marie answered. 'There's my sister. She lives in Lincoln.'

'I'll drive you there, once they've finished with us.'

'Thanks,' said Brad. 'But we've got our own car.'

'Do you have the keys?' asked Beatrice.

'Shit!'

'Bradley!' Marie admonished.

'Sorry.' He took a deep breath, which prompted a coughing fit, waking up the girls, who began sniffling. 'We should ring your sister, let her know we're coming.'

'Oh,' said Marie. 'My mobile's inside. I don't know her number.'

'Perhaps the police can get it for you?' Beatrice suggested.

There was tapping on the driver's window. Beatrice looked up to see a uniformed policeman. She got out of the car, closing the door behind her.

The constable noted Beatrice's personal details and her explanation of why she had been at the pub. 'Can you talk me through what happened, please?'

As Beatrice recited the events, Hardwick, the fire control officer came over and listened.

'That was reckless,' said Hardwick. 'Going into a burning building. We don't do it without specialist equipment, training and backup.'

'They have children,' Beatrice explained. 'When Brad went off towards the fire, I couldn't just leave. I read the reports on the other fires. They had to get out fast, before it spread. I didn't know how long you'd be.'

'Well, what's done is done,' said Hardwick. 'How are you feeling?'

'Fine.'

'Any trouble breathing?'

'No.'

'An ambulance is on its way. You'll have taken in smoke and need to be checked out before you leave.'

'What about the kids?'

'The ambulance crew will assess the whole family. From what you've said the father will be most affected by it.'

'Why is that firefighter filming?' asked Beatrice. She pointed to a young man with an electronic tablet. He'd been recording the small crowd which had turned up to watch, no doubt drawn by the emergency vehicles which would have passed through Louth. What kind of person would get out of a warm bed in the middle of the night to be a spectator to someone else's misfortune?

'He's making a record. Standard procedure. In some cases of arson, the perpetrator returns to the scene to watch.'

'So, he could be here?'

'It's possible.'

Beatrice scanned the crowd, but she hadn't got a good look at the man she'd chased, so wouldn't be able to identify him, even if he was there. She couldn't see any parked motorbikes either.

'Right,' said Hardwick. 'We're getting to grips with the fire, but it will take longer to put it out completely. There's nothing more you can help us with tonight. Make sure you see the ambulance crew.'

'I will,' said Beatrice.

Hardwick left her with the constable, who had continued taking notes. 'You'll have to give a formal statement, I'm afraid,' he said. 'I'll leave it to the officer in charge of the investigation though.'

'Can you be quick with the family, please?' asked Beatrice. 'They're really upset, especially the girls. It was very frightening.'

'I won't keep them any longer than necessary.'

'Marie has a sister in Lincoln they can stay with. Can you get a phone number for her? So, they can let her know what's happening?'

'We'll take care of them. You can leave as soon as you've been seen.' He gestured towards the ambulance which had just arrived.

A paramedic gave Beatrice the all-clear around four o'clock, with instructions to go to her doctor if she experienced a hoarse voice, prolonged coughing or difficulty breathing. When she was ready to leave, the family were being questioned by the police, whilst being examined by the ambulance crew. There was nothing she could say or do to help so she left without speaking to them.

Beatrice entered the house as quietly as she could, not

wanting to see James. She had no inclination to explain the events of the evening, and no desire for his company. In the dark, she stripped off her clothes in front of the washing machine. The smell of smoke they and her hair had absorbed was difficult to ignore. Driving with the windows open hadn't reduced the stench. Bundling everything into one load, she set the washing machine running.

Under the powerful jets of the shower, she shampooed her long, brown hair several times, in a distracted way. At half past five, she fell onto her bed, exhausted. The note from James, asking her to wake him when she got home, remained unread.

I rolled the corpse up in the rug. I wrapped it in a layer of plastic sheeting. I always knew where to lay my hands on the right materials.

In my experience, bodies were almost always found, eventually. The trick was to hide identification as long as possible, and destroy forensic evidence. My thoughts turned to burning. I was already forming a plan which would, with a bit of luck, throw the police off the scent too.

My issue was timescales. I had to act soon, before the corpse could be found in the wrong place. It was too late for disposal today, but I had access to an empty chest freezer, for temporary storage. I'd have to take the risk of hiding him for a couple of days. The sooner the body was dealt with, the better.

As I'd worked, my trembling companion stood white-faced, silent. We'd need a cover story, for both the rug and man. But my new partner in crime was in no state to help. The dirty work would fall to me, as it always did. I didn't know what to say: words of reassurance would be false, so I said nothing.

Chapter 3

After a disturbed night, Beatrice finally gave up on sleep. The cat, who had decided to adopt her when the previous owners moved out, followed her downstairs. She pretended to merely tolerate her, but actually enjoyed the times the furry creature was happy to cuddle. Now though, she was in the kitchen dishing up cat food, being impatiently meowed at. When her phone rang, she put the bowl of food down before answering – the animal's complaints would only get louder. 'You're quick off the mark. It's only nine o'clock.'

'Always,' replied DC Susan Wilde. 'Go on then.'

'What?'

'Give me the low-down on last night.'

'I told the constable.' Beatrice didn't want to have to relive the fire. She'd done enough of it in her dreams.

'Yeah, not much though. So, you can tell me. The full story.'

'It'll be easier if we meet.' Beatrice stifled a yawn.

Susan sighed dramatically. 'Fine. I'm in the office the rest of the day, doing paperwork for court. Why don't you come here?'

'No thanks.'

'You'll have to make peace with Sergeant Fisher sometime.'

'Not today. Besides, he's the one with the problem.' Beatrice paused. 'There's a garden centre in Scothern with a tea room.' It was the right direction, north out of Lincoln, to put her roughly on the route to Spilsby, for her meeting with the brewery owners.

'I know it.'

'How about we meet there, say ten o'clock?'

'OK. You're buying the cake though.'

James appeared in the office doorway. 'Morning.'

Tall, dark-haired and muscular, James was a welcome sight. 'Well, hello.'

He came further into the room, bent down and gave her a gentle but lingering kiss, then sat on the floor, his back against the wall. 'What time did you get home?'

'About five, I think.' Beatrice wondered whether she should get a second chair for her office, but dismissed it. She didn't want to make the room into a shared space. 'Sorry, I only saw your note this morning.'

'You're up early, considering.'

'Yes, I've got a possible new case this afternoon, and this morning I'm at the brewery to explain how I let another of their pubs burn down.'

James frowned. 'It's hardly your fault.'

'No. But I was there and didn't stop it.'

'What happened?'

'I was trying to get a video, but he saw me and ran for it. I followed, but he was too quick and got away.'

'What? You chased him?' James stared at her wide-eyed.

'Maybe.' She looked away.

'Jesus, Beatrice. I thought we'd agreed to get evidence, not risk our necks running after a criminal.'

'It was a spur of the moment thing.'

'What if he'd attacked you?'

She shrugged. 'I saw he got on a motorbike. It's of some use, isn't it?'

James ran his fingers through his hair. He was clearly annoyed with her, but Beatrice was being truthful when she said she'd simply reacted. It had been risky, but hindsight was easy.

'Please don't do anything like that again.'

There was an uncomfortable silence. Beatrice wasn't going to give him any false reassurances. 'I should've been waiting nearer the cellar,' she said finally.

'There was only the car park and you'd have been seen.'

'Did you sleep OK once you got back?'

'Yes. It was lonely though.' His expression softened. 'Shall I cook for us tonight? You will be home? You're not thinking of going out again?'

'No point. The fires have been a couple of weeks apart so far.'

'So, dinner?'

'That would be great, thanks.'

James jumped to his feet, kissed her again, and left.

Beatrice was impressed at the rate DC Susan Wilde polished off her fruit cake. 'It's mine,' she said to the shorter, younger woman, who was casting covetous glances at her half-finished chocolate cake. They'd been through the events of the night before, and Beatrice had explained how she came to be hired by the Browns.

Susan had made notes as they talked, still managing to eat. 'I expect the Sergeant is going to want to speak to you herself.'

'I've told you everything.'

'She'll want to show Inspector Mayweather she's taking action. Send me your video. We'll see if we can enhance it, but I doubt there's much can be done, given how dark it was. If Sarge wants a formal statement, I'll use these notes to write one, and you can come in to check and sign.'

'Sure. What's she like then, the new recruit?'

'Alright, actually. Organised. Knows her stuff. Doesn't get involved in office politics, concentrates on the job. I like her. She's one of these highflyers though. Doubt she'll stay here long. She'll be after a big case to make her name, and then will be off on the back of it as soon as she can. That's why I reckon she'll want to see you.' Susan drained the tea from her cup, peering down into it as if she hoped it would magically refill.

'What's your next move then?' She picked up the teapot to confirm it too was empty.

'I'm not sure. I need to track down the arsonist, but don't have much to go on. I'll go through the video again, see if there's anything I've missed.'

'Be careful, Bea. This guy is happy to set fire to buildings whilst people are sleeping in them.'

'You sound as bad as James.'

'Trouble in paradise is there?' Susan chuckled.

'No. Not really,' Beatrice mumbled. 'He's great.'

'Blimey, it's hardly a ringing endorsement. He's a hunk; tall, handsome, all those muscles. If you don't want him, send him my way.' Susan froze. 'You have jumped him though?'

'Jumped him! You do have a way with words.'

'Well, I would. Mind you, I'm so much shorter than you, I'd have to take a run up to do it.'

The image of her friend doing exactly that popped into Beatrice's mind, and she burst out laughing. She didn't fancy James' chances if Susan did get it into her head to jump on him.

'So, have you?' Susan persisted.

'I'm not going to answer that!'

'Oh, come on. What's wrong with two single people getting it on?'

'Any other charming euphemisms you want to drop in?'

'Fine. Be like that. But if you haven't already, you should get on with it, before he finds someone else. A gorgeous man like James won't be stuck for offers.'

'I'm not used to sharing my home with a boyfriend. We've only known each other a short time.'

'You have done the dirty then?'

Beatrice raised her eyebrows. 'Really?'

Susan grinned. 'So, how's it going?'

'Fine. It's good,' she added at Susan's unimpressed expression. 'He's... Well, he's getting overprotective.'

'It must be terrible having an attractive man in your bed

and watching out for you. I don't know how you cope.' Susan frowned. 'Seriously Bea, he's a good bloke.'

'I know. I don't know what's the matter with me.'

There was a short silence, which Susan broke. 'And how's the search for your mum going?'

Beatrice glared at her friend. 'It's got nothing to do with that!'

'Really?'

'Yes, really.'

'If you say so. Go on, what's happening?'

'Nothing much. I've been in touch with the solicitor who sent the cheques to Rosie and me. I asked to see him, but he's refused, saying he won't discuss a client's private affairs.'

'But if he's controlling your mum's estate, there must be something he can tell you?'

'That's what I thought, but he won't budge.' Beatrice drank the remains of her tea, wondering if she should've had a coffee to help her stay awake. 'I've contacted the probate office, to get a copy of her will, but since she's not been declared…' Beatrice stopped herself. 'Since she's only missing, I can't get the will that way.'

'What's next?'

'I'm not sure. I'll have to think about it, but other than turning up at his office and confronting him, I don't know what options I have. I'm sure he must know something about what's happened to Mum.'

'Have you thought about contacting the officers who checked into her disappearance?'

'Can they help?'

'I don't know. But if you say you're concerned about your mother's money being distributed, without her consent, they might be able to ask questions in an official capacity.'

'There was a Family Liaison Officer. She was good. You know, it's not a bad idea.'

'I'm not just a pretty face.'

Chapter 4

Spilsby, a small market town near to the Lincolnshire Wolds, was thirty miles from Lincoln. As she drove, Beatrice noticed the change in landscape, from very flat to green rolling hills. She enjoyed the journey, the bright blue skies punctuated with white fluffy clouds, but wasn't looking forward to the meeting. The Browns, a serious, middle-aged couple, had hired her in a bid to save their business. Facing them after her failure was making Beatrice's stomach churn.

She parked in a residential street, the centre car park having been taken over for the weekly market. The brewing part of the business was on a light-industrial estate on the edge of Spilsby, but the Browns kept a separate office in the town centre, a short walk away.

Inside the building, with its immaculate façade, the reception area was all clean lines and polished brass. Artistic black and white photos of the brewing process adorned one wall. The other was decorated with copies of the Goose-themed pub signs they'd commissioned a local artist to create.

The Browns were waiting for her when she was shown into their personal office. Zoe stood up and moved away from her own desk to stand supportively behind her husband. 'Thank you for coming,' she said. 'Please sit.'

Beatrice sat and regarded the couple. Smartly dressed, fitting in well with their sleek, modern office, they both had dark circles around their eyes, and a defeated slump to their shoulders. She explained what had happened at the pub, and showed them the video.

'You were there. Couldn't you have done something?' Gareth's voice was hectoring, and he glared at her. Then he leaned forward, placed his elbows on the desk, and his head in his hands.

Zoe put her arm around his shoulders.

'I'm sorry,' Beatrice responded. 'He was too quick.'

'We're not blaming you.' Zoe's jaw tensed. 'We feel so hopeless. Everything we've built is being ruined.'

'You can't think of anyone who might want to do this to you?'

Zoe shook her head.

The Browns' ten pubs were in Lincolnshire, selling own brews alongside national brands. They prided themselves on being a local business, keeping production in the county and using local suppliers whenever possible. Beatrice could understand their anger and frustration at having all they'd worked for attacked.

'Thank goodness you were there,' said Zoe. 'It could have been so much worse.'

'Worse?' Gareth glared at his wife. 'At this rate we'll be bankrupt by Christmas! How could it be worse?'

Beatrice's body became tense. 'Four people could be dead.' She held his gaze until he turned away.

'Yes. Yes, of course,' he backtracked.

Zoe moved from behind the desk and sat next to Beatrice. 'We appreciate what you've done, but given our situation, we can't afford to keep you on.'

'I understand you're worried about money, but there's more I can do, and now we have a basic description of the arsonist. We know he was on a motorbike at a certain time and place. I can follow up any sightings.' Beatrice recalled the fear of the Staines family, and how much they'd lost. Their lives had been at risk, and she wanted to make sure it didn't happen to anyone else.

'It's the police's job,' said Gareth.

Gareth had shown reluctance, when Beatrice was hired,

hinting it was a waste of money, but she was surprised at Zoe giving up. She'd seemed so determined, when they'd found out the first blaze had been arson. Accepting their decision, she pulled her notebook out of her bag, scribbled a few figures and showed Zoe the total. 'This is what's left owing. You can pay now, and I'll send you an invoice.'

After a moment of stillness, Zoe got up and collected her chequebook from her desk drawer.

'I'd prefer card, please.'

Zoe sighed, then nodded.

Beatrice's portable card reader showed the payment had been made. 'You know where I am, if you change your minds.'

'Thank you,' said Zoe.

'Yes, thanks.' Gareth stood up and shook her hand, his demeanour improved, now she was leaving.

Beatrice left the office, uncomfortable at having to press for payment, but the prospect of their bankruptcy had focussed her mind. She was certain their ordeal wasn't over.

'I saw the news online. About the fire.' Rosie, Beatrice's twin, had started talking as soon as she'd opened her front door. Much shorter, of slight build and a mass of fair, curly hair, the sisters were a stark contrast to one another.

'Hello to you, too,' muttered Beatrice, before following into the kitchen.

'Tea?' asked Rosie.

'Please.'

Rosie flipped the switch on the kettle. 'You weren't at the Golden Goose then?'

'Actually, I was.'

Rosie paused in reaching for a mug. 'Did you fall asleep?'

'Thanks for the vote of confidence.'

'Well, the police have said they're still searching for a suspect.' She handed Beatrice a filled mug.

Beatrice glanced down at the weak tea. Her sister knew she preferred it strong. Rosie was distracted and it was more than her interest in the fires. Instead of complaining, she sipped at the hot liquid and tried not to grimace. 'I saw the guy going around the corner of the building. I followed, but he heard me coming and ran off. Not before he'd started the fire though.'

'Did you get a good look at him?'

'It was dark. There isn't much in the way of artificial light there. I did get a fuzzy video. The police are checking it.'

'Let's go into the living room.'

She was glad Rosie didn't ask any more questions. She'd had James telling her she was an idiot, in not so many words. She didn't need anyone else pointing out how dangerous it had been. Beatrice took a piece of paper from her handbag and passed it to Rosie. 'Here's the final expenses on the case. Can you sort an invoice, please? I've already taken payment and the amount is written on there. Let me know if I owe them a refund. I don't think so, if anything my estimate was probably too low, but it's better than nothing.'

Rosie raised her eyebrows. 'You thought they might not pay?'

'It was a distinct possibility.'

Rosie placed the paper on the coffee table and stared into space. Beatrice was surprised she hadn't asked about why she wasn't working for the Browns anymore. 'How are you?' Beatrice spoke gently.

'Uh?'

'What's the matter, Rosie?'

'It's nothing.'

'Come on. Out with it.'

Rosie stared at the floor. 'We had a blazing row last night. The girls are upset. They didn't want to go to school this morning.'

Beatrice's twin nieces, Abbie and Katie were nine years old, and pretty resilient, in her opinion. Rosie and Adam's occasional arguments were like background noise. It must have been particularly bad to upset them so much. 'What was it about?'

'Same as always,' snapped Rosie. 'Sorry. It's not your fault.'

'The ten grand from Mum's estate?'

'Adam wants to put it into the garage, says it will keep it going for the rest of the year.'

'What do you want to do?'

'Treat the girls to a holiday. Nothing expensive, a caravan in Skegness, maybe. And put the rest into our mortgage. I spoke to the bank and if we pay off over five thousand pounds, they'll reduce our monthly payments. Money has been so tight this year.' Rosie put her still-full mug onto the coffee table. 'I thought he'd be pleased.'

'He isn't?'

'He says he has an obligation to his staff.'

Adam's garage had been in trouble for a while, and Beatrice couldn't see it getting better anytime soon. He was a good mechanic, but things were hard for lots of businesses right now. Propping up the garage would be throwing good money after bad. 'How can I help?'

'What would you do with the money. If you were me?'

'I don't know. We've got different responsibilities.'

'No advice then?'

'Do you really want advice?'

'I think I do.'

Beatrice saw moisture in Rosie's eyes. 'OK. Well, it's your money. Not his. Since you can't agree, you should do what *you* think is right.'

'We're married, and supposed to make financial decisions together.'

'That's not what's happening, is it?'

'What do you mean?'

'He's basically telling you to give him the money, so he can spend it how he wants. Doesn't sound like a discussion.'

'I guess.'

'Is there a compromise?'

'I suggested using a few thousand, for the garage.'

'And?'

'He said it wouldn't go far. I was selfish and insulting him by implying he couldn't run the business properly, and if he came into a ton of money, he'd let me have it if I needed it.'

'Really?' Beatrice couldn't keep the scepticism out of her voice.

'Right? We both know where it would go. Thing is, I don't see why we should be paying other people's mortgages, when we might end up not being able to pay ours.'

'Where's the money now?'

'In Premium Bonds, whilst I decide what to do.'

'Sounds sensible.'

'Of course, he doesn't like that either.'

'Why?'

'Because it's not in the joint account. I told him I was going to put it in the bank, the day after it arrived. He went out that night with his mates, and bought drinks all round. Like it was already his.'

'Wow.' Beatrice had considered her sister had a happy marriage. There'd been problems when the girls were born: Adam had left most of the work to Rosie, who'd had to give up her job. Since then, things had seemed fine. But then they'd not had any other big issues, until now. On reflection, the difficulties with the girls had only resolved because Rosie took the responsibility on herself. When their father had died, followed by their mother's disappearance, Adam had been sympathetic initially, but his patience soon ran out. Beatrice had been living in London at the time, and remembered the tearful phone calls from Rosie.

'I'd better get on with this invoice, before the girls get home,' said Rosie, standing up. 'Oh. Would you and James like to come to dinner next week?'

Beatrice, taken by surprise, didn't answer immediately.

'What?'

'It's weird being asked to go somewhere together.'

'Why? You're in a relationship, aren't you?'

'I guess.'

'So? What's the problem? I've only invited you for a meal. It isn't a declaration of undying love.'

'I'll ask James.'

'Let me know soon though. I'll need to go shopping.'

'Call me if you need to talk, or want to get away for a while, won't you?'

'I will.'

Beatrice stood and bent down to give her sister a hug.

'You'd be helping me out,' said Rosie. 'I'm not sure I can cope with many more evenings on my own with Adam. He either starts an argument or ignores me. With you both here he might make an effort to be civil.'

Chapter 5

Charles Sharpe appeared to be in his early forties, with the beginning of wrinkles around his eyes and a few slithers of grey in his hair. The dark suit he wore appeared expensive, and he looked ill fitted to the clean, but shabby pub they'd arranged to meet in.

'Thank you for agreeing to see me.' Charles glanced at the building, his nose wrinkling in distaste. 'It's a nice day. Shall we walk instead?' His piercing blue eyes stared directly at her. Their intensity was unnerving.

'Let's head towards the cathedral.' Beatrice indicated the way. 'How was your journey from Norwich?'

'Good, thank you,' he said. 'Shall we get to it?'

'Please do.'

Charles took a deep breath. 'It's my daughter. I haven't seen her for over a year. I need to find her.'

Beatrice stopped moving. 'How old?'

'Almost two.' He began walking again.

Beatrice followed. 'What happened?' She turned her head to look at him.

'I had an important business trip. To Paris.' He ran a hand across his head, smoothing down his immaculate hair. He smiled at her, showing a brief glimpse of perfect, white teeth. 'I was away for a few days. When I got back, my girlfriend, Lily Taylor, her mother, had vanished, taking Elizabeth with her.'

'She hadn't said she was going away?'

'No.'

'You called the police?'

'Yes. There was nothing they could do. We weren't married, and Lily hadn't identified me as Elizabeth's father when she registered the birth. She'd written a note saying she was leaving, telling me not to search for her. She'd left it with a friend of hers, someone I'd never even met.'

'Who was the friend?'

They both turned to watch, as a noisy group of tourists decanted from a coach. A sense of calm began to return as they filtered through the entrance to the Cathedral.

'Lily started taking Elizabeth to a mother and baby group,' Charles continued. 'Maybe they met there. Other than that, she liked being at home.'

'Where was the group?'

'I don't know. Does it matter?'

'The letter: it definitely was from Lily?'

'The police confirmed it, using writing samples from the house. In the letter she claimed Elizabeth wasn't mine. I had nothing to prove otherwise, and there was no evidence of any crime. The police said Lily had left of her own accord, and if I wanted to argue I was Elizabeth's father, I would need to take it up as a civil matter.'

Beatrice considered his words. He'd no official connection to the girl. 'Why are you searching for her a year later?'

'I tried before, but got nowhere. Honestly, I thought she'd realise she'd made a mistake and come back. We were happy.'

Why had Lily left, if that was the case? 'You tried friends and family?'

'There's only her brother, Andrew, who lived in France at the time. He's in London now and hasn't heard from her either.'

'You believe him? If Lily didn't want you to know where she'd gone, wouldn't she ask her brother to keep it from you?'

'I can be very persuasive.' A fleeting smile appeared on Charles' face. 'I'm sure he was telling the truth, a few weeks back, when he said he didn't know where she was.'

'Why do you think Lily wanted to leave?'

'I don't know.'

'You hadn't argued?'

'No. How is this relevant? It's not going to help you find her.'

They'd come to a stop at the rear of the cathedral. There was something unsettling about Charles, but Beatrice couldn't pinpoint what. She gave herself a mental shake, she was tired, and it's not as though she had to like her clients, just do the job they needed doing. 'Why me, rather than a PI from Norfolk?'

'I think she might be in Lincolnshire. Besides, I saw a report on you in the paper a few weeks back. The murder case. You don't give up easily. I like that.'

Beatrice brushed aside the compliment. 'Why do you think she's in Lincolnshire?'

'Lily and Andrew lived in the county, when they were young, back before their parents died. She mentioned having happy memories, and talked about it being a good place to raise a child.'

'Do you know where they lived?'

'No. Andrew is older than her, he might remember.'

'I take it you want me to find Lily?'

'I want you to find Elizabeth.'

'Then what?'

'I'll get my solicitors involved. We can apply to the court for a DNA test. Once I can prove she's mine, I'll be able to see her. She should know her father, shouldn't she?'

Beatrice nodded. It sounded reasonable. Lily might not want anything more to do with Charles, but at one point at least, she'd told him he was Elizabeth's father. Beatrice's own father had been so important to her, his death had hit her hard. She felt, in the vast majority of cases, a child should have the chance to know both parents. It was understandable he'd want the truth, one way or the other. The solicitors could deal with his rights, if he was Elizabeth's father. If he wasn't, well it was a resolution too. 'You'd better give me some more information.' She pulled out her notebook and pen, self-conscious about working outdoors.

Charles gave her the dates of his Paris trip, and the day Lily had left, according to her letter, which he'd destroyed. He told her they'd met at a party, had a drunken liaison, which then developed into something more. Within a month Lily had moved in with him, and soon after, announced she was pregnant.

'I wasn't sure I was ready to be a father,' he said. 'And Lily and I barely knew one another. But once Elizabeth was born, it was love at first sight. It was amazing to me, seeing this beautiful little girl was mine.' He smiled. 'She was born a month premature, but looked perfect.'

Beatrice jotted down the full names and birthdates of Elizabeth and twenty-five-year-old Lily. Elizabeth was now twenty-two months, which meant she was only ten months old when they left. Charles also gave her a phone number and address for Andrew Taylor, and several photos. One was Lily and Elizabeth, but the baby was too young for it to be any help in finding her. Another was of Charles and Lily together: Lily, wearing heavy foundation, and obviously pregnant, was staring down at the floor, Charles had his arm around her shoulders, beaming. The last photo was of Lily as a child, with her brother.

'What's she like?' asked Beatrice.

'She liked films, the fairground, nice clothes, dancing in clubs, going to restaurants. It changed, once Elizabeth arrived.' He glanced at his watch.

'What's she like, as a person?'

'I don't understand.'

'Was she impulsive? Kind? Affectionate?'

He shrugged. 'Normal really. It's hardly going to help you find her, is it?'

He sounded annoyed, so Beatrice let the subject drop. 'There's not much to go on, and she left a long time ago. It may be impossible to find her.'

'I understand,' said Charles. 'But I have to do something. I need to find my sweet little girl.'

Beatrice's recollection of her nieces at that age was a lot of noise and smells. Hardly sweet. She went through the process of completing the paperwork with him, which he signed leaning against the Tennyson statue, and she took a deposit.

'I'll start with online research, then talk to Andrew.'

Charles smoothed back his hair. 'Let me know if you have any issues with him and I'll have a word.' He paused. 'You know, appeal to his affection for his sister. He must be worried and want her found.'

'After my initial enquiries, I'll let you know if I think it isn't worth continuing, but normally you can expect a report and detailed expenses weekly.'

After Charles left her, she sat on a bench, planning. It wasn't her first missing person's case, but it was the first involving an infant. The only way to find Elizabeth was by finding her mother. Andrew would be a good place to start, and he'd be able to tell her things about Lily which might help her search, as well as about their connection to Lincolnshire. Getting her birth certificate and identifying her parents might give a clue too, if Charles' hunch was correct. It was going to be difficult to find Lily if she didn't want to be found though.

Beatrice was wandering around the market when her phone rang. She answered it, registering it was an unknown number.

'Beatrice Styles?' A man's voice, polite and gentle queried.

'Yes.'

'My name is Percival Simmons, from Condor Insurance.'

'Yes?'

'I'd like to talk to you about some work, in your capacity as an investigator.'

'Hang on.' Beatrice walked away from the noise of the market, to a spot outside. 'How can I help?'

'It's rather delicate. Can we speak in person?'

'Sure.'

'Perhaps you would meet me for coffee, and allow me to explain what we'd like you to do? I can come to Lincoln.'

They arranged to meet at a coffee shop at Brayford Pool the next day. Beatrice had worked for insurance companies before, and they usually paid reasonable rates and on time. It could be good, she thought, to have a small job to keep her busy, whilst waiting for a bigger investigation to come along, now she'd lost the arson case.

Beatrice went back inside the market: she needed oranges and cat litter. It was busy and she moved slowly through the crowds, and negotiated around customers waiting to be served at several stalls. As she neared the fruit and vegetable stall, the crowd parted a little, and she was able to see ahead. She noticed a woman in a wheelchair, with a paper bag on her lap. A figure with his back to Beatrice was handing over apples for the woman to inspect. The ones which passed her careful examination were placed into the bag, those which didn't were returned. It was a well-rehearsed process. Once the bag was full, the man bent down to pick up the whole selection, and handed it to the stallholder for weighing. The three of them had a good-natured conversation whilst the money was passed over, as if the couple were regulars.

As the man moved behind the handles of the wheelchair and prepared to push, his face became visible to Beatrice. It was Detective Sergeant Derek Fisher. He was smiling: almost unrecognisable. She'd only ever seen him looking angry before, usually because of her.

Before she could turn away, Fisher looked up, staring straight at her. His expression changed to its familiar scowl.

Beatrice turned abruptly, causing the man behind her to bump into her and exclaim. 'Sorry,' she mumbled and hurried away.

Chapter 6

Back in her office, with a purring cat on her lap, Beatrice mulled over seeing Fisher. He was usually grumpy or angry when she saw him. Was his homelife difficult? The woman in the wheelchair was the right sort of age to be his wife. Susan hadn't mentioned he was married. A few subtle questions next time she saw the DC would be in order.

Beatrice lifted the cat and placed her on the floor, receiving a protesting meow, then switched on her laptop. A hot bath and a sleep would be preferable, but she had work to do. Starting with finding out more about Percival Simmons. A search on the internet showed he was a senior claims investigator at Condor Insurance. He'd no social media presence she could find. Condor, based in Nottingham, had been established over twenty years ago, and boasted of an impressive insurance book, dealing in all types of cover, mostly in the East Midlands and Lincolnshire.

Next, having been rebuffed by her mum's solicitor, she decided it was time to be more proactive. She'd not tried to find her mum before, relying on the police to have done everything necessary. Now, with experience of finding a missing teenager, she was well aware of the limits of what they would do, especially for an adult. Online she discovered there was no way to get a copy of her mother's will without probate. Her mother had mentioned rewriting it, shortly before her disappearance, and Beatrice assumed it was lodged with her solicitor. She hadn't given either daughter a copy though.

The concept of Guardianship was new to Beatrice. Legislation, dated 2017, allowed someone to apply to the

Courts for an official Guardianship order. If awarded, it would allow them to act for the missing person in financial affairs. Had the solicitor, Simon Atkinson, done that? She'd been told her mother's affairs were being taken care of by her solicitor, and hadn't thought to question it. Forgivable, in the immediate aftermath of her mother's disappearance, but not after all this time and she was frustrated with herself.

Making a snap decision, Beatrice completed an online form, requesting information about any applications to take responsibility for her mum's financial affairs. Surely, she thought, as her daughter, they'd have to give her some information. She also noted the police, and her ex-employer HMRC, could be given information which might be withheld from family. It was certainly worth bearing in mind, if she decided to get the police involved.

Her third and final task - the largest - was to start the search for Lily and Elizabeth. Trying to put her mother out of her mind, she checked over her notes and began.

'Hey.' James appeared in the doorway. 'It's ten minutes until dinner.'

Beatrice checked the time on her laptop. 'Is it that late? I got lost in a bit of a rabbit hole there.'

'You can tell me about it whilst we eat.'

'Sure. I'll be down in a few minutes.'

'Don't get dragged back into the internet,' James warned.

'I'm switching it off now,' she said, closing down the browser with its multiple tabs.

'Good.'

Downstairs, she could see James had made an effort, setting the table, pouring wine and lighting candles. He'd even found the tablecloth she kept in the back of a cupboard. It was obviously intended to be a romantic meal, rather than the quick chat over food Beatrice had been anticipating. Why had her heart sunk a little at the sight, she wondered, as she joined James.

'It looks lovely.' She wrapped her arms around him and they kissed. 'Smells good too. What is it?'

'Coq au van.'

'Very exotic.'

'Not really. Just one of the few things I can cook. You've sampled the whole repertoire now.'

'I'm sure it will be delicious.'

Once they had started eating, Beatrice caught James up with her eventful day, then he told her a little about his day at the garage, where he occasionally worked for Adam.

'Rosie wants us to have dinner at hers.' She glanced at James. 'I said I'd ask, but I can make an excuse.'

'Don't you want to go?'

Beatrice shifted in her seat. 'I ought to go, for Rosie, but it's not going to be a great way to spend an evening.' She hoped James would accept it as the whole story. She was uncomfortable with the idea of them being invited as a couple, as if it was taking their relationship to a new level.

'What's the matter with Rosie?' asked James.

'It's Adam.'

'Well, he's been a miserable bugger at work for a while now. Is he taking it home with him?'

'Yes. He wants Rosie to put the money she got from Mum's estate into the garage.'

'She doesn't want to?'

'No, and he's making it very clear he's not happy about it.'

'We should go then.'

'Are you a masochist?'

James laughed. 'I think it would give Rosie a break. He'll be on his best behaviour if we're there. You'll be able to see the girls too. They're nice kids.'

'Yeah, they are.'

'But not your kind of thing?' James regarded her intently.

It was a serious question. 'I've never seen myself as a mum.'

James concentrated on his food for several forkfuls. 'You

got anything on in the evenings next week?'

'No.'

'I'll sort dinner with Rosie, and let you know.'

'Thanks.'

'So,' asked James. 'What was it you got lost in, on the computer earlier?'

'I started with background on Lily and Elizabeth. I've been able to confirm their names and dates of birth, and ordered their birth certificates. If I can trace Lily's parents, I might find where her connection to Lincolnshire is.'

'Why Elizabeth's?'

'See who's listed as the father.'

'You didn't believe Sharpe?'

'I've no reason to disbelieve him.'

'But?'

Beatrice paused and thought before answering. 'I don't know. I thought I should check. What's on the birth certificate isn't conclusive, but I suppose I want to deal in facts, as much as possible. It can't hurt, can it?' She sipped at the wine. 'I did find out Elizabeth was registered as Taylor, same as her mum.'

'Interesting. Anything else?'

'Lily's not on social media, not under her given name anyway. I did an image search on a couple of the photos Charles gave me, but got nothing. I tried Andrew Taylor, but it's pretty common, so I had too many hits to follow up. If I knew what he looked like it might help, or if I had his date of birth.'

'Why research him?' James put his knife and fork on his empty plate, leaving them askew.

Beatrice did likewise, placing hers neatly together. James didn't notice. She tried to ignore the irritation. 'Thanks for the food. It was wonderful.'

James smiled at her. 'You're welcome. Perhaps you could cook next time?'

Beatrice felt guilty: he was right, it was time she reciprocated. 'To answer your question, because Andrew is the only family she has. If anyone knows where she is, it'd be him. He may have chosen to keep it from Charles.'

'Makes sense.'

'I did some checking on Charles Sharpe too.'

'And?'

'He lives in a large house in the nice part of Norwich. It cost a hefty sum five years ago, probably worth loads now. Judging by that, and his suit, he must be pretty well off.'

'What does he do?'

'He's got connections with a property business and a builder. What he does exactly I don't know.' Beatrice finished the contents of her wine glass. 'There were a lot of pictures of him at parties and functions. Usually with a well made-up young woman on his arm. Looks like he's had a lot of girlfriends over the years.'

'It's not a crime.'

Beatrice raised her eyebrows.

'What? I've not had loads of girlfriends.'

'I don't think I want to know. Anyway, it made me wonder, if he was as ready as he claimed, to settle down with Lily and Elizabeth. Perhaps one woman wasn't enough, and maybe Lily found out and left, not wanting Elizabeth to be involved in his lifestyle choices.'

'Does it help, if so?'

'I guess I wanted to understand their relationship. They weren't together for long and I'm not sure he really knew her.'

'Right,' said James. 'That's enough for tonight. Time to stop thinking about work.'

'What did you have in mind?' The food, wine and candlelight had helped her relax, and James was looking particularly attractive.

'Let's go snuggle on the sofa and watch TV. For starters.' He stood up.

Beatrice pushed her chair back and walked over to him, putting her arms around his neck. 'That's a good idea. For starters.'

I had to rewrap the body to remove the unique and expensive rug. I couldn't risk it being traced back. I wore gloves throughout. The chance of fingerprints surviving was low, but it paid to keep good habits. I put the body in the freezer. I only had to break a couple of bones to make it fit. I would have preferred to keep it intact, but it couldn't be helped. The head wound might have gone unnoticed, and his death put down to the fire, but broken legs were unlikely to be overlooked.

I burnt the rug in the countryside. I didn't need any expertise for that. There was a field I knew of, where no one would be able to see the smoke, or worry about the ashes. I stayed to watch, making sure it was completely destroyed.

Chapter 7

Tuesday 19th June

When most people saw Percival Simmons for the first time, they would probably assume he was an accountant. He'd arrived at the coffee shop before Beatrice, though she was five minutes early. As he rose to shake her hand, she observed his smart, but not expensive, three-piece, navy-blue suit, and a plain navy tie, with a full Windsor knot, tucked into his waistcoat. It seemed out of place for the modern world.

He waited for Beatrice to be seated before lowering himself back down. Although appearing around thirty years old, he'd taken on the formal dress and manners of another age. It suited him.

'Thank you for agreeing to meet with me, Miss Styles,' he said, pushing his black-rimmed glasses back up his nose. They almost immediately slid down to their earlier position.

'Beatrice, please.' She watched him arrange the salt, pepper and sugar bowl into a neat line. 'You said you had work for me.'

Mr Simmons leaned down, picked up his briefcase, and placed it flat on the table. Beatrice was fascinated to watch his careful, precise movements, as he undid the clasps, delicately extracted some papers, closed it up, and returned the case to the floor. He lay the papers down, positioning them so the bottom edge was exactly parallel to the table edge. She noticed, with interest, there were several sheets.

'Can I take your order?' The waitress interrupted.

Beatrice glanced at the menu, ordered a white Americano, with an extra shot, to wake her up. She'd hardly slept the night of the fire, and last night, she'd been occupied with James, before eventually falling into a deep sleep.

The waitress jotted down their order and left.

Mr Simmons took a moment to marshal his thoughts. 'I have looked into you and your business, Miss Styles,' he said. 'I would like to know about the murder investigation you were recently involved in.'

'There isn't anything I can tell you, beyond what was in the press at the time.'

'You found out who the guilty party was?'

'The police made a formal statement. I've nothing to add.'

Mr Simmons nodded. 'Good.'

Beatrice tilted her head. 'It was a test?'

'A brief assessment on your view of client confidentiality. I hope you are able to forgive me the minor subterfuge.' He placed his hands on the papers in front of him. 'We are very careful, at Condor, about who we employ, and expect external consultants to keep to the standards of our in-house investigators, with particular attention to discretion.'

'I understand,' said Beatrice.

They paused their conversation whilst the waitress delivered their order.

Mr Simmons leafed through the pages he had in front of him, and when they were alone continued. 'We were particularly pleased to see your experience at HMRC. You should have the necessary financial understanding and investigative skills.'

Beatrice's curiosity was piqued. The time he'd spent researching her background must either mean a big, potentially lucrative case, or maybe he was considering her as a regular hire. Either option would be welcome.

'You have recently been dismissed from the employ of Mrs and Mr Brown of the Wild Geese Brewery.'

She nodded. 'You're their insurers?'

'Correct. Which is how we know about your involvement.'

'I see.'

'Yesterday they updated their loss claim to include the third establishment.'

'That was quick.'

'Yes.' Simmons cleared his throat. 'Altogether we are talking about a substantial sum of money. They are also requesting an interim payment on the claim. Our position is that we would like to be confident the claim is valid, before releasing funds. From our review of their accounts, and other information, we have concerns. The business is in financial difficulties, and was so before the first fire.' He sat back, steepling his fingers whilst allowing Beatrice to absorb his comments.

'You're talking about insurance fraud?' Beatrice tasted her coffee.

'It is a possibility we have to consider.'

'What do you want from me?'

'A report of the work you have done so far, all you know about the arson attacks. We'd also like an idea of the next actions you'd take, were you to continue investigating. With a breakdown of anticipated costs.'

Beatrice regarded him steadily. 'I have two issues.'

'Go on.'

'Firstly, I have been paid by the Browns for everything I've done so far, and I'm not sure how comfortable I am handing it over.'

'And your second point of concern?'

'It will take time to produce. Time I could be spending on other cases.' She didn't have anything else on, but didn't want to give the impression she wasn't in demand.

'We would, of course, be prepared to pay you to write the report. If we are satisfied with your proposed actions, we will also consider paying further for your services.'

'I don't think they're defrauding you. When I was hired, they were genuinely upset at the loss of the pub. Zoe and

Gareth both seemed baffled about why it was happening.'

'If that's the case, you can think of it as an opportunity to clear their name. We would expect you to remain impartial, however.'

Beatrice raised her eyebrows.

'My apologies.' Mr Simmons dipped his head. 'We would pay you five hundred pounds for the report, to demonstrate our commitment.' He reached into his inside pocket and extracted a cheque. He turned it to face Beatrice, laying it with care on the table. It was from an official bank account in the name of the insurance company.

'As regards your first concern, about sharing the information you obtained whilst employed by the Browns, I am happy to inform you that I have written permission for you to provide it to me.' He showed her a document signed by Zoe.

'Why did she agree?'

'I pointed out, since she was so enthusiastic about catching the culprit, she should surely embrace the possibility of us paying for your services, instead of the business doing so.'

It fitted with Beatrice's assessment of Zoe. She'd wanted to stop the fires and have the arsonist locked up. It was in Gareth she'd sensed reluctance. Though it was perhaps due to their financial problems. 'I suppose it's OK then. I'll need a copy of this for my records, in case I find out something they don't like and decide to cause trouble.'

'You may keep that. I have a contract here for you to sign.' He handed her two copies.

Beatrice chuckled to herself. Mr Simmons was a paperwork enthusiast.

The contract was simple, written in plain English, stating what he had already explained. Beatrice considered. The information she'd gathered so far could easily be replicated by another investigator, so was there really an issue with confidentiality, when Zoe had given permission? Was she being overcautious? She certainly liked the idea of being able to continue to hunt the arsonist. Her nighttime encounter and the thought of what could have happened to the Staines family, was too awful to contemplate. Even remembering it now, made her tense, and her heart rate increase.

She sat back in her chair, decision made. 'OK. I'll do it. But,' she held up a hand, 'I want you to give me the accounts and this "other information" you mentioned you'd seen.'

Mr Simmons, pulled a thick envelope from his briefcase and handed it to her. He pushed his glasses back up his nose. 'I've included contact details for myself and my line manager, and how to submit the report. If you have any reason to get in touch with us, please do not divulge any information to anyone else, even within the company.'

Beatrice nodded her understanding. 'I can have the report with you by the end of tomorrow.'

'Excellent.' Mr Simmons stood. 'I look forward to reading it. I'll take care of the bill for our drinks on the way out.'

Beatrice watched him pause at the till to pay, having enjoyed the meeting. He was such an odd character, especially for someone so young, but she thought he would be easy to do business with: clear and methodical. If she did a good job, it could be the start of a profitable alliance, as well as a chance to find the arsonist, before he struck again.

Chapter 8

Wednesday 20th June

Beatrice spent the early part of the morning rereading the initial draft of the report she'd written for Percival Simmons. She made a few changes – additional lines of enquiry, which had occurred to her during the night – then sent it off. She hoped he'd be impressed enough with her efficient and thorough response to hire her.

She spent a few moments staring at her phone before steeling herself to make the call to someone from the past.

'Sergeant Holmes.' The voice was clear and clipped.

Not how Beatrice remembered it. Her reluctance to call wasn't because of any dislike of Vanessa Holmes, but because the memories of the times they'd spent together were all about the fruitless search for Beatrice's mother. The sense of helplessness she'd experienced back then, returned the moment the phone was answered.

'Vanessa. It's Beatrice Styles.' She waited, to give the other woman time to remember her.

'Beatrice. How are you?' Vanessa's voice softened, and Beatrice could hear her switch into 'family liaison officer' mode.

'I'm OK, thanks.'

'Sorry I was a bit abrupt. I didn't realise it was you. You've changed numbers?'

'I got a new one, when I replaced my phone.' Beatrice had decided to ditch her old number, to stop the unending questions about her mother, from people she knew, but wasn't close to. Recently she'd been able to admit the other reason was to put it behind her. She was angry at her mum, for choosing to leave her and Rosie behind without a word. The police had decided she'd left voluntarily, which Beatrice hadn't wanted to accept.

'You have news?' Vanessa interrupted her thoughts, making Beatrice realise there had been a prolonged silence.

'No. Well, not really.'

'Anything I can help you with?' asked Vanessa. 'I'm not an FLO anymore, but I can arrange for you to talk to one.'

'I wanted advice. About Mum.'

'OK.'

'A few weeks back, I had a letter from a solicitor. With a cheque for ten thousand pounds.'

'Wow.'

'The letter said it was money from Mum's estate. Rosie had one too.'

'Right. What's the problem?'

'Mum can't be declared dead until seven years have passed, and it's not quite two, since she went missing. This solicitor might have applied for Guardianship over her financial affairs, but even so, I don't believe it would give him the right to pass her money on to anyone else. According to the Office of Public Guardian, who monitor these things, he should have told me and Rosie, if he'd applied.'

'You think he did, but didn't tell you?'

'I've been through the rules of Guardianship and Probate, and there's loads of stuff he's not done, if so. I don't think he has authority over her affairs, but I've sent in a request, to find out. The thing is, I think the solicitor either is doing something he shouldn't be...'

'Or?'

'Or he knows where Mum is.'

Beatrice could hear Vanessa expel a long breath.

'That's quite a statement.'

'But possible.'

'I'm not up to date on death declarations or probate law. I'll have to take your word for it. It's possible, I suppose, that she left instructions before she went. Maybe the solicitor is following those?'

'Mm,' said Beatrice. 'But it would mean she'd planned ahead, had time to think.'

'There was no evidence of anyone else being involved in her leaving, Beatrice.'

'I know. It's still hard to accept she *chose* to go. It's not the kind of mum she was.'

'What do you want to do? About the solicitor I mean. Do you want to make an official report?'

'I thought I'd try to speak to him again first. See if I can get him to talk to me, tell me where Mum is.'

'Don't get your hopes up. He may genuinely not know anything.'

Beatrice blinked back her tears.

'Look,' Vanessa continued after a moment of silence. 'Text me the solicitor's details and I'll check him out. See if he's reputable. You try to speak to him, and let me know how you get on. Let's talk again in a few days and exchange information. We can decide the best way forward then. How does that sound?'

'Thank you,' whispered Beatrice. She cleared her throat. 'Thank you,' she said again, more clearly. 'I know it's not your job, but I couldn't face having to explain it to someone new.'

'I understand.'

They moved on to talk about other things. Vanessa described how she'd been promoted, and was now part of a team investigating organised crime. Beatrice filled the policewoman in on how she'd decided to leave her job as a tax inspector, when the opportunity for redundancy arose: how she'd wanted out of London, away from everything that had happened. She was more hesitant in explaining her new role, but Vanessa seemed genuinely interested and unfazed.

'If you ever come back down to London, we should catch up,' Vanessa suggested.

'Sounds great,' said Beatrice, thinking it could be sooner rather than later. If Simon Atkinson refused to speak to her, she was prepared to turn up at his office, and make enough noise to attract attention. Not a good idea to tell a police officer she was planning on disturbing the peace though.

Beatrice paced up and down her small office, listening to the ringing tone from her mobile. She'd been putting off making the call since speaking to Vanessa. She'd tidied the house, done all the washing, even going so far as to clean the oven, but she couldn't keep making excuses. So far, she'd not done much, but if she was going to search for her mum, she had to be committed. She'd finally realised she would never be satisfied, not knowing what had happened. Even if her mum was dead, she needed to know.

'Atkinson and Atkinson. How may I help you?'

'I'd like to speak to Simon Atkinson, please.'

'Are you a client of his?'

'I want to talk to him about a letter he sent me.'

'Your name, please?'

'Beatrice Styles.'

'One moment.'

Tinkling, tinny music came out of the handset. It was almost five minutes before the same voice came back on the line.

'Ms Styles. Thank you for holding. I'm afraid Mr Atkinson is unable to speak with you on the matter. The letter he sent to you is the full extent of correspondence he is able to make, due to client confidentiality. Thank you for calling.'

'Wait! Can you at least give him a message?'

There was a short pause. 'Yes, I suppose I can.'

'Good. You'll need a pen.' The attempt to fob her off had annoyed her, and she wasn't going to let Simon Atkinson get away with it.

'Go ahead.'

'Tell him I know about the rules on declaring missing people dead. I know my mum's body hasn't been found, and she can't possibly have been declared dead, in which case, he is either breaking the law by distributing her money, or he knows where she is. If he doesn't talk to me, and explain things to my satisfaction, I, I…' Beatrice's voice cracked, and she took a steadying breath. 'I will be going to the police, the Law Society and the press.' She hadn't set out to threaten Atkinson, and worried she'd gone too far, but she'd said it now. There was no going back.

'Can you give me your contact details, please?'

Beatrice reeled off her number. 'And tell him if I haven't heard back within forty-eight hours, I won't be keeping quiet.'

Chapter 9

Charles Sharpe's home was a mile south-west of the city centre, in what was known locally as the Golden Triangle: home to Norwich's wealthier citizens. The old sales particulars Beatrice found online showed a detached double-fronted home, with an immaculate interior and tasteful decor.

Beatrice parked a couple of streets away, and walked the area, trying to get an impression of what it might have been like for Lily living there. Had Lily felt at home? It was difficult, knowing so little about her or her background. She hoped speaking to Lily's brother would help.

Walking past Charles' house, Beatrice hesitated. Though it was quite reasonable for her to come to the place Lily had last been seen, she couldn't help but wonder what her client would make of it. Pleased to see the sweeping driveway was empty, Beatrice stopped to look at the house. Like the others in the tree-lined street, it was well maintained, but there was little information she could glean to help her search.

Across the road, a similarly large house commanded a good view of the goings on at the Sharpe home. Beatrice crossed over and rang the bell. The door was answered by a young woman, wearing rubber gloves and a tabard.

'Yes?'

The voice was accented, but Beatrice couldn't place it. 'Hello.'

'The owners not home, they not buy what you sell.' She made to close the door.

'My name's Beatrice Styles.' She held out a business card. 'I'm a private investigator. I was wondering if anyone around here could help me.'

'What about?' The cleaner looked interested.

'A woman used to live across the street.' She gestured. 'She went missing about a year ago. I'm searching for her. I'd like to speak to anyone who might have been here on the day she was last seen.'

'I no work here then. Sorry.'

'When will the owners be back?'

'The Mr, I don't know. Mrs: she come back in afternoon, after wine-lunch with friends.'

'Thank you.'

'She not very bright. Probably not help.' The young woman squinted at Beatrice, assessing her.

'Next door.' She pointed. 'Old lady there. Not go out much. Been here long time. Maybe she see woman.'

'Thank you.'

'You welcome.'

'Yes?' Through the gap in the doorway, limited by the safety chain, Beatrice could see a pale, lined face, topped with grey curls.

'Hello.' Beatrice held out a business card. 'My name's Beatrice. I'm a private investigator. Can I ask you a couple of questions?'

'I won't invite you in. My son wouldn't half go on if he knew I'd let a stranger in the house.' She accepted the card and slipped it into the pocket of her cardigan. 'What is it you wanted to ask about, dear?'

'About a year ago, a young woman who lived across the street went missing. Did you see anything that day? Maybe you saw her leaving?'

'A year ago?' The keen eyes peered through the narrow opening.

'I'm sorry, it is a long time. The woman would have had a baby with her.'

'Oh, yes. The house with the man in the expensive suit.'

Her nose wrinkled in distaste. 'Him. I do remember there was a woman and a baby there for a while. I never saw much of her. The indoors type I suppose. She's not missing though.'

'No?'

'No. The police came around asking about her, and I told them what I saw.'

Beatrice frowned. Charles hadn't mentioned any witness evidence from when Lily had left. Was the older woman getting confused?

'Don't look at me like that. I might not get around as well as I used to, but I've still got all my marbles. Besides, I remember the day, because having to go over it with the police a couple of days later made it stick in my mind.'

'Sorry. What did you see?'

'Why do you want to know?'

It was a fair question. 'I'm looking for her.' Beatrice didn't want to mention who her employer was. The older woman wouldn't be too cooperative, given her clear dislike of Charles. 'I'm seeing her brother soon.' It was the truth, if not the absolute truth.

'Her brother?'

'Yes. Andrew. He lives in London. I'm going there later this week.'

'Oh. Well then. It was a few hours after he'd left in a taxi with a suitcase. Looked like he was going away for a few days. He often does. Work, I presume. Well, she came out of the house, checked up and down the road. Then a white van drove up. She waved at the driver who parked on the driveway.'

'What happened then?'

'The woman helped the driver load some things in the back of the van. There wasn't much: a couple of suitcases, a few small boxes, and the child's pram. She and the baby got in the front. She had one of those car seats. After a minute or two they drove off.'

'Did the van have any markings on it? A name?'

'No. Plain white.'

'What did the driver look like?'

'She was about forty, I'd guess. Shorter than you. Blue hair. Bright blue, not a blue rinse. Wore trousers and a shirt. The practical sort.'

Beatrice's phone vibrated in her handbag, causing her to pause for a moment. 'Is there anything else I should know?' Whoever was calling was being persistent.

'I don't think so.'

'Which way did they go?'

'Up the road there. Towards town.' The woman breathed deeply. 'I'm sorry, I can't stand up for long. I'm going to have to go.'

'I won't keep you, but did the police speak to Mr Sharpe about what you saw?'

'Who.'

'The man in the suit.'

'They must have. He came here asking about it. Very rude, he was. Called me senile. Said I was too old and stupid to know what I was talking about.' She sniffed. 'It was a Monday. My lad was here then. It's his day for spending with me. Such a kind boy to his mum. Anyway, my son soon sent him packing. Talking to me like that.'

'I'm sorry he was unpleasant to you.'

'It's water off a duck's back, dear. The likes of him don't bother me.'

'Thank you for your help. If you think of anything else, my phone number is on the card I gave you.'

As she walked down the drive, Beatrice heard the door close behind her. There wasn't any reason to doubt what she'd been told. The police, according to Charles, had decided Lily left of her own volition, and the description of suitcases and boxes confirmed it. She considered what to do next. The van had driven off into town, but it could have been on its way further afield. Who was the woman with blue hair? Someone Lily had known from before? Charles had said she didn't have any friends in Norwich. The van driver's description was distinctive, but would it help? She'd have to ask Andrew about Lily's friends, and anyone she would have kept in touch with.

Back on the street, Beatrice pulled out her phone. It was James who had been calling. She'd better speak to him.

He answered after a couple of rings. 'Beatrice. Where are you?'

'What?'

'I've got the rest of the day off, so I came back to the house. I thought we could do something together.'

'Sorry. I'm working. I'm in Norwich.'

'Norwich? Oh. You never said.'

The silence stretched.

'When will you be back?'

'I don't know. I've got to make the most of being here.'

'I guess,' said James in a low tone. 'I suppose I'll see you whenever.' He hung up.

Bugger. She thought about ringing back, but decided against it. She'd no idea what to say, and wasn't going to apologise for doing her job.

James soon slipped from her mind, as she checked a map on her phone. It was a little over a mile into the city centre, so an easy walk. Probably a route Lily would have taken many times. Charles had mentioned a mother and baby group. An internet search revealed a surprising number of them, but since she hadn't thought to ask on which day of the week Lily went, she hadn't been able to narrow down the selection. Also, the ones she'd found weren't within easy walking distance, and there had been no mention of Lily having a car. She wouldn't have needed help from the woman with the van if she had, so, it was likely the group was one she'd be able to reach on foot, or maybe bus.

The walk towards the city centre in the sunshine was pleasant, but the succession of private homes couldn't help with finding Lily. Eventually residences started to be interwoven with the occasional business, which became more numerous as she got closer to the centre. Frustrated and aimless, she continued another few minutes. At a newsagent she bought a drink. Taking the opportunity afforded by no other customers, she chatted to the woman behind the counter: a bored twenty-something.

'I'm new to the area. I don't suppose you could tell me what people with small babies do around here?'

'What do you mean?'

'Are there any playgroups? Like mother and baby groups?'

The young woman shrugged. 'I don't know.'

Beatrice took her change. 'Thanks anyway.'

'You could try the community centre, I suppose.'

'Yes?'

'Yeah. It's a little further down the road, towards town.'

'Thanks very much.' A community centre was a good bet, and she left the shop feeling more positive.

Chapter 10

Beatrice ate a hasty lunch of a sandwich and coffee, whilst sitting on the grass outside the cathedral. Maybe it was a sign of being more at home in her new city, or the close proximity of Lincoln cathedral to her house, making her possessive, but she didn't think Norwich cathedral was anywhere near as impressive. Afterwards she checked online for the community centre. Its website showed it was open until late afternoon. If they didn't have a group for babies there, they might be able to point her in the right direction.

The centre was a short walk away, and as Beatrice made her way there, she wondered how to approach it. She wouldn't be able to bluff her way through a claim of having her own baby. She knew next to nothing about them, and didn't want to. What story would sound plausible?

When she got there, a group of senior citizens were making a slow exit, blocking the entrance as they stopped to chat and say prolonged goodbyes. Beatrice stood to one side and waited. She watched with interest as one tall, thin man, with a tuft of white hair sprouting from his head, took the arm of a much shorter woman, and led her down the steps. Is it what Dad would have looked like? If he hadn't died in the skiing accident? She shrugged the unhelpful thought from her mind as the entrance cleared.

Inside, the lobby area had a noticeboard. She started to read the messages.

'What sort of thing are you interested in?' A middle-aged woman looked up at Beatrice, with a welcoming smile. 'We do something for everyone.'

'I'm here on behalf of my sister.' Beatrice had come up with a cover story. 'She's moving into the area soon.'

'She's not with you?'

'No. She's pregnant and suffering a bit.'

'Oh, that's a shame. When's she due?'

'A few weeks.'

'Lovely. She'll be after our baby group then. I've got a timetable back in the office. Would you like me to show you around on the way there? I've got time.'

'Great, thanks.' Not interested in the fabric of the building, Beatrice nonetheless agreed. It could be a good way to get the woman to talk.

'I'm Morwenna, by the way.'

'I'm Beatrice.'

'The hall's not in use for another half hour, so let's start there.' Morwenna led the way.

In the main hall, Beatrice looked at the displays on the wall. It seemed as though each interest group had its own.

'This one's for the baby group,' said Morwenna, standing in front of it.

Beatrice examined the photos showing lots of happy babies and tired parents. She feigned interest. 'Lovely.'

Morwenna talked about the group and Beatrice listened with partial attention, whilst carefully examining each of the photographs for Lily. She couldn't see anyone who resembled her though. 'Is the group leader here today?'

'No. There are contact details on the website though. Your sister can arrange a visit, if she's up to it.'

They ambled around the rest of the perimeter of the room, and Beatrice continued to look, out of politeness. At the section for the women's support group, Beatrice came to a stop.

'We have a men's support group too,' said Morwenna.

There were photos of the women involved in group activities, such as painting, collage and needlepoint. A couple of the images showed them at other locations.

'They have the occasional outing. Going on walks, bus rides, that sort of thing,' said Morwenna.

One photo caught Beatrice's attention. In the background of a group shot, a figure stood with her back to the camera. A woman with blue hair.

'Is she part of the group?' asked Beatrice, pointing. 'She doesn't seem to be joining in.'

Morwenna peered at it. 'Oh, Jules. She's a group leader. Doesn't like to have her photo taken. Lovely woman, when you get to know her.' Morwenna sighed. 'That was her blue hair phase. She's onto red now. Not ginger-red. I mean bright red. Lovely golden blonde hair she has, when the roots grow out. I can't imagine why she'd want to cover it up. Each to their own, I suppose.' She shrugged.

Beatrice made a mental note to research the women's support group. It could be a coincidence, strongly coloured hair was more popular these days, but maybe not.

The tour didn't take much longer and Morwenna finished it at her office. 'Here's the timetable. We're still using the old printed versions, so check the website to make sure the dates and times are correct. There's plenty of information and more photos too.'

Beatrice glanced at the timetable. The women's group met at the same time as the baby group, on a Wednesday afternoon. The blue-haired, now red-haired woman, could have met Lily, if Lily had been coming to the baby group. It was all conjecture, but it was progress. She thanked Morwenna for her help and left the community centre.

Returning to her car, Beatrice stopped as her phone rang.

'Ms Styles. Percival Simmons.'

Beatrice stepped away from the busy road, down a side street where it was quieter. 'You're calling about my report?'

'Indeed.'

'Do you have questions?'

'No. It was all in order, thank you. I've spoken to our

senior manager, and he has authorised me to hire you to do further work on the case. Are you willing to do so?'

Beatrice paused. The Browns wouldn't be happy at her carrying on. Should she say no? As soon as the thought crystallised in her mind, she knew the answer. She wanted the truth, and any discomfort the brewery owners might have, didn't outweigh her desire. 'Yes, I am.'

'Your report gave potential fruitful lines of inquiry. However, I'd like you to bear in mind, please, our aim is to find out whether or not the Browns were involved, even tangentially, in the arson attacks. Our interest at this stage is purely regarding whether or not to pay out on the policy.'

'I understand,' said Beatrice. 'Of course, in order to find what you need, I may have to identify the actual culprit, which the police will be interested in.'

'Should you find out anything which may assist a criminal investigation, we are content for you to pass on information to the appropriate authorities.'

'Thank you.'

'I will send you an additional contract. It is standard for any outside investigators. Please sign and post a copy to me.'

'I'll do it straight away.'

'I will leave you to proceed as you see fit, except we do not wish you to do any more stakeouts.'

Beatrice tried not to chuckle at his tone. He'd spoken the last word as though he couldn't believe he was lowering his standards to use slang.

'We do not like our investigators to take unnecessary risks, and we will not be responsible for any consequences should you go against our wishes.'

Spoken like a true insurance agent, thought Beatrice. 'I understand. I don't think there's anything to be gained from another stakeout.' She enjoyed imagining him wincing at the word.

Simmons cleared his throat. 'I would appreciate updates by email, when you have anything to report.'

'Absolutely.'

'Good afternoon.' Mr Simmons rang off.

Beatrice was pleased to get the work. The money would be useful, but what she'd said was true: she really didn't like leaving anything unfinished, and Condor Insurance had given her the perfect opportunity to continue digging.

Chapter 11

Thanks to being stuck behind a succession of tractors on the Norfolk roads, it had taken two and a half hours to get back to Lincoln. Although tired, Beatrice didn't want to miss her meet up with Susan. The DC was good fun, and she hoped to find out what was happening in the arson case. She didn't want to replicate work the police could do more efficiently and easily. Knowing if she sat on the sofa, she'd probably not get up again, she forced herself upstairs and into the bathroom, hoping a hot shower would perk her up. Under the high-powered jet, the tension from the drive drained away.

'Need any company?' James stood in the doorway watching her rinse the soap off.

He looked particularly handsome, leaning casually, his well-built form and small smile tempting her. Shame. 'Hi.' Beatrice turned off the water and reached for her towel.

'That's a no then?' He looked disappointed.

'Sorry.' Beatrice stepped out of the shower. 'I'm meeting Susan. I need to talk to her about the arson suspect.'

James glanced at his watch. 'It's nearly eight. Have you eaten?'

'No, but Susan's usually hungry, so I'll eat out.' Beatrice brushed her lips against James' cheek. 'I'm not sure how long I'll be. Shall I give you a ring when we're done?'

'No. I've an early start tomorrow, collecting parts for Adam. It'll be a long day. How was your trip?'

'Exhausting. I have a potential lead on the woman who helped Lily leave. It will mean going back there again.' Beatrice felt guilty about neglecting James. 'I'm sorry I didn't tell you I was going. How about we go out together on Sunday?'

James beamed. 'No work?'

'I'll take the day off.'

'Good.' James kissed her, held her for a few seconds, then left, leaving her missing his warmth. She would have to make more of an effort with him, if she wanted their relationship to continue.

Susan flashed a broad grin at Beatrice's mention of food, when they met on Steep Hill. 'I know where we can go,' she'd said, setting off at a pace even Beatrice's long legs had trouble keeping up with.

The Italian restaurant, was hidden in a street off the main drag. Beatrice looked at the small tables, subdued lighting and background classical music. 'They'll think we're a couple,' she hissed.

Susan laughed and shrugged. 'So?'

'It's weird.'

Susan put down her menu. 'I know what I'm having. You decided yet? The lasagne is good.'

'I'll have that then.'

On cue a waitress appeared, and asked for their order. It bothered Beatrice that she hadn't written anything down.

'Stop stressing.' Susan interrupted her thoughts. 'What's the matter with you?'

'I guess I'm tired and grumpy. Sorry.'

'Here comes the waitress with our wine. That'll loosen you up.'

Half an hour later they'd both made significant dents in their food, the wine bottle was nearly empty, and they'd caught up on their private lives, including Susan's amusing tale of a blind date which had gone badly wrong in the restaurant they were currently in.

'So, the lasagne was the only successful thing about the whole evening. He was a bundle of nerves, fumbling about all the time. When he dropped his fork for the third time, we both knew we weren't going to be seeing each other again. I had to leave an extra tip, because the waiting staff kept having to pick up after him.' Susan drained her wine glass and topped them both up again. 'I've decided to give up on men for a while, concentrate on my career. Such as it is.'

'I thought you loved your job?'

'I do.'

'But?'

'It's this high-flying Sergeant. She's younger than me and already a DS.'

'The quick route isn't always the best one.'

'I know. I'm wondering whether I need to get out of Lincolnshire though. Get experience in a big city.'

'As an ex-inhabitant of London, I wouldn't recommend the MET.'

'It wouldn't be my first choice: as a woman.'

'Understandable, given how many of their own officers they've had to arrest recently. How could they have not known what some of them were up to?'

Susan frowned. 'People get too scared to speak up because of the repercussions.'

'It's expensive too. I had to live outside the city and spent a lot of time and money commuting every day. I only stayed there because of my parents.'

'I thought you left because of them.'

There was a moment of silence before Beatrice spoke. 'How's your search for the arsonist going?'

'The Browns giving you grief?'

'Actually, they fired me. I'm working for their insurance company now.'

'Insurance?' Susan pursed her lips. 'Do they suspect fraud?'

'It's a possibility, but not likely in my view. They've asked me to investigate if the Browns had any involvement.'

The women paused their conversation whilst their empty plates were cleared. Susan ordered two portions of tiramisu and coffees. 'They're not both for me,' she shot at Beatrice's surprised expression. 'You look like you need it.'

'What do you know about our fire starter?' Beatrice asked.

'We don't know who it is yet, though we've pulled together a list of known locals who have history. You said he'd headed towards Lincoln, so we searched for a motorcyclist on the route, and we put an appeal out on social media for any witnesses. There aren't many people out at that time in the morning, so we didn't have many replies to check out.'

'And?'

'A motorbike was seen, without lights, at the right sort of time. It was driving erratically towards the city. We picked it up on traffic cameras heading down the eastern bypass. We lost it after that.'

'Do you think it carried on south?'

'We don't know.' Susan finished her dessert and rested the spoon in the bowl. 'There are cameras south of Lincoln, but we didn't pick it up again. There's a good chance he came into the city, but the trail's gone cold.'

'So, what's next?'

'It's up to the Sergeant. We're restricted on manpower, so we may try another appeal to the public. We're checking out reports of stolen bikes: no luck so far though.'

'Have you questioned people in town?'

'The uniformed night shift spoke to a lot of people, but got nothing useful. They'll let us know if they hear anything.' Susan glanced at the bill the waitress had slipped onto the table. 'Halves?' she asked.

Beatrice nodded. They both stood and walked to the bar to pay.

Outside, they continued their conversation. 'I think I'll have a go at asking around in town. I might have more luck,' said Beatrice.

'You can't stop passing strangers.'

'I'm going to walk down to the bus station. There are usually a few homeless people about at night. I've talked to a couple of them before.'

'As long as they haven't been moved on by us,' Susan noted.

'If there are any, they're more likely to talk to me than the police. I won't be telling them to shift out of the prime sheltered spots, or offering them a night in the cells. It's worth a try.'

'I guess,' said Susan. 'Are you going there now?'

'I may as well. James is getting an early night.'

'Do you want me to come with you?'

'No. They might recognise you and clam up.'

'Be careful, won't you?'

'I will.'

'Like running into burning buildings kind of careful?'

Chapter 12

The new bus station was an improvement on the old one, but had continued to attract people with nowhere else to go. It wasn't only the homeless. Teenagers with nothing better to do congregated there too. The groups kept their distance, the homeless eyeing the youngsters with apprehension. Beatrice was wary, as she passed a group of lads. They ignored her.

'Hi, Trev, how's things?' Beatrice had talked to homeless Trevor several times before, sometimes buying him a coffee and sandwich.

'Oh, it's you.' Trevor had wedged himself in the doorway of a shop, with his sleeping bag and blankets tucked around him. 'I don't normally see you here this late.' His dark hair and beard hadn't seen a barber in a long time.

'I'm working,'

'Private detecting, is it?'

'Trying to detect, not succeeding. Perhaps you could help?'

'Maybe, for the right incentive.' He winked at Beatrice.

'What's your price?'

'Big Mac large meal, apple pie, and coffee.'

'But what if you can't help me?'

'Then you'll have made an old man happy, won't you.'

'Old man! You can't be much older than me.'

'You try sleeping outdoors all year round and see how young you feel.'

'Point taken.'

'Sorry, love. It's been a rough day trying to get somewhere proper to stay sorted. They keep bouncing me from one department to another.'

'I'll get your dinner. Back soon.'
'I ain't going nowhere.'

Trevor tucked into his burger, taking a huge bite and chewing with enthusiasm. He swallowed, then washed it down with a gulp of coffee. 'So, what do you want to know?'

Beatrice lowered herself to the floor, resting her back against the shop wall. 'Were you in town Monday night?'

'I'm always here, as long as the police don't lock me up.'

'That happen often?'

'No. Most of them are alright. A bloody nuisance if they've been told to clear the area, but, if you cooperate and don't cause a fuss, they just move you on. They don't want the hassle of arresting anyone. Too much paperwork.'

'I'm interested in the early hours. Between three and five.'

'I've been in this spot every night for the last week or so. I can't think of anything. What you after?'

'A motorbike. Possibly driving with lights off, maybe going too fast.'

'Hit and run?'

'No, something else.'

'I tell you what,' Trevor scratched his chin, crumbs falling from his beard. 'I was talking to Danny yesterday. He was complaining about someone driving fast the other night. The noise woke him up.'

'Danny?'

'He's another one, like me.'

'How do I find him?'

'His usual spot is by the Waterside, where Broadgate crosses the river. There's no cloud tonight, so it'll get cold. He'll probably be tucked up under Scott's Bridge.'

'I know Waterside. Which bridge is it?'

'Stay this side of the Witham, but turn to your right. The footbridge over Broadgate is Scott's bridge. He's probably settled for the night already. He likes the quiet. He won't mind you disturbing him if you give him food and drink.'

'Thanks, Trevor.

'Tell him I sent you. That and some nosh should help loosen his tongue.'

Beatrice arrived at the bridge, but couldn't see anyone initially, though the area was fairly well lit. Then she made out, in deep shadow, what appeared to be a pile of blankets tucked into the corner created by two buildings. She approached slowly.

'Hello? Danny?' She spoke at the bundle. When there was no response she reached out, hesitantly. As her hand touched the pile, a large, dark figure exploded from it. She stepped back, startled.

'Who the bloody hell are you?' The voice bellowed at her, followed by a hacking cough. He wiped the back of his hand across his mouth.

'Trevor sent me.'

'Why didn't you bloody well say so in the first place? Frightening me half to death.'

As her heart rate settled back down, Beatrice could see Danny's grubby face and matted hair. A pervasive odour radiated several feet. Beatrice tried not to gag when it hit her nostrils.

'I brought you this.' She held the bag of food at arm's length.

Danny stared at it, appraising, then snatched it from her. He opened the bag and sniffed. She was surprised his nose still worked.

'Thanks,' he grunted.

He hobbled back to the nest of cloth and plonked himself down. Whilst he rummaged in the bag, she placed the coffee on the floor next to him and stepped back.

'Why've you got me this then? I expect you want something.'

'I saw Trevor earlier, and he said you might like some.'

'Like he cares.'

'He said you'd had a rough time the other night. Disturbed

by a lot of noise, in the early hours. He thought you could do with something to make up for it.'

Danny grunted and chewed his food open-mouthed.

'What was it?'

'What was what?' Danny picked up the cup, pulled the lid off and slurped the hot coffee.

'The noise that woke you.'

'Don't suppose you thought to get any sugar, did you?'

Beatrice pulled several packets out of her pocket and threw them over to him.

Danny emptied three into the drink, and used his grubby finger to stir it. 'It was some idiot zooming about like a racing driver. Made a right racket.'

'Where was it?'

'Sounded like it was going up Broadgate.'

'Towards the top of the hill?'

'Yeah. Went up there, then came back down again a few minutes later.'

'Could you tell if it was a car or motorbike?'

'No.'

Beatrice was disappointed. It wasn't a confirmed sighting, though it could have been the arsonist.

'Course, it didn't come all the way back down.' Danny popped the last chip into his mouth and drained the coffee cup. He began settling himself back under his pile of blankets.

'Do you know where it went?'

'I think it stopped before it crossed the river again. Hard to tell though.' Danny was almost completely cocooned in blankets now, only his face showing in the reflected streetlights. 'Next time you come, bring something a bit stronger to drink.' He turned away from her.

Beatrice picked up the empty fast-food bag, collected the rubbish, and disposed of it in the nearest bin. She then crossed the footbridge to Broadgate, where Danny thought the bike had stopped. Susan had mentioned stolen bikes. It made sense that an arsonist wouldn't worry about committing theft. But what would they do with it afterwards? She knew cars got burnt out by joyriders, but a burnt-out bike would have been reported. Presumably he'd dump it where it wouldn't be found too quickly. The longer the time between the fire and the bike being found, the less likely the two things were to be connected. Which meant hiding it where it wouldn't seem out of place. She turned down Saint Rumbold's Street, walked a short way, and stopped outside Broadgate car park.

Beatrice resolved to walk the whole car park if needed. With no one else around, she pulled her phone out of her bag, thinking it would be a good idea to have Susan's number ready to call. She'd helped Beatrice out of a tricky situation in the past.

There weren't many vehicles using the place overnight. On the first floor she reached the dedicated motorcycle bays. There were two bikes. One had a seizure warning notice placed on it for unpaid parking. The other had a ticket displayed, it expired in a week. Using her phone torch, Beatrice could see the ticket was purchased in the early hours of Monday morning. She called Susan.

'Beatrice. I didn't expect to hear from you so soon.' Susan yawned. 'What's up?'

'I may have found the motorbike.'

'Where?'

'Broadgate car park.'

'What makes you think it's the one we want?'

'I had a lead.'

'And you found a motorbike.'

'Two actually. One has been here a while and is due to be impounded. The other, the one I'm calling about, was parked here at 3.45 a.m. on the morning the Golden Goose was destroyed.'

'Give me the registration. I'll check with the station and call you back. Stay put.'

Chapter 13

Thursday 21st June

Beatrice yawned as she sat down at her desk, with a large mug of coffee. It had been a late night. Susan had called her back, asking her to wait until the police arrived. It had taken almost an hour for a pair of uniformed constables to join her. They took a brief statement before letting her go. She'd managed a few hours of sleep, but with her work, and her mother, constantly running through her mind, she'd given up on a lie-in, and decided to get on with the day.

Her call to the Browns was uncomfortable, but using the insurance company as leverage, she'd been able to persuade Zoe to meet with her that morning. In planning her journey, she allowed time for checking at the petrol stations on the way to Spilsby. It was the route the biker had taken, so there was a good chance he'd bought the fuel for the fires on the way.

Thinking about the search for Lily, Andrew was her best bet. Going to Norwich hadn't helped much: maybe he would. The question on her mind was whether to phone, or turn up at his address on spec, and interview him in person. It was usually better to talk face to face, gauge reactions and assess someone's truthfulness, but London was a long way to go on the off chance he'd be in. If she had a date to visit London, to see Simon Atkinson, she could make it a worthwhile trip. She decided to wait until the end of the day, to see what the solicitor would do about her threat.

On her way to Spilsby, Beatrice stopped at the garage on the main road, the A158. Under cover of topping up fuel in her car and going in to pay, she checked with the man operating the till. He'd heard about the fires, and took great pleasure telling her the police had been to review the CCTV. When Beatrice asked if they found anything, he lost interest. She concluded they'd had no luck. However, it was reassuring the police had been there. She'd have to ask Susan what they'd found.

Beatrice was seated in the brewery office. 'Thanks for agreeing to see me again.'

'We're happy to help.' Zoe's tone suggested otherwise. 'The insurance company told us they'd hired you. I don't know why they don't leave it to the police.'

Gareth grunted. He was standing at the window, staring out, his back to Beatrice. 'I was about to go out when you called.'

Zoe glanced towards him, her lips narrowed and her nostrils widened slightly. She turned back to Beatrice. 'What do you need?'

'Firstly, a list of current and previous employees.'

Zoe nodded.

'And I want to go to the brewery site and talk to the staff there.'

Gareth spun around. 'Why?'

'Because they might know something useful.'

'Like what?' he barked.

Beatrice paused. She carefully kept her voice even. 'Probably nothing, but I can't tell in advance what will be useful and what won't be.'

'Rubbish! They think we're responsible, don't they? The insurers.' Gareth became louder. 'They sent you here to investigate us, didn't they? Go on admit it. They think we'd destroy our own business. Can't they see we're going to lose everything? Why would we do that to ourselves?'

'Gareth, please.' Zoe's voice contained a warning. Her

husband threw her an angry glare, and returned to the window, arms folded.

'For what it's worth, I told them I thought you had nothing to do with it. You could always give them a call. I just want to stop there being another fire, by finding out who is doing this.' She waited a moment, to see if there would be a further outburst. The Browns both remained silent. 'Your business is being targeted, either because it's yours, or because of something to do with the business itself. To find out who and why, I need to understand it better.'

'We're a brewery,' said Zoe. 'I really can't see why anyone would want to destroy it like this.' Her head drooped and she emitted a loud sob.

Beatrice saw Gareth's shoulders stiffen at the sound, but he made no effort to comfort his wife. She reached for the box of tissues on the desk, and handed them to Zoe, who pulled one out and blew her nose.

Beatrice returned to her seat, wondering if there was more going on between the couple than the collapse of their livelihood.

'I'm sorry.' Zoe wiped her nose with the tissue, then tucked it into her sleeve.

'It's fine,' said Beatrice. 'Is there anyone you can think of, who might want to hurt one of you? Maybe who you've disagreed with, either in your personal or professional life, or who might imagine they had some reason to be angry with you?'

Zoe cast a quick glance at Gareth. 'No. Before we started the brewery, we were both employed. I was a sales manager, Gareth a company accountant. We left our jobs willingly, to start the business. There were no hard feelings on either side. No fallouts.' Zoe was bewildered. 'I genuinely can't think of anyone we've worked with who'd want to hurt either of us.'

'OK,' said Beatrice, not dismissing the idea of investigating the Browns themselves. 'Then it must be because of the business itself. Which makes it all the more important I speak to the staff, past and present, and find out as much about your operation as I can.'

'Very well.' Zoe walked slowly to the door. 'Come with me.'

It was clear to Beatrice the woman was exhausted. She followed her into the open plan reception area, where the secretary's desk was situated. The young, attractive woman looked up.

'This is Beatrice,' said Zoe. 'Please give her a list of employees, past and present. All the pub staff too.'

'It'll take about an hour,' said the secretary. 'Do you want paper or email?'

'Both, please,' said Beatrice.

'No problem. I'll get right onto it.'

'Thank you,' said Beatrice. 'I'll use the time to go over to the brewery, and call in again later.'

Zoe sighed. 'I'll give Robert, the manager, a ring and let him know you're coming.'

'Thanks for your help, Zoe. I promise I'll do everything I can to stop this happening.'

'The trouble is, it may already be too late.' Zoe turned and walked away. At the entrance to the office she shared with Gareth, she paused and lifted her chin, as if steeling herself for confrontation, then she entered and closed the door behind her.

Beatrice's eyes shifted to the secretary, who had also been watching Zoe. The young woman shook her head slightly, before turning back to realise she was being watched. She gave Beatrice a brief smile, then busied herself with papers on her desk.

Outside the brewery, Beatrice called Susan.

'I wondered when I'd hear from you,' said Susan. 'You can't think we've found out anything yet.'

'I assumed Lincolnshire's number one detective would be on the case first thing.'

'Well, I need my beauty sleep. I'm not the one with a hunk at home already. Besides, it takes time.'

'Can you at least tell me if it's the bike used the other night?'

'We don't know for certain, but it's a good match for the CCTV images. By the way, we traced the second motorbike you found. It was stolen on the night of the previous fire. It's possible our arsonist used it. We've had them both checked for fingerprints.'

'They aren't likely to lead you to a suspect though, are they?'

'It depends,' said Susan. 'If we find a match to someone already known to us, we can at least ask questions about why their dabs are on the bike. We've contacted the owners to get prints for elimination and asked who had legitimate access. They're both parked on the street overnight, which makes any match weaker, but, with any luck, there'll only be one set which is on both bikes. Whoever our man is will have to have an impressive explanation as to why prints are on both, when they're normally parked a couple of miles from each other.'

'What if they're not in the police system? Or wore gloves?'

'We can collect the evidence and we'll have to try other ways to identify him. We've also been able to narrow down the times when they were stolen. We're going through localised CCTV footage. It gives us another possible way of finding him. To be honest, we're pinning our hopes on him being a repeat offender and careless.'

'Is it likely?'

'The fire investigator says our man has experience. These aren't his first attempts at arson, so there's a reasonable chance he's been caught before, even if not for fires. We know he's a thief, after all. If he was confident the bikes wouldn't be connected to the fires, he might not have worn gloves when he touched the wiring to get them to start.'

'How long will it take?'

'Who knows? Forensics are dealing with them both now.

The sergeant's been reading the riot act, saying they have to prioritise possible threats to life, so they might get results to us soon.' Susan paused before continuing. 'I've only told you all this, because you found the bikes. Do not let on to anyone, that you know anything about it.'

'I'm hardly going to get you into trouble, am I?'

'I hope not.' Susan didn't sound confident.

'Any luck on the fuel?'

'No. Nothing there.'

'If you find the guy, will you let me know? I need to ask him if the Browns had anything to do with the fires.'

'We'll be interested in that too. You can be sure we'll be asking the right questions.'

'But I won't get to hear the answers, will I? I need something to take to my employers.'

'Let's cross that bridge if we get to it.'

Chapter 14

Beatrice walked over to the light-industrial estate on the edge of town. Outside the brewery, there were a couple of large delivery vans and a smaller van advertising a farm shop in Lincoln.

A man in dark blue, overalls came out of the building, accompanied by a grey-haired man in baggy stained trousers and an outsized jumper dotted with holes. The first man nodded at the other. 'Thanks, Neil. See you soon.'

'Right enough. Perhaps we can take longer next time.' The older man walked away and got into the farm shop van.

The overalled man turned to Beatrice. 'Can I help you?'

'Are you Robert? I'm Beatrice Styles.'

'Oh, yes. The detective.' His eyes narrowed and he slipped something into his trouser pocket. 'I'm Robert Jones, manager here. I'm supposed to give you a tour and answer your questions.'

'I'd appreciate it.'

'Come on.' He held the door open for her, standing so he was partly blocking the way. Beatrice had to squeeze past and found herself shuddering as her arm brushed against him. Once they were both inside, Robert closed it firmly behind them and locked it.

Beatrice paused at the uncomfortable sound of the lock.

'Don't worry,' he said. 'It's to stop kids getting in. They think it's fun to steal beer. Idiots. Back when we were trying open fermentation, a couple of them got in. They came prepared with a bottle, stuck it in the tank, filled it and ran off laughing.'

'You saw them?'

'Oh, yes.'

'Too quick, were they?'

'No. I didn't bother chasing them.'

Beatrice frowned, puzzled.

Robert smirked. 'By the time they'd polished off the bottle of unfermented beer they'd have learnt a valuable lesson. Plenty of time to regret stealing, sitting on the loo.'

'Right.' It seemed cruel and Beatrice hoped the lads hadn't suffered too badly. 'You didn't call the police?'

'Waste of time. We keep the place locked now. There's a bell for visitors.'

'That man who just left, I saw his van was advertising a farm shop.'

'Neil specialises in organic meat: he does a good steak.'

'What's the connection with the brewery?'

'I'll show you on the tour.'

The main door opened into a small vestibule, from where a second door led to a large room with high ceilings. The nondescript outside of the building didn't hint at what lay inside.

'Impressive, isn't it?' said Robert, close by her ear.

Beatrice nodded, stepping away from him. The room was painted white, with a bright blue floor. There were large silver tanks, gleaming and shining. Coils of pipes and hoses of different colours were hanging on the walls, and others snaked across the floor connecting various tanks. A high-level walkway was built around the room, allowing access to the tops of the containers.

'Be careful where you walk,' Robert warned. 'We don't want you tripping up and hurting yourself, do we? I'd never see the end of the forms.' He laughed.

Robert gave Beatrice a tour of the room, explaining the brewing process. They started at the milling machines, moved on to the mashing urns, then the boiling and fermentation tanks. When Robert began talking about the maturation process, cask conditioning, and flavours and aroma, Beatrice began to zone out, all the while being aware of how close he was standing, in such a large space. When he finally stopped talking, there was a moment of silence, and she grasped frantically for something to say.

'You said you'd explain the farm shop connection.'

'Oh, yeah. Well, they sell our more exclusive brews in their shop. Plus, once we've mashed the grain, we run off the sweet wort…' Robert peered at Beatrice's puzzled expression. 'The wort is the liquid we get from boiling the grain. But the grains have done their job, so we don't need them anymore. They make good animal feed though: lots of nutrition. Neil buys our used grains and feeds them to his livestock. Reduces waste.'

'Is it worth much?'

'No. We produce about three tonnes a week, and if Neil didn't send his lads to collect it, we'd have to pay to dispose of it. I think Gareth charges Neil a nominal amount, peanuts really, but it gets it off our hands.'

Beatrice considered for a moment. Her tax inspector self was wondering about opportunities for money on the side. She hadn't forgotten Robert's reaction when he realised who she was, or how he had slipped something into his pocket. Maybe I'm too suspicious, she thought. Old habits die hard. Besides, Neil hadn't collected waste grain in his shop van, so why was he there? 'Any other similar waste products?'

'No. Nothing. Our other main waste is used water, but that goes down the drain. The big breweries in America are looking into using it to remove nitrogen in water treatment plants. There's even talk of fish food and biogas from brewery waste. We're small scale though.'

Beatrice nodded.

'Come see the stock room.' He walked off, and after a last glance around the brewing room, she followed.

It was larger than she'd expected. On one side were empty

bottles, casks and kegs. On the other were the finished and labelled products. There were at least half a dozen different types of beer.

'This isn't our full range. Just what we're getting ready to go out. By the time the next batches are ready, this lot will have been delivered to the pubs and shops.' He frowned. 'Or would have been. Don't know what's going to happen now, with three pubs out of action.'

'Do you label on the premises?'

'Yes. This way.' He tipped his head in the direction of the other doorway.

Beatrice followed into what appeared to be a hybrid of an office and packing room.

'We label here. It's what Frankie has been doing this morning. We print them off ourselves, as we need them.' He indicated a large, floor-standing printer.

Robert walked over to the tall, thin man who was hunched over a computer. A spreadsheet, dense with figures and dates, was displayed. The muscles in his neck were taut.

'This is Frankie,' said Robert.

Frankie's fingers paused over the keyboard for a second before typing in a number.

'He's monitoring production stages,' continued Robert. 'To make sure we move things on at the right time.'

'Isn't it the same process over and over?' asked Beatrice.

'Depends on what we're brewing. How long we run each stage makes a difference to the flavour and aroma of the beer. Like the amount of kilning the barley gets, or the quantity of hops we add. It all makes a difference.'

'How do you decide which type of beer to brew?'

'Oh, that's Zoe's job. She monitors stock levels and what sells. At the start of every month, we meet, and she tells us what we need. It changes from time to time, but we're pretty well organised.'

'What's that door over there?' Beatrice asked, indicating across the room.

'An office, for admin. Nothing important.'

Beatrice walked over to the door and opened it. The room was small, with a desk, filing cabinet and two chairs. On the desk were four bottles of beer. Two were open. It seemed she'd interrupted something. 'Is there anything else to see?'

Robert was behind her, shifting his weight from side to side. 'No.'

Beatrice glanced at her watch. 'I'd better be going. If I have more questions, I'll pop back.'

'Better call first,' said Robert, as he led her back towards the way out.

'Thanks for the tour.'

He grunted and shut the door firmly behind her. The lock sounded loud as it clicked into place and Beatrice was glad to be on the outside of it.

As she walked back towards the brewery office, Beatrice's phone vibrated. She pulled out her mobile, peering at the screen in the bright light. It was from Simon Atkinson's firm. Beatrice braced herself for the conversation.

'Ms Styles, I'm calling from Atkinson and Atkinson.'

'Hello.'

'I gave Mr Atkinson your message, and he has asked me to make an appointment with you. We're looking at next month.'

'It needs to be sooner. How about tomorrow?'

'Let me see what I can do.'

There was a short pause and the sound of a mumbled conversation.

'I can squeeze you in for half an hour at ten o'clock. He has another meeting straight afterwards.'

'I can manage that. Thank you.'

'You're welcome. We'll see you tomorrow.'

Beatrice stowed the mobile back in her bag. She was pleased to have the appointment confirmed, but wasn't looking forward to what would probably be a confrontation. She'd speak to the solicitor first, then Andrew Taylor.

Back at the brewery office, the information was ready for Beatrice.

'Here you are.' The secretary handed her a folder. 'The employees with both a start and finish date no longer work for us.'

Beatrice flicked through the pages. 'There's a lot of them.'

'It's the pub staff. We get a lot of part-time, temporary and short-term workers, and we take on extra staff for the summer months. Some of them come back year after year, and I've put a star next to those.'

'That's really helpful, thank you,' said Beatrice.

'No problem.'

'How's Zoe?'

'Worried I guess.'

'Is everything alright between her and Gareth?'

The woman's face stiffened. 'Is there anything else I can help you with? With respect to the employees?'

'No, thanks.'

The secretary turned back to her computer; all her earlier openness gone. If all was well between the couple, wouldn't the previously friendly and helpful woman have simply shrugged it off? During her meeting with them, she'd sensed tension between Zoe and Gareth. The question was whether it was related to the business and the stress caused by the fires, or whether it was something else.

Chapter 15

Friday 22nd June

It was another sunny day, and the walk through London in the warm weather meant Beatrice was overheating when she arrived at the solicitor's office. She'd barely sat down to gather her thoughts when the receptionist said, 'Mr Atkinson can see you now.'

The solicitor was a tall, stocky man with greying hair. He stood when she entered, and came around his desk.

'Hello, Beatrice. Do you mind if I call you that?'

Though taken aback, Beatrice stammered out her agreement. 'No. It's fine.' If he expected by being informal, she would go easy on him, he'd soon realise he was mistaken.

'Call me Simon. Please, take a seat.'

They sat on low chairs, with a coffee table between them.

Beatrice took the initiative. 'I came here…'

'I knew your parents,' he interrupted. 'They often talked about you and Rosie. I suppose it's why I find it easier to think of you as Beatrice. Ms Styles seems inappropriate.'

'I never heard them mention you.'

'I was one of many people they worked with, and perhaps wasn't as significant to them, as they were to me.'

'What do you mean?'

'I first met them when I was a trainee solicitor, specialising in drawing up contracts and representation in contract disputes. Once I'd worked with them a few times, they began to recommend me, and I found a lot of work through them. Without their support, I don't think I'd have progressed as well as I have. When I started working in central London, we began to socialise and got to know each another better. I was very sorry indeed to hear of your father's death.'

Beatrice remained silent for a moment. It was significant he didn't mention her mother's disappearance in the same sentence. Was it because he knew something, or because he was profiting off managing her affairs?

Simon shifted in his seat.

When Beatrice thought he was about to speak, she deliberately spoke first. 'You weren't at Dad's memorial service. I would have remembered.' It had been a strange experience. Her father's body hadn't been recovered from the mountains where he'd been skiing, and without it, the service seemed unreal. Beatrice hadn't been able to express her grief, and her mother had been oddly detached. It had been so surreal, it was etched into her mind.

'No,' said Simon. He crossed and then uncrossed his legs. 'I was out of the country at the time.'

'So,' said Beatrice. 'You've been handling my mother's affairs.'

The solicitor straightened up. 'That's correct.'

'I saw from my father's will you were appointed executor, so it makes sense you would act for Mum too. But I checked. You haven't applied to the Courts for Guardianship, and she's still officially missing, not dead. So, I'd like to know on what basis you thought it was appropriate to make payments to Rosie and me.'

'Was the money unwelcome?'

'That's not the point.'

'Isn't it? Surely you, or at least Rosie, could usefully use additional funds?'

Beatrice paused. Was it a generic statement? After all most people would welcome ten thousand pounds. Or did it have knowledge behind it? Rosie had been struggling and stressing over money, and the cheque had arrived at a fortuitous time, despite the marriage difficulties it had exposed. She cleared her throat. 'Unless her body is found, or she's declared dead, the money belongs to Mum. What legal right do you have to do anything with it?'

'I knew your parents well enough to know they wouldn't have wanted you and Rosie to need money, and for theirs to be sitting uselessly in a bank.'

Beatrice lent forward, making direct eye contact. 'What makes you think we needed the money?'

The silence stretched. Beatrice wondered if he'd realised he'd said too much, and was working out how to backtrack. If he knew about Rosie's difficulties, how did he know? Was he monitoring their lives in some way?

'Doesn't everyone need money these days,' Simon finally answered.

Beatrice's mind was whirring with possibilities, but he'd successfully deflected her earlier question.

'You haven't told me what legal authority you had to make the payments.'

'I'm sorry, Beatrice, but I can't give you private information. She may be your mother, but she is still entitled to confidentiality.'

Beatrice sat back in her seat and glanced out of the window. The sky had clouded over. 'So, we're no further forward than we were before.' She sighed. 'Why did you agree to see me, if you'd already decided not to tell me anything?'

'I haven't "decided". It's legally protected information. My professional status requires I maintain client confidentiality.' He hesitated before continuing. 'I thought meeting you in person would be easier, and I could convince you I was following your parents' wishes. I considered them friends, Beatrice. I wouldn't do anything I honestly didn't believe they wouldn't have wanted.'

'You thought you'd fob me off.'

'No. Not at all.'

'Are you going to explain how what you have done is legal?'

'I have no choice. I can't.'

'Right.' Beatrice stood up and gathered her belongings. 'And you've left *me* no choice.' Her voice waivered and she waited a moment to steady herself. 'This isn't the end of it. I promise I will not be leaving it like this.'

Simon stood up as well, disappointed, but resigned. 'What are you going to do?'

'Whatever I have to.' Beatrice stared at him for several seconds, a last hope that he would relent, but he remained silent. She nodded her head and left the room, closing the door behind her with a soft click.

What was she going to do? Her mind and emotions were all over the place. On leaving the solicitor's office, Beatrice had set off without much thought for where she was going, anger and disappointment spurring her on. Now, she stepped to the side of the path and stood with her back against the wall of a building, to give herself time to think. Crowds of hurrying Londoners streamed past her. She noticed a coffee shop on the opposite side of the road. A good place to rest and put her thoughts in order.

Inside the café, the constant noise of traffic turned into a background hum. She waited patiently in the queue for her turn, enjoying the sense of calm the muted colours and soft furnishings of the shop generated.

'Sorry.'

The man behind Beatrice had bumped into her, as he'd moved out of the way of the opening shop door. She turned to look at him and automatically returned his smile. A little shorter than her, he had dark, wavy hair and warm, hazel eyes. His stubble gave him an attractive and relaxed air. He looked like a man who laughed easily.

'Next, please.'

She stepped up to the counter. 'Medium white Americano, extra shot, please. To drink in.'

Whilst she waited for her coffee to be prepared, the man

from the queue ordered his to go, then stood next to her. They exchanged smiles again.

When it was ready, Beatrice took her coffee to the last free table, in the corner of the room. As she sipped at her drink, she thought back over the conversation with Simon Atkinson. Had she really expected a different outcome? If she was being honest with herself, then no. But she had hoped for something. What did she know now that she didn't before? Simon's explanation of how he knew her parents was feasible, but it was odd they'd never talked about him. Her parents must have trusted him, enough to give him financial responsibility, at least.

'Bye.'

Beatrice glanced up at the interruption. It was the man from the queue again. 'Oh, bye,' she said, puzzled. People in London weren't usually so friendly.

She returned to ruminating on her meeting. Could Atkinson have been lying? Perhaps her parents didn't know him at all. Apart from being executor, she only had his word that he'd known them.

He'd certainly tried to use their supposed relationship to manipulate her into not asking questions. Was it reasonable though, for him to expect her to give up because of a friendship he said he had with them? He couldn't be that naive. So, what was the point of arranging a futile meeting? Was there another reason he'd wanted her here?

Beatrice sighed and drained her cup. She'd call Vanessa. Maybe the police would ask questions, and actually get answers. There was also the Law Society, which Atkinson must be a member of, but she'd give Vanessa a chance first.

Glancing at her watch, she saw there were several hours before she'd be able to meet Andrew, Lily's brother, at the end of his working day. A ten-minute walk away, there was an art gallery she used to visit regularly and hadn't been to since she'd moved out of London. She'd have a slow wander, appreciating the art, get lunch, maybe do some shopping. It would take her mind off her mother. She'd ring Vanessa later, when she was feeling more in control and less emotional.

On the way to the gallery, her phone rang.

'Beatrice? It's Charles Sharpe. I want to know if you've found anything out yet?'

'I've done preliminary work and ordered documents. General background. I plan on seeing Andrew next.'

'Good. I'll phone him, tell him to talk to you.'

'I'd prefer it if you didn't.'

'Why?' He spoke abruptly.

'I know you said you were confident Andrew doesn't know where Lily is, but he is her brother, and only relative. I'm not convinced she'd cut off all contact with him. Even if he doesn't know where she is, he may have a means of communication, which is what you need, for your solicitors. I don't want him to know I'm coming, so he can be prepared. I want to catch him off guard, to get the truth.'

There was a brief silence.

'Perhaps I chose the right investigator, after all. Though I think you could have told me you were coming to Norwich the other day.'

'Where Lily was last seen was the obvious place to start.'

'Maybe. But I thought you'd keep me informed. I could have been here to talk to you.'

'Was there anything else you wanted to tell me?'

'No.'

'I said I'd update you weekly, and I will.'

'I suppose I'm keen for you to make progress.'

'I understand, but I'm afraid this kind of investigation can take a long time. Especially when the trail is cold.'

'Fine.'

'I…'

He rang off, leaving Beatrice nonplussed, and wondering how he'd known she'd been to Norwich.

Chapter 16

Beatrice watched Andrew Taylor unlock the door to the building and slip inside. She'd found his employment address online, using the profile he'd set up on a website for connecting business people. After deciding against a confrontation at his work, she'd followed him from there, along the bustling, noisy London streets.

At the door to the building, Beatrice examined the labels for the flats. Most were faded, and difficult to read. Flat 33 had a handwritten scrawl next to it, which could have said 'A Taylor'. If she used the intercom system, he might not agree to speak to her.

She was reaching for the handle, in case the lock hadn't engaged fully, when inside, a young woman approached the door and mirrored her movements. Beatrice grabbed the door as it swung open and put on a surprised expression. 'Oh, sorry. I didn't see you there.' She held the door wide open for the other woman to pass out.

'Thanks.'

'No problem.'

The woman paused. 'Who are you here for?'

'Andrew Taylor.'

'Oh. OK then. You can't be too careful.'

'Absolutely.' Beatrice's conscience pricked a little, and she made sure the door locked firmly behind her, after all, one trespasser was enough.

Flat 33 seemed like the best place to start. It was one of four on the third floor, suggesting sixteen flats in total. Not too many if she had to go door to door. She pressed the doorbell, hearing it chime inside. The door opened. The man who answered stepped back in surprise. He was a tired, older version of the picture she'd seen online, bearing little resemblance to Lily. He was shorter than average, and thin.

'Hi. You must be Andrew,' said Beatrice.

'Who are you?'

She gave him a business card. 'I'm here about Lily. I have some questions. It'll only take a few minutes.'

'Lily's not here.'

'Can I come in?'

A neighbour came out of his flat. As he locked the door, he stole repeated glances at Beatrice and Andrew.

'We can do it here if you like.' Beatrice spoke loudly.

'Fine, come in,' Andrew sighed.

'Thanks.' She followed him inside, into a cramped hallway which had three doors leading off it: all closed.

Andrew pointed at one. 'In there,' he said, waiting for her to go ahead.

The room was an open-plan living space. It contained a small kitchenette, a two-person dining table, and a carpeted living area, with barely enough room for a two-seater sofa, which Andrew pointed at. 'You can sit there.'

Beatrice sat, whilst Andrew stood next to the door.

'How did you know where I live?'

'I followed you from work. You weren't at the address I was given.'

He frowned. 'Given by who?'

'Charles Sharpe.'

Andrew became still. Judging from the way his eyes were moving rapidly, his mind was working overtime, and his head was slightly tilted, as if there was something on his left he was trying not to look at.

'How did you know where I work?'

'I found you online. And one of the guys at your last place said he thought you still worked there.'

'You wanted to talk about Lily.'

Beatrice nodded.

'Well, I haven't seen or heard from her since she went missing. I'm not going through all this again.' He filled the kettle with water, enough for only one cup, and moved to stand in front of the fridge. He leant back against it. Beatrice's attention was drawn to the postcards stuck to its surface, the opposite effect to the one she suspected he'd intended. The edges of several postcards poked out from behind him, and her fingers were itching to touch them.

'When's the last time you saw Lily?'

'About fifteen months ago.'

'Where?'

'Norwich. She wanted me to meet the baby. Couldn't see the fascination myself.'

'What did you do there?'

He shrugged. 'We had lunch at the house, then took the baby out for a walk.'

'Was Charles around?'

'Yes.'

Beatrice waited.

'He was there for lunch, then went back to work whilst we went out.'

'How did Lily seem?'

'Fine. Normal.'

'Was she happy being a mum?'

'Seemed to be.'

'And what did you think of Charles? He's quite a bit older than her.'

Andrew shrugged. 'He's a nice man.' It was said without conviction. 'I didn't really see her much, once she got together with him. You know what it's like. She got wrapped up in her new relationship. I was surprised, to be honest, when she phoned and invited me to visit.'

'I understand you and Lily lived in Lincolnshire for a while.'

'When we were kids.'

Andrew suddenly moved across to the kettle, his back to Beatrice. She could see the muscles in his shoulders were taut. He flicked the switch and spent time making a drink. Beatrice saw him instinctively reach across to the fridge, presumably for milk, but he stopped himself.

He really was poor at deflecting her attention from those postcards. 'Where in Lincolnshire?'

'I can't remember.'

'You must have an idea.'

'We were young.'

'You're what, five years older than Lily? Old enough to be taught your address, in case you got lost. You must remember the name of the town or village?'

Andrew sipped his drink and Beatrice saw him wince at the lack of milk. She needed him out of the room, to get at the postcards. Andrew was dismissive and hadn't expressed any concern for Lily's safety. He must know something. 'Perhaps you have an address, or old photos with distinctive landmarks.' She hoped he'd take the opening.

Andrew stared at her. 'I keep papers in the bedroom.' He turned and left the room.

Beatrice heard him open then close one of the other hallway doors. She darted across to the fridge. There were about twenty postcards, the pictures were abstract drawings, rather than locations. She picked one off, at random, and read the back.

'Hope you're OK. We're both fine. Settling in.'

She read several more, listening out for Andrew's return.

'Went to see our old friend. Not doing well.'

'Often thinking about when we were young these days. Good memories.'

'We went to the beach last week. Enjoyed the whole day. Looking forward to seeing you. Miss you.'

Andrew snatched the card from Beatrice's hands. 'What the hell do you think you're doing?' His voice was raised and he was breathing hard.

He wasn't physically intimidating to Beatrice, but he was angry, unpredictable. She raised her hands between them, showing her palms.

He stepped back, seeming to realise he was too close. 'I didn't say you could snoop. Those are private.'

'Where's Lily, Andrew?'

'I told you, I don't know.'

'I don't believe you. What about these?' She indicated the postcards. 'They're from Lily, aren't they?'

'No! From an ex-girlfriend.'

'And you keep in touch?' Beatrice allowed scepticism in her tone.

'I don't have to talk to you. Leave. Or… Or I'll call the police.'

She wondered what explanation she'd be able to give the police, if he decided to carry out his threat. 'I'll leave. Of course, I'll have to include this in my report to Charles.' She let the silence hang, suspecting he had a reason not to displease her client.

Andrew's breathing returned to normal, as he thought about her words. 'I found this.' He thrust a scrap of paper at her. 'I don't see why it would help. She's no reason to go back there.'

Beatrice accepted the paper he offered. It had been torn off a larger piece and had a street name in Fiskerton: a village she'd heard of, but couldn't place. She surreptitiously rubbed the writing on the page. The still-wet ink smudged. It was possible he'd copied the address across, but she thought it more likely he'd made it up, to throw her off track. It's what she would have done. 'Did Lily have any close friends? Ones she'd keep in touch with?'

'Not that I know of. We led pretty separate lives.'

'What was she like?'

Andrew looked at her in confusion.

'Did she have any hobbies or things she liked to do?'

He shrugged. 'The usual. Going out. Cinema and bars.

Before the baby, though.' He poured the remains of his drink down the sink. 'Is that it?'

'For now.' Interested in his reaction, she said, 'You won't get your hopes up about me finding Lily, will you? After all this time it's not likely to happen.' She may have been mistaken, but Andrew appeared relieved.

'I'll show you out.'

At the flat entrance, Beatrice paused. 'Can I have your phone number? So I can let you know if there's progress.'

He paused, as though he was going to refuse, but perhaps the thought of Charles changed his mind. She tapped the number directly into her phone and immediately sent him a text. The phone in his pocket buzzed. At least she knew it was correct. 'That's so you can call me, if you think of anything which might be useful.'

'Right.' He opened the door.

'One more thing. You said you didn't want to go through it all again. What did you mean?'

'I already talked with the last guy. It's pointless going over the same ground again. He couldn't find her, so why would you?'

Trying not to let the comment dent her confidence, she pursued the point. 'The last guy?'

'Yes. A detective, ex-police, I think. Charles paid him to find Lily a few weeks after she left. He got nowhere.'

'What was his name?'

'Can't remember. He was a local man though.'

'From Norwich?'

'Yeah.'

As Beatrice left the block of flats, she reflected on the conversation. Andrew knew something and she was sure the cards were from Lily. But why hadn't Charles told her about the other detective? Did he have something to hide?

Chapter 17

Beatrice checked the departures board. The train from Kings Cross to Newark Northgate was running twenty minutes late. She left the station and turned down a side street, off Euston Road. Finding a quiet spot, she called Vanessa again.

'Sergeant Holmes.'

'Vanessa. It's Beatrice.'

'Hi.'

'I'm in London. Can we meet? I'd really like to talk to you about Mum.'

'Where are you?'

'Kings Cross.'

'When's your train due?'

'I've got an open ticket.'

'I'm finishing up here. We could meet for a drink, if you don't mind delaying your return.'

'Thanks. Where?'

Vanessa gave her directions.

Standing at the bar, Beatrice had a clear view of Vanessa's arrival. She was average height, with short black hair, exactly as she remembered her. About forty-five years old, she moved with confidence through the crowded room, having spotted Beatrice above the heads of the other drinkers.

Vanessa grasped the proffered wine glass, taking a large swig. 'That's better. What a day!' She raised the glass in a salute. 'Thanks. I'll get the next one. Come on, let's go out back. It's quieter.'

Beatrice nodded and followed.

In the courtyard they found an empty table. They chatted amicably for a few minutes, but soon moved on to their reason for meeting. After her mother's disappearance, Beatrice had appreciated how Vanessa had treated her, always seeming to be direct, and not hiding the truth about the fruitless search, and the limits of what the police would do.

'How did it go? With the solicitor?'

'I got nothing.'

'Did you expect anything else?'

Beatrice sighed. 'Not really, but I thought it was worth trying. He wouldn't tell me anything, just said he couldn't break confidentiality.'

'Why not tell you that over the phone?'

'He's the one who suggested we meet face to face.' Beatrice shrugged. 'I was only there a matter of minutes. We didn't need to meet in person.' She sipped at her wine. 'He claimed he'd been good friends with Mum and Dad, and he'd known them for years.'

'Claimed?'

'I don't remember seeing him before, or my parents mentioning him, and he wasn't at the service we had for Dad.'

'You think he's lying?'

'I think he was probably exaggerating their relationship.'

'But why?' Vanessa mused.

'I did wonder if he was making more of it, so I'd trust him, and take his word for it that he's done nothing wrong.'

'Well, he clearly knows nothing about you.' Vanessa laughed. 'What's your next move?'

'Is there anything the police can do?'

'We don't have much to go on.'

'Mum's still missing. Her body hasn't been found.' Tears welled up in Beatrice's eyes, and she picked up the wine glass to cover her reaction, draining its contents. As she stared at the table, Vanessa placed a hand on her forearm.

'Sorry,' said Beatrice.

'Don't be. You should know you don't have to apologise

to me.' She squeezed Beatrice's arm gently.

'What's all this then? Have I been replaced?'

Beatrice looked up to see a blonde woman, in casual clothes. She wore an expression of shock, tainted only by a grin she couldn't suppress.

Vanessa chuckled, stood up, slipped her arm around the newcomer's waist and gave her a light kiss on the cheek. 'This is Jan, my girlfriend. Don't let her wind you up, she's not the jealous type.' Vanessa sat back down.

Jan pulled up a spare chair from another table and joined them. 'If I'm interrupting, I can come back later,' she said.

'We're nearly finished with work stuff,' said Vanessa. 'Why don't you get us a bottle, and yourself a glass. 'We'll be finished by the time you get back.'

'Actually,' said Beatrice. 'If I go now, I'll be in time for the next train.'

'Didn't you say you had an open return?' asked Vanessa.

'Yes.'

Vanessa glanced at Jan, who gave a small nod.

'Why don't you come out with us tonight, sleep on our sofabed – you should just about fit - and go home in the morning?'

Beatrice hesitated. She was tempted. She'd missed nights out in London. But James would be expecting her home.

'Go on,' urged Jan. 'You know you want to.'

Why not? She could pay the extra car parking, using her phone and could text James. 'OK, You're on.'

Jan stood up. 'Right, I'll go and get a bottle of red. You have five minutes to wrap up, then it's strictly off limits for the rest of the evening.'

'She means it,' said Vanessa. 'You were saying about your mum being officially missing.'

'Yes, so unless Mum left instructions, specifically authorising it, then he's paying out money without authority. Isn't it potentially theft or misappropriation of funds, or some potential crime?'

'As far as we know,' said Vanessa. 'He's not taken money for himself; he's given it to you and Rosie. I presume you're both beneficiaries of her will?'

'In the outdated copy I have. But,' Beatrice said, 'isn't that "as far as we know" pretty important? Wouldn't it be reasonable for the police to want to make sure everything is above board?'

'Excellent point.' Vanessa's attention moved to something behind Beatrice, who turned to look. Jan was on her way back. 'Leave it with me,' said Vanessa. 'I'll check into it.'

'Right,' said Jan, placing a bottle of wine firmly on the table. 'Work's over, it's time for a girl's night out.'

The landlords were out of town. The relief manager had gone to his girlfriend's for the night. I heard him arranging it. Careless. I was there, out of sight, watching him lock up and leave. I'd an hour to do what I needed, get back to confirm my alibi, and be out of the way when the fire started. Our tame arsonist knew to do what he was told.

I'd parked out back, waiting for ten minutes, to make sure no one else was around. Fortunately, the Browns had sacked the PI. When I was sure it was safe, I started work.

The body was heavy, though he'd been small in life. The plastic liners I'd used for wrapping would melt in the fire. Even if forensics could work out their type, they were a popular brand sold all over. There'd be no fingerprints or fibres to link him to where he died.

The obvious place to put the corpse was the cellar, where the fire would start. I could be certain the body would be burnt to a crisp before the fire brigade could get to it, even if they arrived quickly.

It only took a minute to pick the low-grade lock. They'd assumed the security would prevent a break-in. It didn't bother me though. I knew the alarm code from watching the relief guy open up, when I came to check the venue this morning. He'd been in a rush, finding a customer waiting.

I went back to the car, and heaved the body over my shoulder. Down in the cellar, I dropped him onto the concrete floor, hearing his head crack as it bounced on contact. It's not like he could feel it.

I checked he'd be in the way of the petrol, when it was poured in, then cut open the plastic sheeting and pulled it aside. I emptied the can of petrol I'd brought with me, on to the body. I needed to make sure he was thoroughly burnt. I couldn't tell our arsonist to add more fuel than usual. He'd wonder why. Satisfied the body was saturated, I left, and returned the "borrowed" car back to where I got it. I pulled off my gloves and walked away, into the shadows.

Chapter 18

Saturday 23rd June

The early call Beatrice received, whilst fast asleep on Vanessa's sofabed, from a DC at Nettleham police station, was a surprise. It was also unwelcome. The officer requested, or rather demanded, her presence for interview that afternoon. He'd been reluctant to tell her what it was about, but when she made it clear she'd no intention of turning up otherwise, he'd admitted it was about the arson attacks. The DC sounded relieved when she'd agreed to attend.

Scribbling a note to Vanessa and Jan, she left quietly. On the way to the train station, she made a detour to buy a large, strong coffee, in the hope it would ease her hangover.

Once home, she arranged to have dinner out with James, and confirmed their agreement to spend the whole of Sunday together. It went some way towards soothing his ruffled feathers, when he learnt not only had she stayed out all night, with nothing but a brief text, she was planning to devote the day to working.

Back in her home-office, Beatrice looked again at the news report she'd found online earlier. Written by Pete Evans, it was unusually short on information. What was clear, was there had been another arson attack. This time the Cooked Goose had been burnt to a crisp. Beatrice zoomed in on a photograph of the still-smouldering ruins. Part of the pub, a wooden frame extension, had been completely destroyed. The roof had fallen in on the main part of the structure and it looked like it would have to be knocked down and rebuilt.

So, why had she been called in for interview? She'd been nowhere near the building, having been in London. The change in intervals between the fires was odd. Maybe it had pushed the police into action. Maybe, in the absence of real leads, they wanted to know everything Beatrice knew, and more importantly, to seem like they were doing something active to catch the culprit. The report of a fourth fire would no doubt be front page news in the printed edition of the county paper next week, if Pete had anything to do with it.

She had no concerns she'd done anything wrong in the case. Certainly not breaking the law. Yes, she'd, recklessly chased the suspect, but he'd got away, and there was nothing she could be accused of there. She recalled Susan mentioning the ambitious new DS. Perhaps her approach was formal, and she wanted to get Beatrice's information recorded in a proper setting. The idea of the interview demand, following on so quickly from another fire, was unsettling though.

Turning back to the search for Lily, Beatrice checked online for information about postcodes. The ones she'd seen on the postcards had an LN prefix. She discovered not all UK post received a postmark. Those that did, were often given the mark of the distribution office, rather than the location of posting. It meant there was no way to trace Lily through the cards. She checked her watch. It was time to move on, and come back to Lily another day.

Beatrice pulled out a paper road atlas and began to plan her day investigating the fires. The six remaining pubs in the Wild Geese brewery were spread out, and she figured she could get around them all in what remained of the day, before her trip to Nettleham. She estimated half an hour at each pub and a longer visit for lunch, leaving a comfortable margin for getting to her interview on time.

'Hi, Rosie.' Beatrice was back home, worn out from trailing around the remaining Wild Geese pubs. She was phoning her sister to check in.

'How's things going?'

'Not great. I've been to the rest of the pubs and talked to the managers. I've come up with nothing. It's the same story at all of them. Zoe and Gareth are good to work with, they've no problems, the business is running smoothly.'

'Isn't that good?'

'For them, yes. But it doesn't give me anything to work on. They all clammed up pretty quickly when I tried to get them to talk about the Brown's personal life, but I can't tell if it's because they know something and are keeping schtum, or if there's nothing there.'

'Where do we go from here?'

Beatrice paused at the mention of 'we'. Was Rosie keen to do more? Realising her sister would bristle, if she thought Beatrice was taking pity on her, she tried to find a tactful way of phrasing it, to make it sound useful. 'What would be a great help, would be if you followed up the employees.'

'I can't leave the girls.'

'You don't have to. It's not worth traipsing all over the place. If I email you a list, could you make the calls for me, please? I've made notes on the ones I've already talked to, so you can leave them out.'

'What do you want me to ask them?'

'I'm interested in whether they know of any problems, either in the business, or in Gareth and Zoe's relationship.'

'You're after dirt?'

'Well, yes.'

'I can do that.' Rosie sounded more positive and Beatrice was glad to hear it. 'You can go about it any way you think best, but it might be worth prioritising people who don't work for the brewery or pubs anymore.'

'Because they'll be more likely to talk if they've been fired, or at least their job wouldn't be at stake?'

'Exactly.'

'Sounds like a plan. When do you need it for?'

'There's a lot of numbers, so you'll need a few days. If you could make a start as soon as possible though, I'll give you a ring later tomorrow and see how you've got on.'

'Mum!' One of the twins call out in the background.

'Got to go,' said Rosie, and the line went dead.

Chapter 19

Beatrice was waiting, with increasing impatience, for her interview to take place. After fifteen minutes, the chair she was perched on was becoming increasingly uncomfortable. She was preparing to leave, when a rotund, dishevelled Sergeant Fisher appeared, file in hand. DC Wilde trailed behind. So not the new DS then, just the old antagonistic one. Great. Beatrice steeled herself for the encounter.

'Follow me,' grunted Fisher.

Beatrice glanced at Susan, who was frowning. She followed Fisher into the room and he directed her to sit at the far side of the table.

He banged his mug down onto its surface, causing liquid to slop out, then threw the file down. Beatrice watched as it soaked up the liquid, staining the edges of its cover and contents.

The DS ignored her as he pulled out a chair and sat down heavily. DC Wilde then came into the room, and closed the door behind her. She moved the chair from next to Fisher to the corner of the room before sitting. She was avoiding looking at Beatrice, who watched Susan open her notebook, while waiting for Fisher to start. He leafed through the file, giving the appearance of closely examining its pages.

Not wanting to give him the satisfaction of seeing her impatience, she made a show of examining the room. Beatrice could see it was functional with limited furniture. It was cramped with the three of them. A panic strip circumnavigated the room, in case of violence erupting during an interview. She assumed Fisher annoyed other people as much as she did him, so he was likely a frequent user of the emergency signal. She continued to gaze about the room, though there was little else to notice.

'Thank you for coming, Ms Styles,' Fisher growled.

She turned her attention back to him. 'You're wel…'

'Now,' he pushed on. 'I have questions about your involvement with the Wild Geese Brewery and the fires in their network. You are not being interviewed under caution, but notes will be made and you will be asked to sign a statement.'

Beatrice nodded her understanding.

'Why did you choose the Golden Goose to watch, on the night of Sunday into Monday the eighteenth of June?' asked Fisher. 'Lucky, wasn't it? Or did you know it would happen?'

She really wished the case hadn't been handed back to Fisher, but it appeared Inspector Mayweather had decided that public interest and pressure required one of her more experienced officers. 'It's not luck.' She tried to reign in the impatience and annoyance his close proximity aroused in her. 'There are ten pubs in the chain. Two had already been targets. We covered two out of the remaining eight.'

'So, you did know something.'

'No.'

'You mean out of eight pubs, you just happened to choose the one targeted. You expect me to believe you?'

'I suspected the arsonist was choosing pubs where the cellars were concealed from view, to reduce the chances of being caught.' She folded her arms. 'Out of eight, three are on busy roads with clear views of the cellar doors. Of the remaining five, two are in towns, making the chance of being seen much greater. So, we covered two out of the three most likely targets. We had a good chance it would be one of them.'

Fisher stared at her as if anticipating more.

Beatrice remained silent. She could wait him out.

'Where were you last night?'

'Are you asking for an alibi?'

'Answer the question.'

'I was in London.'

'Not playing at investigating?'

Beatrice ignored the jibe. 'I was out with friends and stayed overnight with them. I caught the train back this morning.'

'Can anyone vouch for that?' Fisher smirked.

'Yes. Detective Sergeant Vanessa Holmes.'

Fisher opened and closed his mouth, unable to deny the validity of such a witness. 'Did you know there was another fire last night?'

'I saw it on the news this morning.'

'What do the Browns think of you swanning off whilst another pub got burned?'

'I don't work for the Browns anymore.'

Fisher sneered. 'Came to their senses? Should've left it to the police from the start.'

'Brad and Marie Staines might disagree with you, considering they and their children could be dead if I hadn't been there.'

'The smoke alarm would have gone off. They'd have been fine.' He waved away her comment with his hand.

Beatrice tried to contain her anger at his casual disregard of the real risk the family had faced. 'The alarm might have gone off. They might even have heard it. They might have got out in time, you know, before there was a massive, potentially catastrophic explosion of the gas and alcohol stored in the cellar. But that's a lot of 'mights.''

'You think you're a hero?'

'I did what anyone else would have done. Even you,' she snapped. 'But don't you dare pretend it was all a lark. You didn't see how scared those little girls were.' Beatrice's voice cracked.

Susan stood up, poured a glass of water and placed it on the table in front of her friend. She refused to make eye contact with her boss, so didn't see the glare of displeasure he directed towards her.

All three sat in silence for a couple of minutes whilst Beatrice sipped at the water.

She finally broke the silence. 'You can't seriously think I had anything to do with the fires?'

'You were at the scene of at least one of them. We have to check out every possibility.'

Beatrice stared at him, incredulous.

Fisher broke eye contact first, to check his notes. 'Is there anything else you can tell me about the man you say you saw at the Golden Goose?'

'Nothing over what I already told you. And, I gave you video evidence, so don't try to make out I made him up.'

'This is a serious matter,' said Fisher.

'I know that. What I don't know is why you're treating me as if I'm a criminal.' Fisher was badgering her even more than usual. What wasn't he telling her? Why was Susan being so formal and refusing to look at her? Fisher wouldn't tell her anything, so there was no point in asking. Susan's behaviour suggested she wasn't able to either. She'd have to find another way of getting information.

'That's all for now. DC Wilde will write up your statement. You can arrange to sign it with her when it's done.' Fisher stood up, gathered his papers and left, leaving the unfinished, now-cold drink behind, and the spillage on the desk.

Susan and Beatrice followed him out of the room. In the reception area Fisher stood at the secured door to the detectives' offices, watching the two women, making it impossible for them to communicate.

The DC accompanied Beatrice back to the front desk where she signed out of the visitor book. They walked in silence towards the door.

'Sorry,' Susan muttered.

Beatrice was about to ask why, when Fisher's voice bellowed across the public area.

'Come along, Constable.'

Relieved to be out in the open air, Beatrice's curiosity drove her to find out what was going on. She knew exactly who to ask. Someone who liked to think he knew everything that went on in the local area. He'd inevitably want a few pints in exchange for information. Being a reporter was apparently thirsty work.

She got into her car before making the call, not wanting to be overheard. It took a while for it to be answered.

'Hi, Pete,' Beatrice paused, listening to the sound of banging and swearing coming from the speaker on her phone.

'Hello?'

'Pete, its Beatrice Styles.'

'Ah. You. After more info, are you? The only time I hear from you, is when you want something.'

Beatrice smiled to herself. The reporter's gruff voice didn't fool her. Since their paths had crossed on her very first case, she and Pete Evans had shared a drink together several times. She knew he was a big softie. 'I know you love me really, Pete.'

'What is it this time, then?'

'The fire at the Cooked Goose. I saw your report online this morning. Fancy meeting up for a chat about it?'

'What's your connection?'

'I've been at the police station. Providing "my whereabouts".'

'Interesting.'

'You free?'

'If you're buying, I am.'

'Usual place at seven o'clock?'

'See you then.' He rang off abruptly, not big on social niceties.

Chapter 20

'Lovely.' Pete Evans had devoured half of his pint in one go, then put the glass back on the table.

'Tasted good, did it?' Beatrice couldn't believe he'd have any idea, since it went down so fast.

Pete laughed. 'Come on,' he said. 'Cough up. Why were you arrested this time?'

Beatrice glared at him. 'For your information, I have never been arrested. I doubt you could say the same.'

'You haven't lived.' He winked. 'You know me: anything in pursuit of a story. So, how was your friend, Sergeant Fisher? You know it's only a matter of time before he actually does arrest you, don't you?'

'Shall we get on with it?'

'I'm waiting for you to start, love.'

'What can you tell me about the fire at the Cooked Goose? I checked online, but figured you'd know stuff you couldn't publish, being such a hot journalist.'

'Trying flattery now?'

Beatrice grinned. 'Is it working?'

'Cheers.' Pete raised his glass in salute and drank. 'Well, it was the same MO as the others, from what I could get out of the fire brigade. The main difference this time seems to have been the ferocity of the fire, because it spread so quickly. They had real trouble getting it under control. Most of the building was lost before they were able to put it out.'

'Any ideas why?'

'Best guess, at this stage, is there was more fuel this time, but they'll be able to confirm, once they've had a proper look.'

He sat back in his chair. 'I'm done. What about you? What's your connection, other than being under suspicion?'

Beatrice sighed. 'After the second fire, the Browns, who own the Wild Geese brewery, hired me to find out who did it, and prevent it happening again.'

Pete raised his eyebrows. 'Aren't we up to four fires now?' He stuck up four chunky digits to emphasise the number.

'Thanks for pointing it out.'

'I'm only stating facts.' He chuckled.

'Well,' Beatrice continued. 'I nearly caught the guy at the Golden Goose, the third fire, but he got away.'

Pete pulled out his notebook. 'Did you get a description?'

'Only a rough one. It was dark.'

'Let's have it.'

'Male, about five-ten. Very slim build. He left the scene on a motorbike, heading in the direction of Lincoln.'

Pete made a note. 'Not much is it.'

'Unfortunately, no.'

'Hang on,' said Pete. 'There was talk of a woman who helped get the family out of the pub.'

Beatrice remained silent.

'Was it you?'

She shrugged.

'Bloody hell, Beatrice. It's a great news story and you didn't tell me. I thought we had an understanding.'

'It wasn't a fun experience, Pete.' She swallowed. 'Besides, the family has been through a horrible ordeal. I didn't think they needed it splashed across the local paper in lurid detail.'

'Fair enough, but…'

'Pete!'

'Hear me out. OK?'

'Fine.'

'I was due to go and talk to Mr and Mrs Staines anyway. The fires are big news, after all. If they agree to talk to me, on the record, and if they say it's alright with them, will you give me your version of what happened too?' He drank the remains of the pint and waggled the glass at Beatrice, who took it reluctantly. 'Think about it,' he continued. 'It would be a fantastic story. It could get picked up by the nationals. You could be famous.'

Beatrice didn't answer but went to the bar for Pete's refill. If the Staines were happy to talk, maybe it would be alright to give her side. The publicity would be good for her business. Pete would probably spin it to make her come off well. And, with luck, someone would come forward with information about the arsonist.

'I'll think about it,' said Beatrice, putting the refilled glass down in front of him. 'But only if they agree.'

'Sure,' Pete replied. 'Carry on with what you were saying.'

'Yeah, right. So, after the third fire the Browns sacked me.'

'Why? You nearly had him.'

'They made excuses. "It's the job of the police." That kind of thing.'

'I've heard rumours they're in financial trouble.'

'They've lost four pubs. I'd be surprised if they weren't.' Beatrice didn't mention the insurance company's view.

'This goes back before the first fire.'

'Where and when did you hear it?'

'I have my sources.' Pete tapped the side of his nose with a fleshy digit. 'It was a couple of months ago now.'

'I thought this was two-way?'

'You know I can't reveal a source. I wouldn't expect you to.'

'Fair enough.' He was right, frustrating, but right.

'Why were you at the station?'

'Fisher started asking about the third fire, but then jumped onto the fourth. I'd seen about it, online, but there was nothing I could tell him.'

'Why was he asking, if you weren't there?'

'I don't know. But he was being heavy about it. It wasn't his case before, and now he's been moved on to it. There was something he wasn't telling me. I thought you might know.'

'I don't.' Pete looked thoughtful. 'You've got police contacts, haven't you? Ask that DC I've seen you with.'

'We're casual friends. We don't talk work.'

'Don't be daft!' Pete laughed at her.

'OK,' said Beatrice. 'She's on the case too, and clearly Fisher has told her not to talk to me. I don't want to ask because he'd get her fired if he could.'

'Right. Well, I've got one person I can try. I'll pop outside and phone whilst you get me another pint.'

'Good grief, Pete. Where does it go?'

Beatrice was staring at Pete's replenished glass when James arrived. They'd arranged to meet once she'd finished with the reporter.

'Hi,' he said, sitting down next to her. 'He hasn't left a full pint, has he? From what you've told me, I wouldn't expect him to leave a beer willingly.'

Beatrice chuckled. 'No. He's outside, phoning a contact.

'Want another drink?' asked James, gesturing at her almost empty glass.

'Yes, please. Red wine.'

James kissed her lightly on the cheek and went to the bar, passing Pete, who was on his way back. The older, scruffy man looked up at the tall, muscular figure of James and frowned.

Pete sat down. 'Isn't he your lodger?'

'James. Yes. You were gone a long time. What happened?'

'Well, my contact came good, and it's really juicy. I wanted to dictate a report before coming back in. I'll pop along to the office in a while, and get it finished before anyone else breaks the news.'

James returned, placing two glasses of red wine on the table. He sat close to Beatrice and casually draped his arm along the back of the banquette, laying his hand on her shoulder.

Pete's eyes widened. 'Pete Evans.' He held out his hand.

'James Marland.' The men shook hands. 'Beatrice has told

me all about you.' James grinned.

'Yeah, well. She's not said much about you.'

'Really?' James turned to Beatrice, who refused to meet his gaze.

'Pete, you were just about to tell me what you found out,' she said.

'What?' Oh, yeah.' He looked around to make sure no one was listening, and leaned forward.

Instinctively, Beatrice and James leaned forward too.

'Turns out, the reason Fisher was put on the case and was coming on so strong, was because of this.' He turned his phone screen towards them.

They looked at it for a few seconds, trying to make sense of the image.

'Bloody hell.' James sat back. 'You should warn people before showing them stuff like that.'

Beatrice continued peering at the screen. The photo was of the burnt remains of a person. The blackened corpse was curled, its arms positioned like a boxer preparing to fight.

'Doesn't seeing that bother you?' James stared at Beatrice in disbelief.

'No.' She sat back and sipped her drink. No wonder Fisher wanted a formal interview. 'Who is it?'

'Don't know,' said Pete. 'I wasn't supposed to know they found it. The police are trying to keep it quiet. It wasn't noticed until the fire brigade had decided the building was safe. They did a preliminary search and uncovered the remains. That's when they called in CID and forensics.'

'Was it a member of staff?'

'No. The landlords were away and they had a relief manager. With the other attacks they'd insisted he stay in the building at all times, but he snuck off to see his girlfriend for a bit of a fumble.'

'A fumble? Really?' Beatrice shook her head.

Pete looked at her, opening then closing his mouth without comment.

'The body isn't him?'

'No. The police got in touch with the landlords and they all assumed it was the relief, until he turned up back at the pub.' Pete drained his glass. 'We do know, the body was in the cellar, at the seat of the fire, where there'd be no reason for anyone to be. As you saw, it was badly burnt and the police are waiting on the pathologist. They know it's a man,' said Pete. 'Otherwise, it's a bit of a mystery.' He was grinning. 'I can keep this story going for days.'

'Do you think the arsonist got too close to his own fire?' asked James.

'I doubt it,' said Beatrice. 'From the report on the earlier fires, our guy knows exactly what he's doing and didn't even need to be in the building to do it. This is someone else.'

Chapter 21

Monday 25th June

James had left early for the garage, leaving Beatrice alone in her office, checking her phone. Another missed call from Charles Sharpe. She couldn't reasonably ignore two attempts.

'Mr Sharpe, it's Beatrice Styles. I'm sorry I missed your calls.'

'I want to know what's happening.'

Beatrice spoke in a deliberate, measured tone. 'Did you get my email, showing what I've done so far?'

'It didn't say much.'

'I haven't found out much, yet.'

'You talked to Andrew.' It was a statement with the expectation of an explanation.

'Yes. I can't say for sure he knows where she is. He gave the name of a village where they spent time as children and I'll be following it up.'

'What else?'

'It's one step at a time, I'm afraid.'

'It's taking too long to produce results.'

'It's been a week. Lily's been gone a year. Cases like this require time. The trail has gone cold, and I don't have access to things the police do, like CCTV. I can't compel people to talk to me. My methods have to be more subtle.'

'I suppose.'

'If you're not happy, I can stop and refund the remainder of your deposit.'

'No. Don't. I'll try to be patient.' There was a short silence.

'I'm sorry. I really want to see Elizabeth again. Since I hired you, she hasn't been out of my mind.'

'I'll tell you if there's any news.'

'Thank you.'

The call ended and Beatrice considered the changeable moods of her client. She supposed it must be hard, not seeing your child for a year, so impatience was understandable. Wasn't she having the same emotions about her mother? Hadn't the payment from the solicitor brought the pain of her mother's disappearance back into her mind. She was thinking about her mum every day now. Wouldn't it be even more reasonable to be worried about the welfare of a child, one you had hoped to take care of, and watch grow up? She didn't have to like her client to do a good job, but she could be more understanding of his situation.

Beatrice's phone buzzed. Whilst she'd been talking to Charles, a voicemail had been left. She listened to it. It was from a solicitor, Louise Prince, asking Beatrice to come to her office at 9:30 a.m., regarding one of her cases. Intrigued, Beatrice checked the time, then the location of the firm. She could easily make it.

The solicitor's office was down a narrow street in the upmarket Bailgate area of Lincoln, and Beatrice found the yellow-stone building easily. Inside, she was quickly shown into an office.

'You must be Beatrice Styles.' Louise, a short woman, wearing a black trouser-suit stood up, behind a modern desk, empty apart from a paper file. The two women shook hands. 'Thank you for coming. Please sit.'

Beatrice sat. 'Your message was cryptic.'

'Sorry. I'm afraid the circumstances required it.'

'Perhaps you could explain.'

Louise took a deep breath. 'In half an hour, I have a meeting with Michael Burgess.'

'I don't know who that is.'

'He asked for you specifically.'

'How does he know me?'

There was a pause.

'If I tell you he's been questioned by the police, regarding recent cases of arson, does that help?'

'Oh. The pubs?' asked Beatrice.

'I'm afraid so.'

'Was it him I chased away from the Golden Goose? The arsonist.'

'Well, I'm not going to answer that, am I? Anyway, he hasn't admitted to being there. He just asked for you.'

'But why?'

'The police said they had an eyewitness. Since your evidence might be used, they disclosed your name. It didn't take a lot to find you. When Michael heard who you were, he got the idea into his head that you'd help him.'

'I don't know why.'

'Neither do I, but here we are.'

'I'm not sure we should be talking,' said Beatrice. 'If he is charged with arson, I'll be a prosecution witness.'

'I doubt it.' Louise glanced over a piece of paper from the file. 'You can't reliably identify whoever did it. Besides, he insisted. He's only been questioned so far, not arrested or charged, so if you want to speak to each other, I can't stop it happening, and I'd rather I was present.'

'Is he denying involvement?'

'He's not saying anything much. He's clearly an old hand at police interviews. Lots of "no comment" to questions. Until Sergeant Fisher got to the body. Did you know one was found at the latest fire?'

'I heard on Saturday.'

'Whatever else he may or may not be, Michael insists he's not a killer, and there wasn't anyone in the building.'

'He must have made a mistake.'

'I'm not sure. The police are being cagy about the evidence. Anyway, Michael wants to speak to you. He's scared. He thinks the police have set him up. Ridiculous, I know.' She shook her head. 'He believes you can prove he's innocent.'

'How? I don't think he is innocent, if he's the one from the Golden Goose.'

'There could be a charge of manslaughter. It's best case, up to nine years if he's found guilty. Arson could add up to another eight. They could run consecutively. He's done a few weeks here and there over the years, in minimum security. He's terrified of what will happen if he's put away for manslaughter.'

'I don't see what I can do.'

'I realise you can't go into the details of what you know about the fires, or why you were hired, but I can probably guess most of it. Which means it would be useful for you to talk to Michael, wouldn't it?'

'It would help.' If Michael admitted to setting the fires, perhaps she could find out why, and if someone, possibly the Browns, had paid him to do it.

'So, you'll stay, and see him?'

Beatrice hesitated.

'This could be your only chance. He could be arrested at any time.'

'It won't be much use for me though, will it?'

'Why not?'

'Even if he wants to open up, maybe admit something, anything I learn I wouldn't be able to use as evidence.'

'No. But he might be able to point you in the right direction.'

'What do you mean?'

'Can we talk hypothetically?'

'Sure.'

'Well, if someone committed a crime because they were put up to it, would it really matter, to say, a private investigator, if the police were dealing with the person who'd committed the crime? Wouldn't said investigator be more interested in who set the ball rolling, so to speak?'

Beatrice considered the solicitor's words, which echoed the thoughts she'd had herself. What did she have to lose? Just time. 'OK,' she said.

There was a knock at the office door, and the receptionist came into the room, closing it behind her. 'Michael Burgess is here.'

'Well, let's see what he's got to say for himself.'

Beatrice was looking forward to seeing the nimble arsonist face to face. Not only to get answers about why he'd set the fires, but to see if he realised the impact of what he'd done.

Chapter 22

Michael's age was difficult to estimate. Whilst his skin was well tanned, likely from years of working outdoors, he had the pent-up energy of someone much younger. On entering the room, he'd nodded at Louise, sat down, uninvited, and looked Beatrice up and down with an expression of interest, whilst avoiding her face. His left leg kept bouncing up and down, as if he was incapable of sitting still. From what she could tell of his build, he was a good match for the man she'd chased at the Golden Goose.

Beatrice stood up and moved her chair, so it was positioned at the corner of the desk. It put distance between her and the man, whilst giving her the chance to observe him and Louise. The distance also had the added advantage of lessening the strength of the miasma of cigarette smoke, which hung around him.

The solicitor raised her eyebrows at Beatrice's actions. 'Michael,' she said. 'This is the woman you wanted to talk to.'

He sniffed and wiped his nose with the back of his hand. Beatrice hadn't knowingly met an arsonist before, but his demeanour didn't indicate any consciousness that he might have done something wrong.

'As your lawyer, although Ms Styles isn't with the police, you need to think carefully about what you say to her.' Louise regarded her client steadily. 'Do you understand, Michael?'

'I'm not bloody stupid.' He pulled out a packet of tobacco and began to roll a narrow cigarette. His left leg jittered at an even greater speed. 'I'm not admitting to nothing.'

'What did you want from me?' asked Beatrice.

Michael looked directly at her face for the first time. 'I've heard about you.'

She waited.

'You found out about the lassie, the one who killed the big fat bloke.'

Beatrice shifted in her seat. 'And?'

'Well. Shows you don't just believe what people might want you to.'

'You didn't start the fires, then?'

Louise appeared as if she was about to intervene, but Michael waved a hand at her. 'Don't worry so much.' He turned back to Beatrice. 'The thing is, I've never hurt no one. Whatever I may or may not have done, I make sure no one gets hurt. You get me?'

'I think so. But whoever started the fire at the Golden Goose, did it with people inside.' Beatrice's pulse rate increased. 'They could have died.'

'That's different.'

'How?' Beatrice snapped. 'There were children in there!'

Michael shrank back in his chair.

'I'm sorry.' Beatrice took a calming breath. 'I didn't mean to shout, but they could have been killed.'

'Perhaps if you hadn't chased the person what did it, they might have been able to stick to their plan of phoning the fire brigade.'

Was he trying to say the danger they faced was her fault? 'And what if the fire engine didn't turn up soon enough?'

'Well, a responsible person would hang about, and make sure everything was alright, wouldn't they?'

Beatrice tried to remain calm, and forced herself to focus. If she had understood him correctly, he'd started the fires, but would've taken steps to make sure anyone was out safely. Presumably he meant he'd intervene himself, if there was imminent danger. She was shocked at his arrogance and willingness to gamble with the lives of other people. He was looking at her, unconcerned, wearing an expression of someone who takes pride in his work. Perhaps it was his idea of arsonist ethics.

'A body was found, in the latest fire,' said Beatrice.

'Suppose someone had had a close thing, like say happened with the Golden Goose. They'd probably want to make sure it was safe, if they had to do it again.'

'Had to?' Beatrice noticed the attempt to pass blame, again.

'Right, cards on the table…'

'Speaking hypothetically,' Louise interjected.

Beatrice raised her eyebrows. 'Fine.'

'So, hyper-whatsit,' he gestured at Louise. 'If someone was asked to do a little damage, they'd only agree to it again, if they was sure no one would get hurt.'

Beatrice ran her fingers through her hair, exasperated.

'It's nothing personal, love. Just business.'

Translating, Beatrice thought Michael was saying he'd done the latest job, at someone else's direction, with the insistence the building was empty. Was it coincidence the relief manager had gone out that night, or had someone arranged for him to be absent? 'I think I understand you, Michael,' she said. 'But what do you want me to do?'

'You're looking into the fires, aren't you?'

'Yes.'

'So do your thing. Go beyond the obvious. I don't want to go down for manslaughter. The dead bloke was nothing to do with me.'

'Where should I look?'

Michael's leg jumped even faster and higher than before. 'You're the detective.'

'You've got to give me something.'

Michael shrugged.

Beatrice sighed. 'Should I be looking at the Browns?'

'Who?'

'The couple who own the brewery.' From his response, it didn't seem likely they'd hired him.

'There's nothing I can say.'

'Then how do you expect me to do anything? And why would I?'

'You want the truth, don't you?'

Beatrice folded her arms. 'Are you going to tell me who told you to start the fires?'

Michael stared at her for several long seconds. 'Seriously, it's more than my life's worth.'

Beatrice stood and turned to Louise. 'I'm sorry, but there's nothing for me to work with.'

'Thanks for coming.'

'You are going to carry on investigating?' asked Michael.

'I'll do the job I've been paid for.'

A short, brisk walk back to her house had a calming effect on Beatrice. Michael could have easily told her who set him up for the arson attacks, but he was being obstinate, despite the threat of a long stretch in prison hanging over him. Was he really so scared?

She let the cat out into the back garden, then went to her office. At her laptop, Beatrice turned her mind to finding Lily and Elizabeth. Reviewing the website for the Norwich community centre, and the page for the mother and baby group, she jotted down a few details. On her next visit there, if she saw Morwenna again, she wanted to be able to show she'd done research. The page for the women's support group had links to photos, similar to those she'd already seen. Scanning them carefully, it was hard to find the blue-haired Jules, as if she were avoiding the camera, often being captured in the process of turning away, so her face was out of focus.

Beatrice checked the meeting dates for the group. They ran twice a week. One in the afternoon, at the same time as the mother and baby group, the other on a morning. She decided to focus on the morning session, thinking Morwenna might wonder why she wasn't in the mum and baby group if she went to the other.

The contact number for the group was for a mobile and

had the name "Jules" next to it. Exactly the woman she wanted to speak to. Deciding Jules might be more open, if she was expecting Beatrice, she dialled the number. Plus, it was a long way to go if Jules sent her packing after a few minutes.

'Hello?'

'Is that Jules?'

'Yes. Who is this?'

'I'm Beatrice. I got your number from the community centre website. I was interested in your women's support group. Morwenna told me about it.'

'Oh, yeah. Morwenna.' The mention of the manager's name seemed to relax Jules and her tone softened. 'What can I tell you about it?'

'I was hoping to come and see what you do. This Wednesday. Is that alright?'

'Sure. We're painting then. You can join in.'

'Well…'

'It's all for fun. You don't have to be good at it. We try to have an activity which means the women can still talk together. It wouldn't be much of a support group, if we sat there in silence.'

'My sister likes art. It's her who would be joining.'

'I'd be happy to talk to her.'

'Actually, I was going to come on her behalf. She lives in Lincoln now, but she's moving into Norwich soon. Her husband's idea. She's pregnant, you see, and can't travel.'

'Nothing seriously wrong, I hope.'

'No.' Beatrice had absolutely no knowledge of pregnancy and its possible complications. When Rosie really had been pregnant, their mother was still around, which had saved Beatrice from having to hear all the gory details of the pregnancy and birth. She'd no intention of ever becoming familiar with either experience. What could she tell Jules? Something unrelated. 'She had a bit of a fall, I'm afraid. The doctor says they're both OK, but she needs to take it easy until the baby's born.' It sounded plausible to her, at least.

'A fall?'

'Yes. Nothing too bad, thank goodness.'

'Were you there when it happened?'

'No.' A strange question.

'Was she alone?' asked Jules.

'No, her husband was with her, so everything got sorted quickly.'

'And it's his idea to move?'

'Yes.'

'You have other family down here?'

'No. He thought it would be a good place to live.'

'I see.'

Beatrice didn't. Her made-up story appeared to have significance for Jules, but she couldn't see it herself. 'Is it alright if I come on Wednesday, then?'

'Yes. Definitely. Please tell your sister she's welcome to come too, if she's up to it.'

'Thanks, I will.'

Beatrice rang off. It had been an odd conversation, but she'd got what she needed. Jules had sounded friendly, and with luck, would be even more talkative when they met in person.

Chapter 23

'Hi Rosie.' Beatrice was sitting outside the address Pete had given her, where the Staines family were staying. The small terrace was well cared for, with a hanging basket in full flower by the shining red door. How Pete had found the address, she didn't know, but he'd been eager to pass it on, hoping it meant she'd give him an interview.

'Hi. Everything OK?'

'Just checking in on how the brewery calls are going.'

'I've done quite a lot, since Adam spends almost all his time at the garage now. Even when they're closed.'

'I'm sorry. I wish I could help.'

'I don't think anyone can.'

'Do you want to come out for a meal with me soon? My treat. Sounds like you could do with getting away.'

'That would be great, but there's no one to watch the girls. It's not like their father would do it.' Rosie sounded bitter.

There was a silence and Beatrice desperately tried to think of something to say.

'Like I said,' Rosie continued. 'I've spoken to a good range of staff. Some temporary, some returnees and longer-term ones, and I made sure I covered every pub.'

'Great.'

'The results aren't much use. Most of the staff didn't have a lot to do with the Browns. That was the job of the managers. There have been no rumours of trouble, either with the business or in the Brown's marriage.'

'Well,' said Beatrice. 'It's good in one way, but doesn't help me find out why they've been targeted.'

'Sorry.'

'No. Thanks for doing it. You've saved me a lot of time.'

'Shall I carry on? Try to finish the list?'

'Leave it for now. I'll have a rethink once I've spoken to a few more people myself. I'll talk to you again soon, and Rosie?'

'Yes?'

'If you can figure out a babysitter, let me know.'

'Sure.'

'I've brought these.' Beatrice felt a little foolish as she held out a pair of identical stuffed, toy dogs. 'For the girls.' She shrugged. 'I thought since they lost most of their things in the fire…'

Marie smiled. 'Thank you. They'll love them. Come in.'

She showed Beatrice into a small living room, furnished with a three-piece suite, a coffee table and a TV. Brad was watching a football game with the sound turned down so low, it was barely audible. Maisie and Betsy were kneeling at the table, colouring.

'Girls, come and see what Beatrice has brought for you,' said Marie. 'Isn't that nice?'

The girls looked up, then, in silence, scrambled to their feet. Each girl accepted a dog. Betsy, the youngest, stared into her dog's eyes, gave it a quick kiss on the nose, then hugged it tightly. Maisie simply tucked hers under her arm, stared up at Beatrice and blinked.

'What do you say?' Marie prompted.

The girls mumbled indistinct thanks and returned to colouring. Betsy showed her dog what she'd been doing. Maisie began colouring with vigour.

'Sit down,' said Brad, switching the TV off.

'I'm sorry to disturb you,' said Beatrice.

'It's fine.' He gestured at the TV. 'It's just something to do. Passes the time.'

'My sister has been so good, letting us stay,' said Marie.

'But with us, and her family, well, it's difficult.'

Beatrice sat in an armchair. 'How are you all?'

Marie sat next to Brad and clasped his hand. 'OK, I guess. It could have been worse.'

A woman, similar in appearance to Marie, came into the room. 'Everything alright?' she asked. 'I heard the door.'

'This is Beatrice,' said Marie. 'This is my sister, Mandy.'

'Hi,' said Beatrice.

'Oh, you're the one…' Mandy glanced at Maisie and Betsy. 'Thank goodness you were there,' she said quietly. There was a brief silence. 'Girls, would you like to go to the park?'

'Can I bring my dog?' Betsy piped up.

'What a lovely little creature,' said Mandy. 'Of course she can come too.' She held her hand out, which Betsy grasped. 'Come on, Maisie. Let's get your coats and shoes on. We'll be about half an hour,' said Mandy, as she closed the door behind them.

The atmosphere in the room relaxed a little. Brad put his arm around Marie.

'The girls have been so quiet since the fire,' said Marie. 'They wake up every night crying. It's usually Maisie who starts, then Betsy joins in. The doctor said to get them to talk about it, but they get so upset.'

'Perhaps it'll get better with time?' Beatrice was out of her depth and didn't know what else to say.

'What did you want to talk to us about?' asked Brad.

'I'm still investigating the fires,' Beatrice explained. 'I wanted to find out about events before it happened.'

'Like what?'

'I don't know,' said Beatrice. 'The arsonist was targeting the business. It must be to do with the brewery, or Zoe and Gareth. Has anything out of the ordinary happened recently, or seemed a little odd?'

'I can't recall anything,' Brad replied. 'We'd been at the pub a couple of years, so we knew the ropes. Everything was running as it should. No trouble.'

'It's why we were glad when we didn't have to leave,' said Marie. 'I don't know what we'll do now. Or where we'll live.' She choked off a sob, burying her face in Brad's shoulder.

'We'll find something, love.' Brad kissed his wife's cheek.

'Sorry,' said Beatrice. 'Did you say you might not have been able to stay at the pub?'

'Oh, it was nothing in the end,' said Brad.

'What was?' asked Beatrice.

'Someone wanted to buy the brewery. He sent people to ask questions about our finances,' Brad explained.

'I assume Gareth and Zoe knew.'

'I called them, to check,' said Brad. 'I thought Gareth didn't know about it to start with, but then he said to show them around, tell them what they wanted to know. So, I did.'

Marie interjected. 'I was surprised they'd even consider it. They built it up from scratch. It was their baby.'

Brad nodded.

'Who was it that came?' asked Beatrice.

Brad shook his head. 'Sorry. They gave us a business card, but I put it in a drawer at the pub. There'll be nothing left of it now.'

'One of the guys was called Jack, I think.' Marie sniffed and wiped her eyes. 'It wasn't the same as the name on the card though.'

'How do Gareth and Zoe get on?' asked Beatrice. 'Any disagreements?'

'No more than any other couple,' said Marie. 'Nothing serious, I'm sure.'

'Was there anything else?' asked Brad, glancing at the TV.

'Just one thing. I was talking to a friend, who's a reporter. His name is Pete Evans.'

'I've seen his stuff in the paper,' said Brad.

'He'd like to do a feature on the fire at your pub. He wants to interview you both, and me too. He thinks people will want to read about your experience. I told him I'd mention it, to see if you were interested.'

'What's in it for us?' asked Brad.

'I don't know whether he's allowed to pay you for your story, but maybe you could use it you your advantage.'

'How?' Brad frowned.

'Well, he could write about how you've nowhere to live and need jobs. Perhaps something will come of it.'

'Handouts, you mean?' asked Brad.

'Help. A job, or somewhere to live, maybe. You're out of work and home, through no fault of your own. Would it really be so bad to accept a bit of support, to get you on your feet?'

'It couldn't hurt, could it?' Marie looked up at Brad.

'Give me his number. I'll talk to him.' He turned back to Marie. 'I'm not saying yes, mind. We've got to think of the girls, what's best for them.'

'Our own place and making a new life is what's best for them, Brad.'

'But how we go about it matters.'

Beatrice pulled out her notebook, referring to her phone, she wrote on a page, then tore it out. 'Here's Pete's number and mine too. If you think of anything which might help, please call. No matter how insignificant it seems.'

'We will,' said Marie.

They heard the front door open and the clatter of children's footsteps.

'I'll leave you to it.' Beatrice stood.

Brad made to get up.

'It's fine. I know the way out.' Beatrice said goodbye to the girls who were in the hall removing their shoes. Betsy gave her a small wave. Maisie watched her leave, eyes wide.

Chapter 24

Tuesday 26th June

The 'For Sale' sign at the top of the long, private driveway was unexpected, but Beatrice was more surprised by the empty stables. Not only was there no horse, there was none of the usual paraphernalia associated with horse riding. The short row of holiday homes and the main house looked essentially the same as when she'd last been there.

She hadn't seen Marina Bayfield since they'd discussed the murder of her husband, Simon. It had been Beatrice's first investigation, and she'd been crucial in helping the police identify the person responsible for Simon's death.

'Beatrice! Come in. I was so pleased you called.' Marina stood back to let her into the hallway. 'Let's go to the kitchen. Tea?'

'Yes, please.' Beatrice followed her and sat down at the kitchen table. 'How are you?'

'Good.'

'What happened to your horse?'

Marina continued making a pot of tea. 'I sold him.'

'I'm surprised.'

'I can't take him with me.'

Beatrice regarded the other woman who had her back to her. 'I saw the "For Sale" sign.'

'Yes. I've had an offer. It's not great, but I've accepted it. I need to leave.'

'Where are you going?'

'The US.' Marina placed a steaming mug in front of

Beatrice. 'It's why I was glad you called. I wanted you to know what my plans are.' She ran her fingers through her hair. 'It might sound strange, but with you being so involved around Simon's death, I wanted you to know what's next for me.'

'Why America?'

'To make a fresh start. With Simon gone there's no reason for me to stay in England. I've no relatives, the friends I had here were really his friends, and I need something new.'

'What will you do?'

'I'm buying a ranch. It's already set up, with cattle and horses, so I can move in and take over.'

Beatrice chose her words carefully. 'That's a huge change.'

'I know what you're thinking, but I have thought it through. I'm not getting any younger and it's time I did what I want with my life, instead of fitting in with other people.'

Investigating Simon's death had shown Beatrice the businessman could be ruthless, frequently riding over the wishes of others. Being married to him couldn't have been easy for Marina. 'I hope it works out.'

'Thanks. Even if it doesn't, at least I'll have tried.'

'What does Simon's mum think about it?' asked Beatrice.

'After his death she seemed to give up. Lost her spark. I'd arranged for carers to help out, but she's had to go into a care home now. They don't think she has long.'

'I'm sorry.'

'We never got on. But for Simon's sake I wanted to make sure she was taken care of.' Marina sighed and gazed out of the window. 'I went to see her a few weeks back. She didn't even seem to know I was there.' She looked at Beatrice. 'I don't plan on ending my days like that.'

Beatrice imagined no one did, but admired Marina's willingness to do something positive.

They talked more about Marina's plans. Beatrice could tell she intended to leave and cut all ties to her old life. She'd hoped they could have become friends, in time, but it seemed the older woman had other priorities.

'Sorry,' said Marina. 'I've talked non-stop. You must be fed up of listening to me.'

'I'm glad you're excited about your move.'

'You wanted to pick my brains. How can I help?'

'Well, you and Simon were immersed in the business world here, so I thought you might be able to tell me about a business I'm interested in. And the owners.'

'I was just the dutiful wife, but I'll help if I can.'

'It's the Wild Geese Brewery, owned by Zoe and Gareth Brown. I'm investigating the arson attacks on their pubs.'

'The name rings a bell. Hang on.' Marina left the kitchen and came back a few minutes later with her laptop. 'I thought this might jog my memory.' She fired it up and searched for the brewery online.

Beatrice moved her chair closer, so they could both see the screen.

Marina clicked on the link for images and the screen filled with thumbnail pictures. She scrolled through, until she found a clear one of the couple. 'Oh, I do know them,' said Marina. 'Not well, but we've been at the same events.'

'What do you know?'

Marina carried on flicking through the photos whilst she talked. 'She seemed nice, though intense. He was quiet. Simon tried talking him into putting solar panels on his pubs, but he wasn't interested. Hang on.' Marina had stopped on a photo of the Browns with another couple.

'Zoe doesn't look happy, does she?' said Beatrice. The photo had been taken at a party. Two couples were front and centre, with other people in the background. The second pair were an odd match. The man was about sixty, and dressed in a dark, well-cut suit. The glamorous, much younger woman, was in a low-cut, figure-hugging dress. Gareth had been captured staring at her cleavage, which possibly explained the angry expression on Zoe's face.

'What?' asked Marina, who had been lost in thought. 'No, I don't suppose she was. Not that he'd have a chance with

Astra, anyway.'

'Astra?'

'Stupid name, isn't it. I assume she chose it herself.' She grinned at Beatrice.

'Who's the man?'

Marina sat back. 'Victor Malone.'

'Go on.'

'Businessman, he calls himself.' Marina pursed her lips. 'I don't know too much about him, in terms of specifics, but Simon didn't like him.'

'Did he say why?'

Marina shook her head. 'He seemed wary of him.'

'How do you mean?'

'Simon was always very careful to be polite and acknowledge Victor's presence, but didn't like talking to him. Normally Simon would be in there with any opportunity to make a sale, but not with this guy. He avoided him.'

'What kind of business is Victor Malone in?'

'He owns and rents out houses, I think. Possibly other stuff, but I don't know what.'

Beatrice wondered if the Browns had any connection with Malone, beyond being at the same social events.

Marina had begun searching the photos again and stopped at a photo of Zoe alongside another woman. They had their arms around each other and were laughing. 'It looks like Zoe is friendly with Lesley Wilson.'

'Who's she?' asked Beatrice.

'Another dutiful wife.' Marina rolled her eyes. 'She's a terrible gossip though. By which I mean she's really good at it. Do you want me to find out what she knows about the Browns?'

Beatrice hesitated. Could she rely on information from a gossip, and was it fair to Zoe and Gareth? She had no other source of material on them personally.

'You can come with me, if you think I won't ask the right questions,' Marina interrupted. 'If I go on my own, she's more likely to talk, and to be honest, she can be a bit much, so I wouldn't recommend it.'

'Is she reliable?'

'Spot on, in my experience.'

'Then, yes. Please find out what she knows. I appreciate the help.'

'I owe you.'

'You don't,' said Beatrice.

Marina shrugged. 'I can use the opportunity to tell Lesley my leaving plans, in confidence, of course, that way the whole county will know in a few weeks, and it will save me having to tell anyone.'

Beatrice stood up, to leave.

'Are you after something in particular?' asked Marina, as they walked to the front door.

'Anything would be useful, but when I last saw them there appeared to be tension between them. It could have been to do with the fires and the investigation, but maybe not.'

'It's the kind of thing Lesley specialises in.' Marina pulled Beatrice in for a hug. 'It was really nice to see you.'

'You too. I'm sorry you're leaving, but I hope you have a fabulous time.' Beatrice stepped out of the house, taking her car keys from her bag.

'I'll give it my best shot.'

Beatrice walked away, then turned back towards Marina. 'You will try to be subtle, won't you? The Browns know I'm investigating, and they're not happy about it. If they find out I've been asking their friends about them, even indirectly, it could get difficult.'

Chapter 25

Back home in her office, Beatrice repeated the internet search Marina had done. She pulled up the photo of the Browns alongside the mis-matched couple. It had been taken at a charity ball held in Lincoln the previous year. She browsed through other photos of the same event. Victor Malone and Astra featured in many, but she couldn't find more of Zoe and Gareth.

There was one image with a familiar silhouette in the background. She was fairly confident the rumpled figure was Pete Evans. She'd not get anything out of him if she went empty handed though, and she had just the thing to sweeten him up with.

Before she could message Pete, her mobile rang. She glanced at the caller ID, answering with a mixture of hope and trepidation. 'Vanessa. How are you?'

'Busy. I'll have to be quick.'

'No problem.'

'I spoke to a friend of mine who works in fraud. He said it's not something they'd get involved with themselves, right now, because there's no evidence of any crime.'

'But he's dishing out Mum's money…'

'Beatrice, let me finish.'

'Sorry.'

'He said it would be legitimate to make initial enquiries, if an official complaint is made. Do you want to do that?'

Beatrice was reluctant to create trouble for Atkinson, but he was her only connection to her mother. 'Yes. Yes, I'd like to make a formal complaint. Someone needs to ask him questions. I tried doing it myself, so he's had a chance.' She was trying to justify her decision, but what else could she do?

'Right. I'll talk to my Inspector, and see if he has any objections to me approaching Atkinson. It saves having to explain everything to anyone else.'

'I'd really appreciate it, Vanessa. I trust you to do it right.'

'Hold on. You need to know I won't be able to tell you anything confidential.'

'What do you mean?'

'Suppose he can explain how what he's doing is legal, but he has to reveal confidential information. All I'll be able to tell you is *I'm* satisfied he's done nothing wrong, and not say why. Is it going to be good enough, because I have rules to follow?'

'I trust you, and if you say it's OK, I'll believe you.'

'Good. It might be a while, but I'll get back to you as soon as I can. Bye for now.'

'Bye.' Beatrice ended the call and put the phone on her desk. Would she really be happy with someone else's reassurance, but no actual information? She knew she wouldn't, but whatever Vanessa could tell her, no matter how little, it would be something. After that, she could decide for herself what action to take. But it wouldn't be the end.

'Hi Frankie,' said Beatrice. She was meeting him at the pub she usually met Pete in. She'd not been there in the middle of the day before, and the daylight highlighted the grubby carpet and shabby décor. Maybe she should have suggested a different place to meet, but Frankie had seemed happy with a location far away from the brewery. 'Thanks for coming.' She'd noticed his discomfort around Robert and was hoping he might be willing to open up about him.

The young man shrugged.

'Can I get you a drink, Frankie?'

'Lager, please.'

A few minutes later, Beatrice returned from the bar. 'Here you go.' She'd noticed whilst walking back to the table that

Frankie's shoulders had returned to a slouch. His moods appeared to be changeable. Or maybe he wasn't used to being treated kindly?

'Thanks.' He smiled at her as she sat down opposite.

Beatrice pushed a packet of crisps towards him.

Frankie opened the crisp packet, tearing along the side so it lay flat then pushed it to the middle of the table, to share. 'You wanted to ask about the brewery?'

'Yes. As you know I've been investigating the fires at the pubs.'

'What do you want to know?'

Beatrice asked Frankie about his job, and how the brewery was run. She was softening him up for the questions she really wanted to ask. Before tackling them, she bought him a second pint, banking on him not wanting to leave until it was finished. She set the drink down on the table in front of him. 'Robert and Neil seem friendly.' She sat back down.

'I don't think they see each other outside Neil's visits to the brewery.'

'He come often?'

'Every couple of weeks.'

'Does he stay for long?'

'About an hour or so. They usually go into the small office, taking a few beers with them.' Frankie grinned. 'They had to cut it short the day you visited though.'

Beatrice remembered the bottles she'd seen on the desk. 'So, you don't know what they talk about?'

'I'm not interested. I know something *you* might be interested in though.'

'Yes?'

'I looked you up, after you came. You were involved in sorting out the dead businessman a while back. I saw in the article you used to be a tax inspector.'

'That important?'

'It means you'll understand what I'm talking about.'

Frankie went into a detailed explanation about how he'd

137

discovered Robert was selling part of the waste wort to Neil, at a reduced price, for cash in hand. Clearly proud of his detective work, he explained how part of it went through the books, otherwise Gareth and Zoe would have noticed, but they left the brewing details to Robert, so hadn't realised what was happening.

'Until I told Gareth.'

'He knows?'

Frankie nodded.

'When did you tell him?'

'About two months ago.'

'And? What did he say?'

'He'd look into it. I offered to show him the records and how Robert was hiding it, but he never came back to ask me about it. At first, I thought, he was biding his time, until Neil was due again, but nothing happened that visit or since.'

'Perhaps he thought there wasn't much at stake. What does it amount to, maybe a hundred pounds a month.'

'Roughly. But why have someone dishonest working for him? I know how to run everything. I'd just need an assistant. That's what I told the guy who came and was thinking about buying the place. Robert doesn't do much anyway. I know all the brewing side of things, and I'm good with the numbers and admin.'

'You were hoping Gareth would fire him and let you take over running the place?'

'Yeah. But he hasn't, and now it seems like the whole business is going to go down the pan. They should have sold, whilst they had the chance. I've started looking at other jobs. I'm hoping Zoe will give me a reference. I wouldn't want one from Robert.'

'You get on well with Zoe?'

'She's alright.'

'Do Gareth and Zoe get on?'

Frankie shrugged. 'Fine.'

Beatrice couldn't think of anything else to ask, but checked

Frankie had her phone number, in case he thought of anything else. At least he'd given her a couple of leads.

Beatrice had gone back home, where she'd left the list of Wild Geese employees and contact details, and spent time ringing around. She ended her final call, and reflected on the conversations she'd had. She'd managed to speak to another three landlords. They all confirmed someone had been thinking about making an offer to buy the brewery and pubs, but nothing had come of it.

Michael Burgess had seemed convinced the fires were to do with the business, with his insistence it was "nothing personal". Was that an assumption, or real knowledge? What had whoever put him up to the fires said to him about it? Beatrice knew Gareth would be uncooperative, but perhaps Zoe would be willing to talk to her.

Zoe answered after two rings. 'Hello?'

'Zoe, it's Beatrice Styles.'

'Oh. I'm expecting a call. Can you ring back later?'

Afraid Zoe wouldn't answer next time, Beatrice ploughed on. 'It will only take a minute.'

'Go on then.'

'Did someone approach you about buying the brewery?'

'How do you know…? Never mind. It wasn't serious. A businessman had a look, asked a few questions and made an offer.'

'You turned it down?'

'Yes. Gareth was in two minds about it, but we hadn't been planning to sell. The business was doing well; growing, in fact. The offer was way below market value too. Valued the goodwill at nothing. We turned it down and that was that. Why does it matter?'

'Could the buyer have held a grudge about you not selling?'

'It's business. Of course not. We've seen him several times since, with no issues.'

'Who was it?'

'A man called Victor Malone. He's well-known locally. A very successful businessman who knows a good thing when he sees it. It was a compliment he thought our brewery worth taking on. I've got to go now. Is that it?'

'Yes, thanks.'

Beatrice checked her watch, she had time spare, and there was someone she really wanted to talk to.

Chapter 26

The farmyard was a series of dips and ditches. No doubt easy for a tractor to navigate, but Beatrice didn't want to risk her car. She parked in the lane and walked back down to the farmhouse. Her ring of the doorbell precipitated a cacophony of barking, from several dogs by the sound of it. The door swung open, and three black and white balls of fur shot out. Ignoring Beatrice, the border collies began to chase one another around the yard.

'Can I help you?'

Beatrice turned to look at the woman who'd spoken. She was short and slim, in her forties. Her pretty face was marred by dark circles under her eyes. 'Is Neil in, please?'

'He's out.'

'Can you ask him to call me?' Beatrice passed over a business card. The woman read it and peered up at her. 'What do you want him for?'

Had there been a spark of recognition at her name? Had Robert, the brewery manager told Neil who she was? And then Neil mentioned it to this woman? Beatrice couldn't think why either of them would bother. 'Who are you?' she asked.

'Yasmin, Neil's wife.' She folded her arms.

'I'm looking into the fires at the Wild Geese pubs.'

'What's it got to do with Neil?'

'I'm talking to anyone connected with the brewery, in case they've seen or heard anything useful. I understand Neil goes there regularly, and I thought he'd be worth talking to.'

'Haven't the police caught the guy who did it?'

'No one has been charged yet. It's still an open

investigation.' It sounded thin, even to Beatrice.'

'I'll tell him you came, but there's nothing he can tell you. We don't have much to do with the Browns.' Yasmin whistled loudly, the dogs stopped playing and ran back into the house. Yasmin closed the door.

Walking back to her car, Beatrice checked her watch. There was plenty of time to get home, shower and walk back down to the pub, to meet Pete. Perhaps she could encourage him to develop an interest in coffee and cake so they could meet somewhere else in future.

'Have you got anything for me?' Pete growled, as Beatrice placed a pint of bitter in front of him.

'Isn't a beer enough?' She sat down.

'No. It isn't. Have you seen the Staines yet?'

'Yes.'

'And?'

'They're thinking about it. I gave them your number. It's the best I can do. I did try to say you might be able to help them out. To encourage them.'

'You didn't make any promises, did you?'

'I said maybe you could write the story in a sympathetic way.' Beatrice decided not to tell him she'd raise the idea of a fee. 'They've lost everything, including their home and only source of income.'

'Hmm. I suppose I could talk to them about setting up one of those donation pages. We occasionally get offers from the public, wanting to help.'

'Thanks.'

'They still at the sisters?'

'Yes. They've nowhere else to go.' Beatrice sipped at her orange juice. 'Don't go badgering them though, will you?'

'As if I would!' Pete took out his notebook. 'Go on then. Tell me about the night of the fire. We need this online as soon as. People are already losing interest.'

With reluctance, Beatrice told Pete the story of how she

came to be at the pub and chase down the fire starter.

'Don't look so worried,' said Pete, closing his notebook. 'You're the heroine of the piece. I'll make sure you come off well. You'll be Lincolnshire's most in-demand private investigator by the time I've worked my magic.'

'We'll see. I need information from you now.'

Pete looked down into his empty glass.

Beatrice sighed and went to get another pint. When she returned, she started asking questions before handing it over. 'What do you know about Victor Malone?'

'Blimey.' Pete puffed out his cheeks and regarded her for several seconds.

'What?'

'Bit out of your league, isn't he?'

'Is he?'

Pete gestured at the beer and Beatrice passed it across. He had a long swig, then leaned forward. 'I don't know anything for certain. Not certain enough to publish, anyway, but what I do know isn't good.'

'Go on.'

'He has legitimate business interests. He popped up out of nowhere about ten years ago and bought a load of rental properties, mainly cheap terraces. Where he was before, and where he got his money from, I don't know.' He sipped his beer whilst thinking. 'Since then, he's widened his interests. He spots a successful business he wants and buys it.'

'What if they don't want to sell up?' Beatrice was thinking of the Browns, who'd turned his offer down.

'Victor Malone is not someone you say no to.'

'You think he'd do anything? Get revenge?'

'I don't know, but he's not a nice man.' Pete regarded her with an unusually serious expression.

'What aren't you telling me, Pete?'

'Just rumours. In fact, you're probably better off talking to your friendly police officer. She'll know more than me.'

'I will, but what have you heard?'

'Word is, he's involved in trafficking.'

'Of what?'

'Drugs and people.' Pete paused. 'Women. Girls, really.'

'For prostitution?'

'I should think so.'

Beatrice stared at the tabletop, trying not to imagine what life would be like for those women and girls forced into the sex trade.

Pete placed a hand on her arm. 'Be careful, Beatrice. He's dangerous. You should keep well away.'

She patted his hand, distracted by the idea Victor Malone could have decided to take revenge on the Browns.

Beatrice parked outside Rosie's Sudbrooke home and turned to James. 'Ready?'

James laughed. 'It won't be that bad. Come on.'

The door was answered by the twins, dressed in pyjamas. 'Hooray!' they cried. Each grabbed a hand of Beatrice and James and dragged them inside.

'At least we've got a warm welcome,' James whispered in Beatrice's ear.

'Mummy said we could stay up until you came,' said Katie.

'And Mummy said you'd have to go straight to bed, too.' Rosie had emerged from the kitchen, drying her hands.

'Can Auntie Bea and Uncle James read us a story?' asked Abbie.

'Please, Mummy?' added Katie.

Beatrice turned to James and silently mouthed 'Uncle James?'

He grinned and shrugged.

'One story only,' said Rosie in a stern voice, then looked at Beatrice. 'The food will be ready in fifteen minutes.'

'Yes, Ma'am.' Beatrice saluted as she and James were pulled up the stairs by the twins.

'Where's Adam?' Beatrice and James, were sitting at the dining table. Rosie had taken several trips to bring in plates and dishes of food.

'Hiding in the garage,' said Rosie. 'I'll get him. You two start serving yourselves.'

When Rosie returned, Adam followed.

'Hi, Adam,' said Beatrice, with forced cheerfulness.

There was no reply, just a frown.

'Alright, mate,' said James.

Adam grunted, then sat down.

Beatrice complimented Rosie on the meal before turning to Adam. 'How are you? I haven't seen you for ages.'

He looked at her for a few seconds, before deigning to answer. 'Fine.' He returned to eating.

After several more direct attempts, Beatrice fell into silence. Rosie and James made a spirited attempt to fill the quiet with light-hearted chat until they were interrupted by Adam noisily pushing his chair back.

'I'll see you at work tomorrow.'

'Er, sure,' said James.

'Where are you going?' demanded Rosie.

'I've done,' Adam replied.

'We have guests.'

'Yours. Not mine. I don't get to have a say in things.' With a glare, he left the room.

Rosie picked up her and Adam's plates and went through to the kitchen. James stood, about to follow her.

'I'll go,' said Beatrice. She found Rosie trying to push a plate into the dishwasher with considerable force. Beatrice took it from her, placed it on the side, and wrapped her arms around Rosie, holding her until she ran out of tears.

'I'm sorry.' Rosie blew her nose.

'You've nothing to be sorry about.'

'I shouldn't let him get to me.'

'Is he always like that?'

Rosie nodded. 'He spends even less time with the girls now, too. It's not like he was ever going to win a father of the year award, but he's managed to get more useless.'

'What can I do?'

'Nothing. We have to sort it ourselves, but I can't go on like this much longer.'

After saying goodbye to Rosie, Beatrice and James sat in the car and shared a look.

'Wow.' Beatrice shook her head.

'I know, right.' James pulled on his seat belt. 'Shall we get out of here?'

With a last glance at the house and a pang of guilt at leaving her sister, Beatrice started the car and pulled off the drive.

'You and Rosie did well, trying to keep talking.'

'She's easy to get on with. You were quiet.'

'Maybe. You know you didn't have to agree with her when she told me I work too much.'

'Sorry. I do know your work is important to you, but I enjoy spending time with you and…'

'What?'

'Sometimes it feels like, when we're together, you're busy thinking about work.'

Beatrice had to concede he had a point. She did have a tendency to be single-minded when it came to her investigations, finding it hard to let go of them. 'How about, when we get home, I give you my full attention?'

James placed his hand on her knee. 'Now that sounds good.'

Chapter 27

Wednesday 27th June

Beatrice arrived at the community centre early. In the hall she found a woman with bright red, short hair. Jules. Average height, wearing loose fitting trousers and a checked shirt, she was setting up for the women's group. Half a dozen tables had been put into a large rectangle. Jules was struggling to cover them with vinyl tablecloths.

'Can I help you?' Beatrice asked.

Jules spun around. 'I didn't hear you come in.'

'Sorry I startled you.' she smiled. 'I'm Beatrice. We spoke on the phone.'

'Of course.' She walked over and held out her hand. 'I'm Jules. Good to meet you.'

'Thanks for letting me come.'

'No problem at all. If you could help with these,' she gestured at the pile of tablecloths, 'it would speed things up.'

'Sure.'

Beatrice helped Jules cover the tables in overlapping pieces of plastic, and take out several boxes from a storage cupboard set in the corner of the room, containing paint, palettes and brushes. Afterwards they placed chairs at the tables.

Jules glanced at her watch. 'The others will be here soon,' she said, regarding Beatrice, thoughtfully. 'What's he like? Your sister's husband?'

'Adam?' She was surprised by the question, and thought it best to stick to the truth; the lie about the pregnancy was big enough to trip her up already. 'He's alright, I suppose.'

'You don't like him?'

'I don't know him well. He's moody.'

'He gets on with your sister though?'

Beatrice hesitated. After the dreadful dinner, the answer would have to be no.

'Why do you want her to join the women's group?'

'She doesn't know anyone here. I thought it would be a way for her to make friends. I talked to Morwenna about the mother and baby group too.'

'It would be good for her to have people she can talk to. Especially with a baby. It is her first I presume?'

'Oh, yes.'

Jules nodded. 'She should come to us as soon as she can. It will help her settle in.'

Women began to arrive. Soon there were fifteen of them, seated at the tables, wearing oversized shirts, splashing paint around. Beatrice joined in and, to her surprise, enjoyed herself. The painting she created was a mess, but she'd enjoyed the process, and felt comfortable with the easy way the women chatted. A lot of it was casual, but now and again one of the women would mention something, like an argument with a husband, or difficulties with a child, and the others would sympathise and offer advice. Joining social groups had never seemed like her kind of thing, but she had a new appreciation for the mutual support they offered.

Two hours passed quickly, the only interruption being for tea and biscuits. At the end Beatrice stayed to help clean up, hoping to get Jules talking about Lily, but she couldn't think how to subtly introduce the subject.

Once the hall was tidy, Jules turned to Beatrice. 'Do you fancy a drink? There's a pub around the corner.'

'Yes, thanks.'

'Great. There's something I'd like to talk to you about, but not here.'

They made their way to the pub in silence, Jules leading. Beatrice wondered if she'd said or done anything to make the other woman suspicious of her.

Inside the pub Jules indicated a quiet nook. 'You sit there. What can I get you?'

'Orange juice, please.'

Jules returned a few minutes later. She began talking as soon as she sat down. 'I know you've got to get back to Lincoln, so I'll come straight to the point. I'm worried about your sister.'

'Rosie! Why?'

'I've heard the same story before.'

'What story?'

'Woman gets into a relationship, becomes pregnant, boyfriend or husband isolates her from family and friends, takes control of her money, watches her every move...'

'But...'

'Trust me. Your sister sounds like a classic case. The fall she had. Was it really a fall? No one was there to see.'

'Adam was.'

'No one else, I meant.' She raised her eyebrows and inclined her head. 'How do you know what really happened? That he didn't do something?'

'I... Rosie would tell me.'

Jules shook her head. 'That's not true. You don't know how it affects women, in these situations. They're ashamed, embarrassed. They think it's their fault, and they've done something to deserve it.'

'But Rosie and I are close.' Beatrice was starting to lose sight of the fact Jules' assessment was all based on the lies of a pregnancy and a fall. And there was Adam's behaviour at dinner. What was really happening in her sister's marriage? She gave herself a mental shake. Rosie would tell her, if anything was going on, but she could use it, maybe to lead on to talking about Lily.

'I had a friend once. Lucy.' Beatrice changed the name on instinct. 'She met a man and soon moved in with him. After a couple of months, she told us she was pregnant, and I saw less and less of her.' Beatrice stared into her orange juice and left a silence she hoped Jules would fill.

'Your friend could have been in the same position. Just because Rosie is your sister, doesn't mean it's not happening to her.'

'Lucy disappeared after the baby was born. Her boyfriend came looking for her, but I hadn't seen her in ages.'

'There you go, then. Sounds like she had a lucky escape.'

Beatrice sat in thoughtful silence. Charles had told her how quickly the relationship with Lily had developed, and Andrew said he'd heard less from Lily as time went on. Was that why Lily had left? Because she was afraid of Charles? Had Jules known her situation, and helped her? 'You said you'd heard the same story before.'

'Unfortunately.'

'From women in the group?' Beatrice ventured.

'Yes, and the mother and baby group.'

'Why don't they leave? I wouldn't stick around, if a man was hurting me.'

'It's not always physical violence. Usually, the husband or boyfriend likes to control the woman's life: her access to money, to family and friends. I've been doing this for a few years now, and I've seen men walk their wife to the baby group, and be there waiting at the end.'

'You don't think they're just being supportive?'

'Not always, no.' Jules leaned forward, elbows on the table. 'You might like to talk to your sister.'

Beatrice nodded. 'Thanks.' She paused. 'What do I do? If there is a problem?'

'Give me a ring. I can put you in touch with people who might be able to offer her support and practical assistance. Every situation is different, but there's a good chance they could help her. If she wants them to.'

'Is that what you've done with the women you mentioned?'

'Yes. I try to steer the women who need it towards official organisations. There are charities, who do what they can to help them stay safe.'

'You don't get involved yourself?'

'Not if I can help it.' Jules hesitated, as if having an internal debate about how much to reveal. 'But sometimes, yes.'

'How?'

'I help them get away. To disappear.'

'Isn't there an easier way to deal with things? Rather than give up their lives?'

'I only get involved with the really desperate ones. When they can't or won't go to the police, family or friends for help, if they're worried about the lengths their abuser will go to.'

'How do they disappear? Don't families want to find them?'

'It only works where there's not much in the way of a family. The woman has to be prepared to cut ties with everyone in her life. Completely. It's a huge step. Imagine how scared you'd have to be, to be willing to do that.'

Beatrice couldn't imagine it, but believed Jules was sincere. 'How do you stop the police getting involved? If someone disappears, they're going to ask questions?'

'You get the woman to write a letter, saying she's leaving.'

Beatrice thought back to her conversation with Charles. He'd said Lily had left a letter with a friend, but hadn't mentioned having a copy himself.

'But not why she's leaving?'

'No. The idea is to go, not give the police a reason to search. These women just want to get away. They want to be safe. Their children to be safe.'

'How do you know the abuser will hand over the letter? Couldn't they lie and get the police to search for them?'

'They could. So, we make a copy and give it to the abuser. The original goes to the police, but not straight away. It's always interesting to find out if he'll pass it over. And, if it later becomes an issue, the police have evidence of the woman's desire to get away, and of his trying to hide things.'

'What do you mean, become an issue?'

'These guys don't tend to let go easily. They're persistent. Especially ones who like to think of women as their property.'

'And sometimes they find them?'

'Yes.'

'And then?'

'Depends on the man.' Jules stared into her drink. 'Once, one of the women I helped had things go as bad as they can.'

'What happened?'

'She'd got careless.' Jules looked directly at Beatrice, emphasising the seriousness of what she was saying. 'We tell them to stay away from family, stay off social media, not to go back to places where they might be recognised. This woman, she missed her family and created a false account on social media, started following her siblings. He was watching out for it, saw her account appear on the brother's and sister's profile, and became suspicious. He took on a false name, followed her profile, and they began exchanging messages. He was clever, never pushing it too far, and he was patient. After a while, they agreed to meet for coffee.' Jules straightened up and wiped her damp brow.

'And?'

'Her body was found a few days later.'

'Jesus!' Beatrice sat in silence for a minute. 'Did the police catch him?'

'Eventually. But it wasn't any help to her, was it?' Jules finished the last of her drink. 'The charity side of things at the centre is a place for women to meet and do activities together. The other side, that's just me and a couple of others, nothing official.'

'But it's how you find women to help?'

'Yes. We're not actively looking, but can often tell which ones are in trouble. We let them know they can talk to us and build up trust. We don't tell them to leave, but if they want to, we offer help and advice.'

'You and the others, you have personal experience?'

Jules regarded Beatrice steadily. 'You ask lots of questions.'

'Sorry. That was too personal. I guess I was wondering what motivates you.'

'We all have our stories, and enough bad experiences to want to help other women caught up in something they can't get out of.'

Chapter 28

The conversation petered out, with Beatrice distracted by what Jules had told her. What did she actually know about Rosie's marriage? Was Adam the kind of man to raise his hand to her? The way he'd been over their mother's money certainly suggested a willingness to bully her, and the prolonged sulking and refusing to talk about their problems weren't the actions of someone trying to be reasonable, or reach a compromise.

'I've got to go,' said Jules.

'Thanks for the drink.' Beatrice drained her glass.

They walked the short distance back to the community centre in silence.

In the car park Jules pulled out her keys. 'Talk to your sister. It's all you can do, apart from making sure she knows where we are. She can come anytime.'

'Thanks.' Beatrice felt guilty lying to Jules, who seemed genuinely concerned about the fictional Rosie. 'I will.' The conversation had helped her to think about Lily's situation more critically too, which she was grateful for.

Jules nodded, climbed into the van, and drove away. Beatrice, watching from the car park, noticed a small sticker on the back, bearing the name of a van hire company. Was it the same van Jules had used to take Lily from Charles' house? The lettering was so small it was unlikely the neighbour could have read it from across the road. Once out of sight, she jotted down the company name and registration plate. A quick internet search on her phone showed the firm had an office and storage yard on the outskirts of the city.

Walking back to her car, Beatrice wondered whether to go

to see if Charles was in, and update him on progress. She was reluctant to do so. Everything Jules had told her made her more wary of him. She didn't feel physically threatened by him, partly due to her own size, partly because if he was the kind of man Jules had described, he'd be likely to select a target he knew wouldn't report any assault. Bullies were good at choosing victims.

Was that Rosie? A victim? The idea wasn't going away. She'd have to ask Rosie, no matter how difficult the conversation would be. She owed it to her sister to watch out for her, and make sure she knew she could count on Beatrice. As for Charles, she'd need to think about what to tell him, once she'd checked into the situation further. She needed to be confident she was doing the right thing.

Beatrice parked in front of the van hire office, and once inside, walked with fake confidence, up to the reception desk, to address the woman seated behind it. 'Hi. I wonder if you could help me?'

'I'll try.' The young woman, flashed a broad smile.

'I've come from the community centre in town. Morwenna, the manager, was wondering if you could give us a copy of an invoice from last year. I realise it's a pain, but we've mislaid the original.'

'I don't know,' said the secretary. 'Last year, you say?'

Beatrice nodded. 'It would have been arranged by Jules,' she offered, hoping the more information she gave, the more convincing she'd sound.

'Oh, I know her. She's a regular customer.'

'This would have been for a van.'

'Why do you need it?'

'It's the auditors. They get twitchy when there's paperwork missing. It's not like it's even for a large amount. If you could print a copy, we'd really appreciate it.'

'I'll have to see if we've archived the records. When was the van hired?'

Beatrice told her the date of Lily's disappearance and waited, whilst she searched the computer. After a few minutes the printer sprang into life.

'You're in luck.' She walked over to the printer and picked up the sheet of paper, checked it then handed it over.

'Thank you so much.' Beatrice quickly skimmed the document. The invoice was made out to Jules Kegan, using the community centre address. It had the date, vehicle and milage. 'That's perfect.'

'You're welcome.'

'We'll make sure we file the invoices properly in future.' Beatrice made a quick exit. As she left, another customer entered and started up a conversation with the receptionist. She hoped it would be enough of a distraction for her to completely forget about the invoice. There was a small chance she'd mention it to Jules, and Jules would check with Morwenna, but it was worth the risk for the information.

Lying made Beatrice uncomfortable, but not as uncomfortable as realising how easy she'd found it. But she couldn't have got the information otherwise. She had an unexpected protective instinct about Jules and her desire to help other women, and wouldn't want to do anything to draw attention to what she was doing. The suspicion Lily had been abused by Charles was one she couldn't ignore, and she considered telling him Lily couldn't be found, but concluded he'd only hire someone else to do it. After all, according to Lily's brother, Andrew, she wasn't the first detective he'd sent looking for her.

Chapter 29

Thursday 28th June

The morning was bright and sunny. Beatrice picked up a coffee at the top of Steep Hill, and strolled down through the town, enjoying the sun and fresh air. Neil Trews farm shop would be open by the time she reached it. She'd telephoned first thing and asked how she could get in touch with Neil. The employee she had spoken to had told her he was due in that morning.

The shop was in a good position, just off the high street, with a colourful A-frame sign. There was a large window with piles of vegetables on display, and a sign declaring organic eggs and meat were on sale.

Inside, the shop walls were covered in white tiles, creating a clean and bright image. Neil was behind the counter, talking to one of the employees when Beatrice entered. The change in his facial expression suggested he recognised her.

'Hello. Neil, isn't it?'

He nodded.

'I'd like a word.' Beatrice glanced at a waiting customer. 'In private would be good.'

With reluctance, Neil indicated an archway, which led to a room behind the shop. 'You'd better come back here.'

The second room was set up as an office and stock room. A large chest freezer occupied a big space at the back. Neil sat at the desk. He didn't offer Beatrice a seat, but she pulled out the chair opposite him and sat anyway.

'What do you want? Make it quick, I've got customers.'

'As you know I'm investigating the pub fires and I'm sure Yasmin told you I went to your house. I was hoping you'd call me. I left my number.'

'I've got a business to run. I can't be messing about with other stuff.' Neil pulled out a large handkerchief from his sleeve and noisily blew his nose. 'Ask your questions then.'

'Did Robert ever tell you if there were any problems with the brewery?'

'No.'

'Were there any issues between Gareth and Zoe?'

'How would I know?'

'You're friendly with Robert. Has he said anything?'

'No. Nothing.'

'Did you know earlier this year someone was thinking about buying the brewery?'

'Robert mentioned it.'

'What did he say?'

'Nothing much. Some guy thought about taking it on, but the Browns didn't want to sell.'

'Was Robert worried he'd lose his job, if it was sold?'

'All I know is that he said the guy who wanted it, Malone, had promised to keep him on when he bought the business. So, no, he wasn't worried about his job.'

'Why would this Malone reassure him?'

Neil shifted his weight and looked away.

'Neil?'

'What?' He snapped.

'I know what you're both up to, with the waste products. I thought I'd pop in and speak to Gareth and Zoe. Make sure they know what's what.'

'I don't know what you're talking about.' His expression implied otherwise.

'You've nothing to worry about then.' Beatrice waited.

'Alright. Just don't tell them, please. It's nothing much. They'd only have to pay to get rid of it, if I didn't take it off their hands.'

'So, you're doing them a favour?'

'Maybe.'

'What is it you know about Robert and Malone?'

'Robert agreed to pass information to Malone.'

'What kind of information?'

'Harmless stuff. About the pubs, how much beer was sent to them, what was sold.'

'And in exchange he'd keep his job?'

'That's how I understood it. Look, I've never met this guy, but I've heard of him.'

'And?'

'If he'd told me to do something, like give him information, I'd do it. I wouldn't tell him no.'

Beatrice had exchanged texts with Susan on the walk back up Steep Hill. She'd planned to visit Rosie and wanted to speak to Susan on the way. They'd agreed to meet in the police station car park.

The policewoman was stressed. 'I've only got a few minutes. What did you want to ask me?'

'Victor Malone,' stated Beatrice.

Susan raised her eyebrows.

'He's come up in connection with an investigation,' Beatrice explained. 'What do you know? I'm told you have quite a file on him.'

'It's all on computer, these days,' said Susan, absently.

'You know what I mean.'

'This wouldn't be to do with a certain investigation I've been told not to discuss with you, would it?'

'How could it be?' Beatrice shrugged.

Susan sighed. 'Between you and me, we've been interested in Malone for years.'

'In connection with what?'

'We'd be happy to get him for anything, even in your old arena of tax evasion, but we suspect him of money laundering, distributing drugs and running a prostitution racket.'

'The person I spoke to mentioned trafficking.'

'It wouldn't surprise me.'

'Is he under investigation currently?'

'Not that we know of, but, if we get any evidence of him being involved in any crime, we're supposed to pass it on.'

'Who to?'

Susan shrugged. 'Above my pay grade. I was told not to take action and let Inspector Mayweather know.' Susan frowned. 'You're not investigating him, are you?'

'Like I said, his name came up. I've nothing on him. As far as I can tell his only association is trying to buy the brewery, and there's no crime in that.'

'He does have genuine businesses, and could be trying to expand. It won't be worth much now, though.'

'That's a very good point.'

'Tread carefully, won't you?' said Susan.

'Of course.'

Susan didn't look convinced, but she glanced at her watch. 'I've got to go,' she said. 'See you.'

Beatrice watched Susan leave. She was getting fed up of people telling her to be careful. If she was going to do her job properly, she had to ask questions some people would rather she didn't ask. If she constantly worried about upsetting people, she might as well close her business and open a flower shop. Besides, she was sure Pete and Susan were being overly cautious about Victor Malone. Her investigation into the fires wasn't going to bother him.

Chapter 30

'Auntie Bea! Auntie Bea!' Rosie's twin girls bounced into the room. Katie held a newspaper, Abbie a pen. They halted abruptly in front of the sofa, where Beatrice was sitting. Rosie watched from an armchair on the opposite side of the lounge.

'Can we get your autograph?' asked Katie, almost out of breath.

Abbie nudged her. 'Please,' she said in a stage whisper.

'Please,' echoed Katie, nodding in rapid motion.

Beatrice took the newspaper and pen. 'How are you, girls? Still enjoying Brownies?'

'Oh, yes.' They said in unison.

'We're going to take the paper to Brownies and tell everyone you're our auntie,' said Abbie. 'You're famous,' said Katie.

'And school,' Abbie chipped in.

Beatrice skimmed over the paper. The report by Pete Evans was a double page spread. She didn't have time, or the girls the patience, to read the article, so she focussed on the photos. The largest was a picture of the Golden Goose in its burnt-out state, with its pre-fire image inset for comparison. There was a portrait of Marie and Brad Staines. The picture which drew more attention was the one next to Pete's byline. She'd not seen it before. Barely recognisable, with smoothed back hair and a neatly trimmed moustache, he looked at least ten years younger.

'What shall I write?'

The girls held a whispered conversation, which took several exchanges. Finally, Katie spoke. 'Sign your name and put you are the auntie of Katie and Abbie.' The girls nodded in sync.

Beatrice did as requested, and handed the paper back.

The girls bent over it, checking. 'Thank you, Auntie Bea,' they chimed, grinning broadly, then they ran out of the room. Beatrice could hear their footsteps on the stairs, then a bedroom door close.

'So, you're famous then,' said Rosie. 'Don't think I'll be asking for your autograph.' She sounded annoyed.

'They're kids,' Beatrice appeased. 'Let them have their fun. Everyone will have forgotten about it by next week. Including them.' She rummaged in her handbag and pulled out an envelope. 'I've brought over receipts and notes of what I've been doing. Can you update the records and invoices, when you get the chance, please?'

Rosie remained silent, staring into space.

'There's no hurry.' Beatrice placed the envelope on the side table. 'Why don't I make us a cup of tea?'

'Sure.'

When Beatrice returned with steaming mugs, Rosie was still in the same position, curled up in the arm chair. She accepted the drink in silence.

Beatrice sat back down, looking at her sister. Always smaller than Beatrice, today Rosie seemed even more reduced, as if she were turned in on herself, hiding from the world. Marriage guidance wasn't something she knew anything about, but the situation couldn't be ignored, and she had a difficult, related topic she wanted to address. It was best to get it over with. 'How are you doing?'

Rosie glanced at her and shrugged. 'You know.'

'No. I don't. That's why I'm asking.'

Rosie opened and closed her mouth several times. 'I don't really know. I can't carry on like this. I don't want to. You saw what he was like.'

Beatrice nodded. 'What are your options?'

'Give him the money? Let him have his way?' She shook

her head. 'Not this time. I want to do what's best for all of us. He wants what's best for him.'

'He still won't accept a compromise on how your money is spent?'

'No.'

'So, what are you thinking?'

'Whether or not to try to save my marriage.'

'You've had rough patches before. And got through them.'

'Only by me giving Adam whatever he wanted. I'm not prepared to do it anymore. I basically parent the girls and run the house alone. He doesn't seem to care about any of it.' Her voice cracked. 'Or me.'

'I'm sorry. You know you can come to me any time.'

'You can't fit all three of us in your place. Besides, I don't think it's a good idea for me to leave the house.' Rosie frowned at Beatrice's concerned expression. 'I'll deal with it.'

'Actually, I had something I wanted to ask you. It's kind of related and I wasn't sure if I should, except…'

'Except?'

Beatrice let out a long breath, walked across the room and knelt next to Rosie. 'OK. You know I've been searching for Lily and her daughter?'

Rosie nodded.

'I've been talking to a woman, who helped Lily to leave Charles' house.'

'And? Come on Beatrice, spit it out. Don't make me drag it out of you.'

'Right. Does Adam hurt you?'

There was a silence.

'Wow,' said Rosie. 'I did not expect that.'

'I'm sorry. This Jules I was talking to, sees a lot of women in abusive relationships.'

'And it made you think that Adam's been hitting me?' Rosie didn't seem angry, more surprised.

'He's been so off with you lately, bullying really. Not talking to you. Jules said women can be really good at hiding what's going on.' Beatrice reached for Rosie's hand and held on tightly. 'It had never entered my head that Adam would physically harm you, but she got me worried, and I couldn't stop thinking about how he's been. I'd never forgive myself if I didn't ask.'

Rosie squeezed her hand. 'It's OK. He is being an idiot, but he doesn't hit me. I promise, I'd tell you if he was.'

'OK. I want you to know I'm here for you. Whatever happens.'

'Thank you.' Rosie managed a brief smile. 'I know things will have to change, at some point. Anyway, you've got enough going on. I can sort this.'

The detective is still sniffing around. I thought she'd done investigating. Turns out the insurers hired her. Could be a problem. She was in the paper again this week. The report made out she was some kind of hero.

I had a word with people in the know. Seems she's not bad for a PI. Maybe too good. Made the police look stupid over the murder last month. I know the type, won't let sleeping dogs lie, keeps on until she knows the truth. I may need to do something about her. She can't have any real evidence. I've been careful. Best to find out what she knows, then I can decide if more direct action is needed.

Chapter 31

Friday 29th June

Gareth scowled at Beatrice as she was shown into the brewery office. He was alone, sitting at the desk with his arms folded. 'What do you want this time?' he barked.

Realising he wasn't going to be civil, no matter how she approached him, she didn't bother with any preamble. 'Why are you letting Robert steal from you?'

'Don't be ridiculous. It's none of your business.' He waved the question away.

'Robert's been selling waste products to Neil Trews, and only putting part of it through the business. He's been pocketing the rest.'

'I'll look into it. You finished?'

'You were told about it, months ago. You said you'd look into it then, but you've let him carry on. I'd like to know why?'

'How we run our business is nothing to do with you.'

Beatrice noticed Gareth's reddening face. She'd expected him to be unhappy about her raising the subject, but not to this degree. 'What's going on, Gareth? Why won't you tackle him? Or Neil?'

'We're done.' Gareth jumped to his feet, walked to the door and opened it.

Beatrice turned to look Gareth right in the eyes and said, 'I *will* find out what's going on.'

'Out.'

Back home, in her office, Beatrice checked over the

invoice from the Norwich van hire company. It was dated the day Lily left Charles, and the milage showed Jules had driven 230 miles, which would have included the return journey, so a range of 115 miles. Beatrice switched on her laptop and found a mapping website.

She started with the assumption Charles was correct about Lily heading back to Lincolnshire. The distance between Norwich and Lincoln was 104 miles by the direct route. This meant, if Jules had taken Lily to her final destination, she couldn't have got much further than 10 or 15 miles beyond Lincoln. It narrowed down the search considerably. It also meant Andrew's note with the Fiskerton address was a possibility.

Beatrice's musings were interrupted by her mobile.

'Hello, Beatrice.' Marina's voice was cheerful.

'You sound happy.'

'I am. I finally exchanged on the sale of the house and cottages. We complete in two weeks. Three days after that, I'm on a plane to the US.'

'Congratulations.'

'Thank you. I'm really looking forward to it. A chance for a fresh start.'

'I hope it all works out for you.'

Marina laughed. 'I'm determined to make sure it does. I'm actually excited.'

'That's great, but I assume you're ringing about Zoe and Gareth Brown? Did you find out anything?'

'A bit. Lesley started getting suspicious, so I couldn't push it too far.'

'What can you tell me?'

'They say a picture paints a thousand words, and the one we saw with Gareth ogling Astra sums him up, I'm afraid.'

'Gareth and Astra?'

'Not her. But rumour is, there is someone, and has been for a while. Besides, Astra has minders. She'd never get the chance to have an affair, even if she wanted to.'

'Minders?'

'Astra always has some man or other following her, driving her places. Supposedly for her protection, but I think Malone wants to keep tabs on her.'

'He sounds lovely.'

'I know.'

'Did Lesley have any idea who Gareth is seeing?'

'Nothing definite. But the woman is married too, and Lesley mentioned Gareth's frequent trips out west.'

'I wonder what she meant. London's West End?'

'I got the impression it was more local.'

'So maybe west relative to where they live?'

'Or where the business is,' Marina suggested.

'Good point.' Beatrice was thinking of Yasmin, the farmer's wife. Had she been after excitement, away from her daily grind? Neil and Yasmin lived west of Spilsby.

'Are you still there?' asked Marina.

'Yes. Sorry, I was thinking. Does Zoe know about the affair? Assuming it's true.'

'I don't think so.'

'Thanks for talking to her, Marina. I appreciate it.'

'Glad to help. Anything else I can do?'

'No, thanks. You're going to have your hands full for the next couple of weeks.'

'I'm having a party on Saturday, at the house. A sort of goodbye. I know it's short notice, but I'd be glad if you could make it.'

'Send me the details,' said Beatrice, flattered to be asked, given the kind of illustrious company Marina was used to keeping. 'If I can make it I will. I'd really like to be there. Do I need to bring anything? Food or a bottle?'

'No, nothing at all. Just yourself.'

'Great. See you, then.'

'Bye.' Marina rang off.

Beatrice was pleased for Marina, getting to achieve a lifelong ambition, but she would be sad to see her leave. She only had Susan as a friend in Lincoln so far, and was sorry to lose the chance to get to know Marina better. It was interesting what she'd found out through Lesley though. If true, it could provide a suspect for who set up the fires. A jealous husband, for example.

She needed to gather real evidence, and wondered about Gareth's failure to challenge Robert and Neil about the stealing. Was it because it meant he knew when Yasmin's husband would be busy at the brewery for an hour or so?

Beatrice texted Frankie. *Hi Frankie. It was good to talk last week. I'd appreciate it if you could let me know when Neil is due at the brewery again, please. But don't get yourself in trouble finding out.*

The reply came back within minutes. *Tuesday morning at ten.*

Beatrice made a note in her calendar. What are you up to Gareth? Something you shouldn't be? Is that why you were reluctant to hire me?

Chapter 32

'I've got something for you.'

Beatrice laughed 'Wow! Pete Evans volunteering information! With not even a pint of beer to show for it. Whatever next?'

Pete had appeared, unexpectedly, at her home. They were now sitting at the dining table with mugs of tea. Pete stared at his, as if he didn't know what it was. He sniffed and took an experimental sip. 'I figured I owed you. The article about you and the Staines family was a big hit. I even got a mention in a few nationals.'

'Go on then, spill.'

'The body in the Cooked Goose has been identified. With help from yours truly.' He looked smug.

'Who is it?'

'Not so fast. Let me tell it in my own way. I am a master of words, after all.'

Beatrice rolled her eyes. 'Fine.'

'There is this woman, Janice. A bit rough looking. Mouthy. You know the type.' Pete grinned. 'So, she goes to the police about a week ago.'

'Before the body was found?'

'Yep.' Pete had another sip of tea and pulled a face. 'So, at the station, she reports her husband missing. Kicks up a fuss and makes a lot of noise. Thing is, it's not the first time she's claimed he's gone missing, is it? On previous occasions, he's eventually turned up with no explanation.'

'Another woman?'

'You'd be forgiven for thinking so, but he's an ugly little

bastard. Hard to imagine he'd talk anyone, other than Janice, into taking him on.'

'So, where's he been these other times?'

'We'll come back to that.'

Beatrice performed an exaggerated sigh.

'The police think it's the usual, and he'll be back in a few days. But she's actually really worried this time and gets extra mouthy with them. They're none too happy and tell her to sling her hook, or they'll arrest her. That's when she comes to talk to me.'

'Why you?'

'That's a bit rude!'

'Sorry.'

'It's because I was the only one who'd listen, and I know how to talk to people like her. These new graduate types look down their noses at people like Janice.'

'Can I refer you back to your use of the word "mouthy" just now?'

'I wouldn't say it to her though, would I?'

'That makes it OK?' Beatrice shook her head. 'What did you do?'

'I listened, made notes, told her to go home, and I'd follow it up.'

'And you found out...?'

'Her husband went out to work on Sunday the seventeenth. Everything seemed normal. He had plans to play pool with his mates later the same night. Janice says they talked about going to Skegness on the weekend. She waved him off in the morning, said he was happy, almost excited. The thing is, he never came home, and hasn't been seen since. Not by anyone I've talked to. His phone's gone dead too.'

'Did he arrive at work?'

'Don't know.'

'Why not?'

'I didn't ask.'

Beatrice frowned. 'That's not like you.'

'There's some places even I don't go sticking my nose in.'

'Where does he work?'

'A building maintenance firm. Or at least that's what it claims to be.'

'Why wouldn't you go there?'

'Because it's owned by Victor Malone.'

Beatrice folded her arms. 'He works for Malone?'

'I'm not making a mistake telling you this am I?'

'Of course not. What do you know about him? The victim.'

'He's called Lee Chambers. Thirty-two years old. Been knocking about with Janice for a few years. He's been done for minor stuff, nothing too serious and has managed to stay out of jail, apart from a brief stint a few years back.'

'What for?'

'He was part of a group picked up for an assault in a pub. I don't know more than that. You'd need to ask your friendly detective.'

'As opposed to the unfriendly one.'

Pete grinned at her. 'You can ask the pretty one, anyway.'

'Can't. Fisher has warned her off.'

'You need to cultivate more sources in the police, if she isn't giving you the goods.'

'You're probably right. I like Susan and I don't want to get her into trouble.'

'You need to keep business and pleasure separate, too.' He gave her a glance, then turned away. 'Mostly.'

Beatrice was still trying to fathom his meaning when he spoke again.

'How's your boyfriend doing?'

'James? He's fine. Why?'

'No reason.' Pete pushed his almost full mug of tea away from him. 'Thanks for the tea.'

'Looks like you enjoyed it.'

Pete stood up and pulled on his coat, despite the heat of the day.

'You know anything else about Lee Chambers?'

'If you're going to ask about him, you should know he went by Bugsy.'

'Like Bugsy Malone? Seriously? Because he thought he was a gangster? Or because he was close to Malone?'

'The likes of him don't get cosy with the Malone's of this world. They're tolerated whilst they're useful.' Pete shrugged. 'Word is, he liked to think it's why he's called that. Made him feel important. It was actually because he bugged the hell out of everyone. They were laughing at him.'

'Anything else?'

'He's a non-entity. One of Malone's hangers-on. Docs stuff for him.'

'Like what?'

'Fetching, carrying. Anything.'

'Keeping an eye on Malone's girlfriend?'

'Probably. Malone likes to keep the younger, good-looking ones away from her. In case of temptation. They'd have to be bloody stupid to try anything though.'

'Not worth losing their job over?'

'If it was only losing their job, they might think it worth the risk.'

'You think he'd hurt them?' Beatrice was shocked.

'Or worse. Malone's a bastard. A very dangerous man. You should stay well away.'

'I know.'

Pete sighed. 'You're not going to listen, are you?'

Once Pete left, Beatrice considered what he'd told her. Clearly, he thought Malone was the kind of man to physically harm or maybe even kill anyone who crossed him. Which meant arranging for Michael Burgess to burn down a few buildings was a real possibility.

If Bugsy was one of Astra's minders, had he tried to get too familiar with her? Beatrice couldn't see it. Astra was an attractive woman, but Bugsy would've known Malone wouldn't be forgiving if he'd overstepped the line. There must be a reason he wound up dead and was in the fire. Had he done something to anger Malone? Serious enough to get him killed? Or did he know something he shouldn't? She needed to talk to Astra. In the meantime, the other person she could talk to was an unnerving option. But he'd have all the answers, even if he didn't want to provide them.

She searched on the internet for a phone number and found one listed for his office. Her call was answered on the second ring.

'Malone's Property. How may I help you?' The woman's voice was calm and assured.

'I'd like to speak to Mr Malone, please.'

'I'm sorry. That won't be possible. What's it about? I could try to put you in contact with an appropriate person.'

Beatrice hesitated. How far was she willing to push it? She could hardly accuse him of murder, but could she say enough to make him agree to see her? 'I assume Mr Malone has a personal assistant or secretary?'

'Er, yes.'

''Well, it's rather a delicate matter. Can I speak to them about it?'

'Your name, please?'

'Beatrice Styles. I'm a private detective.' She heard a small intake of breath on the other end of the phone.

'Please hold.'

It was a couple of minutes before the voice came back on the line. 'I'm putting you through to Mr Malone's personal assistant.'

'Thank…' There was a click, a purring ringtone, then a new, male voice came on. One which was smooth and cultured.

'Miss Styles?'

'Yes.'

'You wished to speak to Mr Malone?'

'That's correct.'

'I'm afraid Mr Malone is a very busy and important man.'

'I'm aware of who he is.'

'Then you understand he can't be disturbed with trivial matters.'

'I don't think the murder of one of his employees, and the arrest of another for arson are trivial matters.'

There was an extended silence.

'I'm going to put you on hold for a moment.'

Beatrice was left waiting for ten minutes, listening to a snippet of the Vivaldi's Four Seasons on a repeating loop.

'Miss Styles?'

'Yes?'

'Mr Malone will see you today at six p.m. I have your number. I'll text you the location.' The call ended abruptly and was immediately followed with the promised text.

Beatrice searched the address on the internet. It was a large building, set in several acres of garden, surrounded by farmland. Presumably it was Malone's home. With several hours until she needed to head out, she spent the time planning her interview. Feeling a little foolish, she left a note for James, explaining where she was going.

Chapter 33

On arrival at the mansion house, Beatrice was greeted with closed gates and an intercom system. Once the voice on the other end had confirmed her meeting, the gates swung open in a majestic arc. She parked in front of the building, as instructed, and got out of her car. A man in a dark suit, holding an ipad, came out of the house. The PA, she assumed.

'Miss Styles,' he said. 'You're early.'

'The traffic was lighter than I expected.'

The man sniffed. 'Come in, but you'll have to wait until Mr Malone is ready for you.'

'Of course.' Following him along an immaculately decorated double-height hallway, to the rear of the house, she walked past several closed doors, and many original oil paintings of the long-dead. It was unlikely they were ancestors of Malone; more likely they were bought to complete the image of the well-to-do country house. At the end of the hallway, outside a solid oak door, several chairs were arranged along the wall.

'Remain here.' He knocked lightly on the door and slipped inside the room.

For the twenty minutes she was kept waiting, Beatrice rehearsed the questions she planned to ask, trying to stifle a nervousness she was determined to keep at bay. When finally invited into the office, she was calm and prepared.

Beatrice was curious about Malone. The photographs hadn't prepared her for his presence. He stood, straight-backed and square shouldered, in front of a large oak desk. He was of average height and had a trim figure. His well-lined face would have been pleasant enough, if it weren't for the dark, brooding nature of his eyes. He regarded Beatrice for several seconds, his eyes ranging up and down her body. His expression of disdain suggested she wasn't a woman he could have any interest in.

'Sit,' he spoke curtly, then returned to the other side of the desk, placing himself in the dark-green leather chair.

Beatrice sat on the hard wooden seat placed opposite.

'You wanted to see me.' The businessman took immediate control of the conversation.

'Yes. Thank you for agreeing…'

'What do you want?'

'I'm investigating the fires at the Wild Geese brewery.'

'So?'

'You know the owners: Zoe and Gareth Brown.'

He shrugged.

'I heard you had made an offer to buy their business.'

Malone's eyes became slits. 'Where did you hear that?'

'Is it right?' She regarded him steadily, despite his glare. Beatrice sensed a shifting to her left and couldn't help but glance that way. She caught a glimpse of a large figure, before Malone demanded her attention again.

'I occasionally buy businesses. If it's worth my while. The Browns turned down my offer.'

'Were you upset about it?'

'It's just business.' Malone dismissed the question with a wave of his hand.

'Some people might be offended.'

'Don't be ridiculous.'

Was his annoyance due to being challenged? Everyone she'd talked to suggested he liked to be in control, and expected to get whatever he wanted. She doubted he would take a refusal so calmly. Would he seek revenge?

'I'm a busy man. Anything else?'

'Did you know there was a body found in the fire at the Cooked Goose?'

'I have no interest in other people's businesses. I have enough to deal with in my own.'

'You wouldn't know who the dead man was then?'

'How could I?'

'His name was Lee Chambers.' Beatrice watched for a reaction. There was none. 'Known as Bugsy.' Had his eyes narrowed a little at the nickname? And had the large figure off to the side shifted briefly? She resisted the temptation to turn her head, focusing on the man behind the desk.

Malone shrugged.

'He worked for you. Until his death.'

'Lots of people work for me through my various businesses. I can't be expected to know them all.'

'Are you saying you didn't know him?'

'I couldn't be sure.'

A non-committal answer. 'He was last seen on his way to work. For you. Did he turn up?'

'Why would I know?'

'Sunday the seventeenth was the date his wife last saw him.'

'If you say so.'

'Did you see him that evening?'

Malone grunted. 'I was in another part of the country, so I couldn't have.'

'Where were you?'

'That's not your concern.'

Doubtful she was going to get any more out of him, Beatrice nonetheless continued. 'The police have been questioning someone in connection with the arson attacks.'

Malone's gaze remained steady.

'His name is Michael Burgess. He's been known to work for you too.'

'Your point?'

'It seems rather significant that both the victim and the arsonist were employees of yours.'

'Not to me, it doesn't.'

'So, when the fires happened and when Bugsy was killed,

they wouldn't have been working for you, then?'

Malone leant forward. 'I don't like what you're implying.'

'I'm not implying anything. I'm asking questions.'

'This meeting is over.' Malone looked across at the man standing sentry. 'Jackson.'

In two steps the large figure towered over Beatrice and she was very aware of his presence. She turned to look at the man called Jackson. Her racing heart thundered in her ears and her palms became clammy. She'd never been as close to anyone so huge and intimidating. He was tall with large, powerful muscles, and emanated a sense of danger. The bend in his long nose and the scar above his right eye, hinted at a violent past.

'Really?' she asked, relieved by the lack of tremor in her voice. 'What's he going to do? Throw me out?'

'If you make it necessary.'

'I've been perfectly civil.'

Malone stood and came around the desk. He bent forwards over her, placing his hands on the arms of her chair. His face stopped inches from Beatrice's. She felt trapped and vulnerable, but kept her expression still.

'You've all but accused me of arson, murder and setting up someone else to take the fall.' Malone glared at her. 'Using the façade of polite words and questions doesn't make their meaning any less insulting.'

'I'm a detective. It's my job to ask difficult questions.' This time her voice did tremble on the last words.

'Don't play games with me, Miss Styles. I always win.' His words were almost a growl. Malone held her gaze for a long moment then stood upright and stepped back.

Now with space to move, Beatrice stood and Malone had to raise his head to continue glaring at her. 'If you really had nothing to hide, you'd answer my questions.'

'You call yourself a detective, but you have no standing. Neither I nor anyone else is obliged to indulge your impertinent interrogation.' He returned to his chair. 'Jackson. Show this individual out.'

The huge figure took a step towards Beatrice. She turned to look at him. 'I'm going. You touch me, and the police will be here questioning you about assault.' She wasn't sure the police would care, but hoped the threat would make the mountainous man hesitate to get physical. She turned and walked to the door of the study, aware of his heavy footsteps close behind her. She tried to walk with a sense of calm and nonchalance she didn't feel.

Accompanied all the way to the front door, Jackson opened it for her, staring in silence as she exited. He continued to watch as she got into her car and left.

Away from the estate, Beatrice found a layby and pulled over. She turned the engine off and got out. Looking down at her hands, she noted their shaking, and leant against the car, taking several slow, deep breaths, until her heart returned to a steady rate.

The tone of the meeting had taken a sudden turn when she'd pushed Malone. There had been an air of menace from him, and a sense of a real threat from his sidekick. Malone would likely make sure to keep his hands clean by getting someone like the impassive Jackson to do his dirty work for him. A man with huge strength, and capable of violence. He'd responded immediately to just a word from Malone, no doubt used to doing whatever was asked of him, regardless of possible consequences.

Beatrice sat in her car. Everything she'd found out about the arson attacks and the dead man pointed to Victor Malone. Or his circle, at least. The police were unlikely to help her, and from what Susan had said, they wouldn't thank her for causing any disturbance there. What if Malone had contacts in the force? Did that happen in real life, or only in TV programmes?

Whatever, if she was going to get to the bottom of the fires and the death, she'd need to be more circumspect. No more direct approaches to Malone. Perhaps she should have heeded the warnings from Pete and Susan. She'd have to get what evidence she could, and pass it on to her employer and the police. Beatrice chose to ignore the small voice in her head, which told her she already knew what she'd been hired to find out. After all, Michael had strongly implied the Browns hadn't arranged the fires. But stopping now would be leaving the job half done. Something she'd never been good at.

Chapter 34

James was out for the evening, so Beatrice looked forward to watching TV and cuddling the cat. In the fading light, she was putting the key into the lock of her door when there was a noise from behind her.

'Alright?'

Startled she turned, raising her hand to her chest to still her rapidly beating heart. A figure stood before her and she let out a long breath of relief. 'Michael. What do you want? And how do you know where I live?'

'I got these.' Michael thrust a sheaf of papers towards Beatrice.

'What are they?' She leafed through the pages, whilst keeping a wary eye on the jittery man.

'From my solicitor. Stuff from my file. I can't make head nor tail of them.'

'Does Louise know you have them?'

'They're to do with my case. I'm entitled.' He sounded petulant.

Beatrice doubted he came by them through legitimate means. 'Why are you giving them to me? I'm not working for you, Michael.'

'I know you said there's nothing you could do, but no one else will help. Thing is, I'm going to be arrested tomorrow. Probably charged soon after.'

'What charges?'

'Arson and manslaughter, I should guess.'

'You didn't answer my other question. How did you know I lived here?'

'You're not difficult to find. You do tend to stand out, you know.'

Beatrice pushed the comment away for later consideration. 'Are you going to tell me anything useful? Like who hired you to start the fires?'

'You know I can't say anything.'

'Come on, Michael. You've got to give me something.' Beatrice found his reluctance to speak exasperating. How was she supposed to investigate, if the person who knew the most wouldn't provide any answers? Why couldn't he see it was in his own interests?

'I said I wouldn't do it again, after the Golden Goose,' said Michael. 'Not if there were people inside. I burn things, but I don't want to kill anyone. I'd no idea anyone was in there. It was supposed to be empty. I wouldn't have done it, otherwise. Not that I had a lot of choice.'

'You need to come clean. How am I going to help, if you won't tell me anything?'

'More than my life's worth to talk. You're the detective, you figure it out. I promise you though, it wasn't my fault. I didn't kill anyone.'

Was he exaggerating his fear? Or did he have good reason to be afraid? 'You work for Victor Malone, don't you?'

Michael bounced up and down on the balls of his feet. He looked down the street. 'So what?'

'Has he threatened you?'

'Leave it.'

'Then what do you expect me to do?'

He gestured at the papers in her hand. 'You could find something in there?'

'Louise would have found it, if there was anything useful.'

'Maybe.'

'Don't you trust her?'

'I don't trust anyone.'

'But you've given these to me, and you've basically confessed to arson.'

'Nothing you can use as evidence though, is it?' Michael grinned, then his expression returned to its serious aspect. 'You'll keep investigating until you get the truth. It's the only thing that'll help me now. I can't go down for manslaughter. They'll give me serious time for it.' Michael looked at her earnestly. 'You will check the papers, won't you?'

'Fine.'

Michael turned on his heel.

'Wait.'

He turned back. 'What?'

'Did you know Bugsy?'

He shrugged. 'I didn't have much to do with him, but I saw him around. I don't know what he was doing in the pub. Stealing maybe.'

'So, you know it was him? The body?'

'Yeah. I read it in them papers.' He gestured at the pages.

'He worked for Malone too?'

'One of the regulars. Was allowed to go to the house.'

'Malone's?'

Michael nodded.

'What sort of thing did he do?'

'Whatever he was asked?'

Beatrice let out an exasperated sigh. 'Such as?'

'Getting stuff, or people, you know, driving Malone's visitors about.'

'Did he have anything to do with Astra?'

'He was allowed to drive her places.'

'Keeping an eye on her?'

'Yeah. Malone likes to have a close watch on his valuable property.'

The disrespectful reference to Astra no doubt reflected Malone's attitude towards her. 'Would Bugsy have tried anything? With Astra? She's very attractive.'

'No chance. He made comments, you know, to the guys, but he'd never do anything. He liked breathing.' He tilted his head. 'That it? I'm off to the pub. It'll be my last chance, for who knows how long.'

'Sure.'

Without another word, Michael set off down the street with an irregular, quick step. Beatrice looked at the bundle of papers. Louise Prince clearly had too much work, perhaps there was something useful in them she'd missed.

In the house, Beatrice spread them out on the dining room table. They were in a muddle and it took a while to sort them into complete documents. There were seven of them, including an autopsy report, police report, interview notes and transcripts of Michael's interview with the police.

There were also Louise's case notes, which Beatrice checked first. She learnt Louise was going to argue there was only circumstantial evidence to connect Michael to the fires. She'd referred to inconclusive eyewitness testimony, presumably Beatrice, which couldn't positively place Michael at the Golden Goose fire.

The autopsy report was ten pages long. After several pages of preamble, of no use to Beatrice, she came to the thrust of the report. All Bugsy's clothes had been destroyed and the body itself badly damaged. The pathologist concluded a high likelihood of an accelerant being used on and around the body. It was possible Michael had done it, if he'd killed Bugsy, but she couldn't see him as a killer. The off-hand way he'd said Bugsy might have been in the pub to steal, didn't suggest any antagonism towards him.

The pathologist described injuries to Bugsy's skull: two impacts, one peri-mortem, one post-mortem, the first having been of sufficient force to cause death, the second happening several days later. There was nothing showing where on his head the wounds were. Louise had scrawled a note next to the section of the report: *Dead before being put in fire. Poss. Murder?*

So, it seemed Bugsy was murdered then dumped at the pub. Michael had been expecting manslaughter, but a murder charge was a distinct possibility. Other than Michael, who would have known when the fire was going to happen?

Chapter 35

Saturday 30th June

'I'm so glad you could make it.'

As Beatrice stepped into the hallway, Marina enveloped her in a hug.

'Come through, everyone's here. If you hadn't been able to come, I'd have had to question them myself.'

'Question them?' asked Beatrice.

'About your investigation. It's the perfect chance to find out what they know. This lot are married to influential men, and know far more than they should. They've nothing better to do than swap gossip.'

'This is supposed to be your party.'

'It is. And the entertainment, for me, is you getting them to help you. They're not really my friends. Come on. I'll help you get them started.'

A dozen women stood around the kitchen island, wine glasses in hand. They stopped talking when Beatrice and Marina entered. Looking at the other guests, Beatrice felt out of place with her jeans, and t-shirt. The other women wore stylish dresses, heels, rigid hairstyles, manicures and layers of make-up. They looked her up and down with disdain, as if she was clearly failing at womanhood. Beatrice wanted to turn and run away.

'Everyone, this is Beatrice, a good friend of mine.' Marina was either oblivious to the atmosphere, or too good a hostess to acknowledge it. She passed Beatrice a glass of wine. 'You aren't driving, are you?'

She wished James hadn't offered to drop her off. Now it would be harder to make a quick escape when she'd had enough. 'Erm, no. I got a lift.'

'Lesley lives in Bailgate.' She indicated one of the look-alike women. 'She can drop you off in town later, can't you Lesley? When your car comes for you.'

Lesley gave a small, unenthusiastic smile.

'You've probably all heard of Beatrice,' Marina ploughed on, grinning as if she were enjoying herself.

Beatrice's heart sank. Please don't mention... Too late.

'She was in the paper this week.'

An interested murmur rippled through the room.

'She's the woman who saved that family from the fire in the pub.'

'Oh, my goodness,' said Lesley, who looked at her keenly. 'How exciting. You must tell us about it.'

There were nods and mutterings of agreement, as they all turned to look at Beatrice, expressions eager.

Marina sipped her wine, enjoying the sensation she'd created. She nudged Beatrice and whispered in her ear: 'Go on. After a bit more wine, they'll tell you anything you want to know.'

'Aren't you a private detective?' asked a petite, dark-haired woman, who was impossible to age, due to her painted-on face. There were more excited gasps.

Half an hour later Beatrice had been thoroughly questioned about her career and the fire.

Marina opened yet another bottle of wine. 'You know the Browns, don't you Lesley?'

'Oh, yes.'

'Lesley knows everyone.' Marina said to Beatrice.

She took the opening and pretended she and Marina hadn't already discussed Lesley's information. It would be a good way to start everyone on the topic. She tried to sound casual as she pointed out the Browns seemed to be a nice, happy couple. After a few non-comital comments, the women began to warm up, dishing the dirt on the brewery owners. Through them, Beatrice confirmed Gareth was having an affair, and had been for months. One of the women hinted at it not being his first, but no one else could confirm that.

Having exhausted all they knew about the couple, Beatrice steered the conversation to her other area of interest. 'I heard someone tried to buy the brewery a while back. They must be wishing they'd sold up, now.'

There was an uncomfortable silence and some shifting amongst the women.

Beatrice looked around the room. They had become very interested in their wine glasses and nails.

'Come on, ladies,' said Marina, pouring out more wine. 'We're all friends here. It's not like Beatrice is going to tell Victor Malone anything you say.'

'Who's that?' asked Beatrice.

'He's not a man to upset,' said the petite woman, who Beatrice now knew was called Anne. 'I go to the same yoga class as Astra, his girlfriend. She has all the best clothes and loads of expensive jewellery, but I wouldn't be in her shoes for anything.'

There were a few nodding heads.

'Why not?' asked Beatrice.

'She's got no freedom,' said one woman.

'Can't go anywhere alone,' said Anne. 'There's always a man bringing her to yoga. Watching her. Victor treats her like she's a piece of decoration.'

Talk turned to more general topics, but Beatrice was later able to speak to Anne alone.

'I was thinking of trying yoga,' said Beatrice. 'Where are your classes?'

Anne mentioned the name of a gym. 'It wasn't me who told you, though. OK?'

'Sure,' agreed Beatrice, surprised simply mentioning a gym had Anne concerned. 'Is there anything else I could have not heard from you? About the Browns or Victor Malone?'

Anne checked no one else was near enough to overhear. 'Its second or third hand information,' she said. 'But I heard when Malone sets his mind on having something, he doesn't take "no" for an answer. Whether its property, women or a business.' Anne looked at her pointedly on the last word.

'You think he'd…'

'I'm saying nothing else.'

'Understood. Thank you.'

The party was breaking up, and Lesley's car arrived. Beatrice joined her, after giving Marina a hug goodbye.

'I hope it was useful.'

'It was, thanks.'

'When I'm settled,' Marina said. 'Perhaps you could come out to visit. It's an amazing place, and I'd love to see you.'

Beatrice was pleased to receive the invitation and said so. She resolved, if Marina kept in touch and repeated the offer, she would definitely go.

Chapter 36

Loud knocking woke Beatrice from her snooze on the sofa, where she'd flopped, after Lesley had dropped her off. It was a few seconds before she realised someone was at the door. She staggered across the room, picked up an envelope which had been delivered whilst she slept, and opened the door. The cat scooted in and ran upstairs.

'Rosie! What on earth?' Beatrice was startled by the red face, puffy eyes and tear-stained cheeks of her sister. 'Come in.' She ushered her into the lounge, closing the door.

'Where are the girls? Are they alright?'

'A friend is watching them for a couple of hours.'

'What's happened?' She dropped the envelope onto the coffee table.

'It's over. We're getting divorced.' Tears streamed from Rosie's eyes.

Beatrice wrapped her sister in hug, holding her until the sobs subsided, then she led Rosie to the sofa. 'I'm going to make us a cup of tea, and get you some tissues.'

When she returned with their drinks, biscuits and a box of tissues, Beatrice could see Rosie was calmer. She placed the tray on the table. 'Are you really getting divorced?'

'Yes. I've been to a solicitor.' Rosie took one of the mugs and dunked a biscuit in the hot liquid, before pushing the whole thing in her mouth.

'And it's what you want?'

'I'm upset about it ending,' said Rosie. 'This isn't how I hoped things would be, when we got married. But I know it's the right thing to do. For all of us.'

'Would talking to someone be useful?'

'I've done all that.' Rosie wiped her face with one of the tissues and blew her nose noisily, shoving the used tissue up her sleeve. 'I made us an appointment with a counselling service. I wasn't getting anywhere trying to deal with it by myself, and Adam wasn't helping. I told him I was going and I wanted him to be there.'

'How did he take it?' Beatrice suspected she could predict the answer.

'He said I was being stupid. That's the word he used! Made an excuse about having to be at the garage. I knew he would, so I'd already asked James if he was available to cover for Adam, and he was.'

Beatrice was surprised James hadn't mentioned he'd talked to Rosie, but she pushed the thought to one side, to concentrate on her sister.

'I told Adam it was serious, and if he wanted our marriage to continue, he had to put in the effort. We needed to sort our problems out, together.'

'And?'

'He said I was being ridiculous. We didn't need a stranger poking their nose in our business. Do you know what else he said?'

'No.'

'That if I wasn't being so selfish, about Mum's money, everything would be fine. That it was all my fault.' Rosie folded her arms. 'Can you believe it? I nearly lost my temper then, but I stayed calm. I told him where and when the appointment was, and I was going anyway. It was up to him whether he came too.'

'And did he?'

'No.'

'So, that's it?'

'Yep. Don't worry, I talked it all through with the counsellor. But I've had enough. I've done my best to keep my marriage going, but I don't want to anymore. I'm still relatively young, not as old as you anyway.'

'It's thirty minutes!' Rosie's old jibe was a good sign she was regaining her composure.

Rosie gave her a brief smile. 'I still have a lot of life ahead of me, and I don't intend to spend it with a man one who doesn't even seem to like me. To him, I'm just the person who does all the cooking, cleaning, childcare. I think he'll be happier too, if we aren't together anymore.'

'What about practical things? The house, kids, money?'

'We'll have to sort it out. In the meantime, I'm staying in the house with the girls, and he'll keep contributing to the bills. We'll probably have to sell and I'll have to look for a job. I don't want to leave you in the lurch, but I might not be able to carry on doing your admin.'

Beatrice waved her hand. 'Don't worry about it. If necessary, I'll do it myself until I make other arrangements.' She would be happy enough doing her own record keeping and invoicing, but didn't want to draw attention to how she created the job to help Rosie. 'Also, I still have Mum's money, so…'

'Thanks, but I'll be fine.'

'I mean it. You can call it a loan if you like, but you and the girls need to get on track as soon as possible.'

'OK.'

'How did Adam react when you told him you wanted a divorce? Was he expecting it?'

'It went about as well as you'd imagine, and no, I don't think he did expect it. He didn't believe me at first and thought I was trying to manipulate him.' Rosie shook her head. 'I don't want to go through it all again. It was bad enough having to do it.'

'He understands you mean it though?'

'Yes. He knows I won't be changing my mind, that I've had enough.'

'Have you told the girls?'

'I did it last night. They're upset. But that's no change, with

Adam like he has been. One of their friends has divorced parents, so it's not a totally new idea to them.'

'They can always stay with me and James for a few days, to give you time to sort things out.'

'I'll think about it.' Rosie checked her watch. 'I'd better get going. I've got things to do before I go home.'

After Rosie had left, Beatrice sat back on the sofa. She'd known of their troubles, but she'd assumed everything would be OK. She hoped James would be home soon, his strong arms around her were exactly what she needed. Her gaze fell on the letter she'd placed on the table earlier. She picked it up and opened it. It contained the birth certificates for Lily and Elizabeth.

Up in her office, the first one she checked was Elizabeth's, the child. There was nothing unexpected. Her mother was listed as Lily Taylor, the space for father was blank. She'd been born in Norwich and was approaching two years old. All consistent with what Charles had told her.

Lily's birth certificate showed her full name was Lily Evangeline Taylor. Her parents were listed as Parker and Grace Taylor. She was born in Lincoln, with Parker, who had registered the birth, giving his address in the village of Bardney. Beatrice searched online and found it was to the east of the city, a half hour drive away. It wasn't large and would be a good place to go and see if she could find out more about the Taylors. The piece of paper Andrew had given her had the name Fiskerton on it, which was near Bardney. Had Andrew chosen a village close by, to deflect from where they had actually lived, choosing the first name he could remember?

Now possessing the full names of all the family, Beatrice tried general online searches again, thinking such unusual names might stand out. She began with the parents', but even with names she'd thought were uncommon, there were too many results. She combined all the names into one search: 'Parker Grace Lily Andrew Taylor'. This time the search was successful.

Contained in a newspaper archive, which had been digitised and added to the paper's catalogue, she found a headline relating to a car accident. She couldn't access the article, because it was too long ago, though she was able to work out the date it was published. She found out it was possible to view copies of the actual paper, it being county based, at the central library in Lincoln. The University of Lincoln website, where she obtained the information, advised contacting the library in advance, with details of which papers were wanted. Beatrice glanced at her watch. It was too late today, the library was now closed, but it was a job for next week. She made her way to her bedroom and joined the cat on the bed.

Chapter 37

Monday 2nd July

Yesterday, Beatrice and James had gone for a walk in the arboretum, which was enjoyable, until he started to talk about the future and their relationship. He made oblique references to children and families. It had caused a sinking sensation in her stomach when he'd returned to the topic several times, despite her deflections. James had been quiet as they cooked and ate dinner together, but when they'd decided on an early night, he'd seemed more like his usual self.

Beatrice had awoken to find James had already left for work, despite it being very early. Feeling uneasy about what it meant for them, she pottered around the house until it was time to tackle the first job of the day.

At 9.05 a.m. Beatrice made a call to the library about the newspaper report which featured the Taylors. The woman she'd spoken to had been very helpful, confirming the papers she wanted were available, but would need to be retrieved from storage. The librarian promised to message as soon as she had them.

Afterwards Beatrice drove straight to the address listed for the Taylors on Lily's birth certificate. The terrace of unadorned brick homes was nondescript, apart from a few flower pots and hanging baskets.

She found the house and knocked at the door. No answer. She tried again, but still no response. Beatrice walked up and down the street. One house appeared grubby, compared to the others. The window frames hadn't been painted in a long time, the scrap of lawn was overgrown, and a low fence leaned at an angle. Speculating it could be occupied by an older, long-term resident, she pressed the doorbell. A small dog barked from within, and the sound of a slow progression, marked by muttering and shushing of the dog, could be heard. Beatrice waited patiently until a short, lean man opened the door.

'Hello?' The smell of overcooked vegetables wafted outside from behind him. A Jack Russell peered up at Beatrice, wagging its tail.

'Good morning,' said Beatrice, stepping back to avoid towering over him, and to dilute the smell. The dog followed her and sniffed at her ankles. 'I'm trying to trace my family tree, and was hoping you could help?'

'I don't know nothing about that sort of thing.' The man bent double as a spasm of coughing overtook him.

'Sorry, I should have been clearer. A relative used to live in this street, about twenty-five years ago. I was hoping there might be someone who remembers them.'

'I've been here forty years. Who was it?'

'Parker and Grace Taylor. They lived three doors down.' She pointed.

'Taylor?' The man frowned. 'I'm not so good with names, these days.'

'They had a son and daughter. The boy would have been about five.'

'Five, you say?'

'Yes.' Beatrice gave him time to collect his thoughts.

'There was a family with a girl and a boy. The girl was only a baby. I'm not sure which year it was, though.'

'That's OK. Can you remember anything about them?'

'He was a nuisance, the lad.'

'How?'

'Riding up and down the path on his trike. Didn't care who he knocked over. Making lots of noise too.' The man coughed again, longer this time. It sounded painful, but he didn't acknowledge the interruption. 'I spoke to his parents about it.

They apologised, but it didn't stop him.'

'I expect he settled down when he got older.' What she'd seen of Andrew as an adult didn't suggest a particularly disruptive or inconsiderate person.

'Wouldn't know. They moved away.'

'Where did they go?'

'Back where they came from, is what I heard.'

'Do you know where?'

'How would I?'

'Thanks for your time.'

The man, nonplussed by the quick dismissal, turned around and made his way back inside. 'Scamp!' The dog gave Beatrice a final sniff, then ran into the house.

Back at her car she considered what to do next. She could knock on other doors, though the absence of cars meant most people were probably at work. It seemed sensible to come back in the evening, if she had no luck with the library search.

She called in at Rosie's on the way to Lincoln, to see how her sister was doing, but the house was empty. If she was really going through with the divorce, Rosie would have a lot of things to organise, and she'd need to do it whilst the girls were in school. She sent a brief text to her sister, planning to call her soon.

Having been to the library before, Beatrice found it easily. She gave her name at the information desk and, after a few minutes, was approached by a woman in her thirties.

'Hello, are you Beatrice?'

'Yes.' She smiled at the librarian. 'Thanks for calling me back. I was pleased you'd been able to get the papers so soon.'

'You were lucky, they were easy to find.' She led Beatrice to a table with several large volumes on it. 'I've taken a few out, since you said you were interested in the general time period.'

'Thank you so much.'

'I'll leave you to it. When you've finished, tell someone at the desk.'

The younger woman left and Beatrice settled herself down at the table. She checked the spines of the volumes for the date that covered the article headline she'd seen online. Finding the edition easily, she turned to the relevant report. *Tragic Double Death* was the main headline, with *Family Day Out Makes Orphans of Brother and Sister.*

Beatrice read the piece several times, making notes. It was a sad story. The family were returning from a day at the seaside, Lily and Andrew in the back of the car, when a fully laden truck shot through a junction, and collided with the front of the Taylor's car. An ambulance crew had tried to save Parker and Grace, but they died at the scene. The children escaped with minor injuries. Beatrice was moved by the story, imagining the young children injured and shocked in the midst of all the chaos, and witnessing the deaths of their parents. What had happened to them after the crash? Who had looked after them?

Helpfully, the article referred to the village of Cherry Willingham, as the Taylors' home and place of burial for the couple. It was where the family must have moved to from Bardney. Beatrice checked over every page of the paper and those for the following three weeks. The crash had quickly fallen out of the interest of the newspaper editors.

The churchyard in Cherry Willingham had a section for more recent burials, so Beatrice didn't have to check every grave. She walked along the rows until she found what she was after. The headstone was black with gold lettering, and named both of the Taylors and the date they died. The inscription read: *'Beloved Parents of Lily and Andrew'*, and *'Taken Too Soon'*. She took a photo.

Beatrice contemplated the grave and its fresh flowers. Who had paid for the headstone, and who had left the bouquet? She bent down to read the card tucked into the centre of the arrangement. On one side was the name of a florist in Welton.

The reverse had a handwritten note *'Love always xxx'*. Having taken photos of each side of the card, she checked online for the florist. It was open until 5 p.m.

The newspaper report hadn't said exactly where the Taylors had lived, and there were too many houses for her to go door-to-door. When she'd arrived, she'd seen a rotund man with a limp unlocking the church. If he was still around, perhaps he'd be able to help.

Inside the church the older, grey-haired man she'd seen, was tidying hymn books.

Beatrice coughed, to get his attention. 'Hello?'

He turned. 'Hello.'

'Hi. I wonder if you could help me? I'm trying to trace some relatives.' Not hers, but her description was suitably ambiguous. 'Their parents are buried here.'

'You want to find the grave?'

'I've already seen it. I was hoping you'd know if anyone in village might remember them.' She selected the photo on her phone and held it out for the man to see.

'It's what, eighteen years ago?'

Beatrice nodded.

'Best ask at the pub, up near the shops. A few of the older villagers go in at this time of day. If not, ask the landlord, he'll set you in the right direction.'

'Thanks very much.'

'You're welcome.' He turned back to the hymn books.

Beatrice dropped a few coins in the collection box as she left the church.

Chapter 38

Beatrice parked outside the small shopping centre and walked over to the pub, which was more modern than she'd expected. Inside it was quiet. A man in his forties sat behind the bar, reading a newspaper. He looked up as she entered.

'What can I get you?'

'I'm searching for relatives. A couple of them are buried in the churchyard, and a man there sent me here,' said Beatrice.

'Why here?'

'He thought your older customers might remember what happened to the rest of the family.'

'You're early.' He checked his watch. 'They'll start coming in soon, if you want to wait. Do you want to see the menu?' He grinned at her.

'Sure.' Beatrice glanced at the menu, and ordered a sandwich and fruit juice.

The food arrived quickly, and by the time she'd finished, three older men had come in and set up in a corner of the pub.

The barman came over to clear her plate. 'Come on. I'll introduce you.' He tilted his head in their direction.

'Thanks.' Beatrice followed him across the room.

'Alright fellas.' The men cast curious glances towards Beatrice. 'This lady is hoping you can help her.'

One of the men drained the last part of his drink and pushed the empty glass across the table in her direction. It was proving to be an expensive day.

Beatrice handed the barman money, and a few minutes later, he brought across three pints of bitter for the men, by which time she'd explained what she wanted to know. Of the three, only one had known the Taylors, and did all the talking.

'Tragic, it was,' he said.

'What happened?' Beatrice was interested in his version.

'Road accident. That's what. A truck driver, who didn't know the area, shot through a T-junction. Clipped their car, and spun it around, ended up under the wheels of the truck. It was one of those really big ones, with a full load. They don't stop easily. They were all still alive when the kids were pulled out by other motorists. The parents were stuck, because of the way the bodywork had been crushed.

'The ambulance arrived quickly, but they didn't have a chance. It would have been more merciful if they'd died straight away. The kids were still young. One day they had parents, then the next they didn't. Hard.'

'What happened to the children?'

'Someone in the family looked after them. An Aunt. Related to the mother, if I remember rightly.'

'Local then?'

'Oh, yes. Families of both of them, been here for generations.'

'Where are the children now?'

'I don't know. Gone. They moved away I imagine.'

'What about the aunt?'

'In Louth, is what I heard. She's got early dementia. I was told a while back she'd been taken into a care home. Younger than us lot.' He gestured at the three of them. 'I don't want to end up that way.'

'Can you remember her name?'

'Her name was Hope. An old-fashioned way of naming kids, even back then.'

Beatrice decided she needed to go home and do more research. If she could identify the care home Hope had been taken to, it would save a lot of legwork. First, she made a detour to the florist in Welton.

The shop was small, but crammed full of flowers. The

scent was overpowering.

'Can I help you?' The woman behind the counter gave a welcoming smile.

'I want a small, inexpensive bunch of flowers.'

'How much were you thinking of spending?'

'Er. Twenty pounds?'

'Any particular type of flowers?'

'No. I don't know much about them.'

'How about I put you something together?'

'Yes, please.' Beatrice watched her. She couldn't work out how the florist was deciding which flowers to select, but she was taking her time. 'I saw a bunch from here on a family grave at Bardney.'

'Oh, yes?'

'It gave me the idea of coming here.'

'It's nice to be appreciated.'

'I'm tracing my family tree.'

'Like the TV programme?'

'Yes, but no royals in my family.'

The florist gathered the small bunch and moved them into different positions until she was satisfied. She then wrapped them in a thick patterned paper. What had seemed to Beatrice a handful of random colours turned into an attractive bouquet. 'They're lovely.'

'Thank you. It's all in how you put them together.'

'Well, you're in the right business.' She pulled out her wallet. 'If I showed you a photo of the flowers I mentioned, do you think you'd remember who bought them?'

The young woman paused at the request.

'I was thinking they might be a relative too.'

The florist finished securing the bouquet. 'I'll have look.'

Beatrice paid for the flowers then selected the right photo.

'I do remember those. She always has the same flowers. Lilies and roses. Comes every month.'

'Do you know her name?'

The florist shook her head. 'Sorry. She pays cash.'

'The cousin I'm searching for has a small child. A girl.'

'She came in once with a toddler. I remember because the child commented on the woman's hair being the same colour as one of the flowers.'

'She dyes her hair?'

'She's been a couple of different colours. I hardly recognised her the first time she changed it.'

Beatrice smiled at the woman. 'Thanks for these, they're really lovely.' The comment about hair colour reminded her of Jules. An adopted disguise?

Back in her office, Beatrice checked her file for Lily. The bouquet lay on her desk. She was reluctant to take them out of their wrapping, knowing if she put them in the solitary vase she owned, they would definitely look worse.

Checking her papers, she'd remembered correctly that Grace's maiden name was on Lily's birth certificate, and made a mental note to photograph documents in future, so she'd always have them on her phone. So, she was searching for a Hope Walker, in a care home, in the Louth area. If she had no success there, she could widen her search later.

She checked online and made a list in her notebook of the care homes in and around the market town of Louth. She'd decided to approach the calls to the homes with confidence, to avoid explaining who she was.

'Good morning. Is it possible to speak to your resident Hope Walker, please?'

'I'm sorry, we don't have anyone here by that name.'

'I must have misremembered the name of the care home. I'm sorry to have troubled you.'

All of the calls to Louth care homes went the same way. The busy staff didn't linger to ask questions. Beatrice widened her search to homes within twenty miles of the town. She was halfway down the second list when she got a result.

'I'm sorry, you can't speak to her on the phone. Her condition makes it too difficult.'

Beatrice sat up straight in her chair and circled the name of the care home. 'I understand she has dementia.'

'I'm afraid so. She can communicate well enough, but the telephone confuses her, because she can't see who she's talking to.'

'I live in Lincoln. Can I visit?'

'Are you a relative?'

'I've been tracing my family tree. I think she's related on my mother's side. I was hoping to ask about her sister, Grace, who died about eighteen years ago.'

'Oh, I see. She doesn't get many visitors, so I can't see the harm. She'd probably enjoy talking about the past.'

Beatrice arranged to be there within an hour, feeling lifted by making progress at last.

Chapter 39

The care home was several miles west of Louth. An old building set in a large garden. The warmth of the day meant a number of elderly people were sitting on benches dotted about the grounds. Staff were easily identified by the single-colour tunic and trouser sets they wore. Beatrice signed in at reception and was directed to the back of the house, with the warning not to upset Hope. 'If she starts getting confused or getting things wrong, let her. Don't try to correct her. It keeps our residents with dementia calmer.'

She found Hope drinking tea, in the shade of a large parasol.

'Hope?' She looked down at the woman. About sixty, she was physically healthy apart from the pronounced asymmetry of her face. Her eyes shone brightly.

'Yes?'

'My name is Beatrice. Is it alright if I sit and talk to you for a while?'

'That would be nice. Everyone here is so busy.'

Beatrice sat beside her. 'I brought you these.' She held out the bouquet.

Hope beamed with delight. 'Thank you! They're beautiful.' She reached out for them with one hand, the other lay flopped in her lap.

They spent a few minutes chatting about the flowers, the gardens and the weather. During the conversation Hope asked her to repeat her name several times. A care worker asked Beatrice if she'd like a drink, poured two coffees then left. Wondering how to broach the subject of Hope's family,

Beatrice allowed a silence to develop.

'Such a shame I have to be here,' said Hope. 'I can't manage on my own anymore.'

'I'm sorry. It must be hard, having to leave your home.'

'It belonged to my parents. It wasn't large, and could be cold in winter, but it was home.' Hope smiled at her memories.

'Was it near here?'

'Not far. Middle Rasen.' It was a village to the west of Louth.

'Were you a large family?'

'No. Mum, dad, me and my younger sister, Grace.' Hope's mouth drooped. 'They've all gone now.'

'Including your sister?'

Hope nodded. 'Even her.'

'I'm sorry.' Beatrice hesitated, but needed to ask. 'What happened to Grace?'

'Died in a car accident. She was only thirty-five. Terrible. I don't want to talk about it.'

'You've no other family?'

'I've a niece and nephew.'

'Grace had children?'

'Yes. They were only young when their parents died.'

'What happened to them?'

'They lived with me.'

'It can't have been easy.'

'Not for any of us. It was that, or a children's home. I couldn't let them be taken away.'

'Are you still in touch with them?'

'No. They couldn't wait to leave. Too many bad memories. Kids at school teased them.'

'Why?'

'Why do kids do anything? I never understood them.' Hope stared off into the past. 'I wasn't the best person to take them on. I'd never wanted children of my own and didn't know what to do with them. I can't blame them for wanting to get away.'

'I'm sure you did your best.'

Hope wiped a tear from her eye. 'I did it for Grace.'

They sat in silence for a few moments, then Hope leaned in towards Beatrice. 'Don't tell anyone, but she comes to see me sometimes.'

'Who?'

'Grace.'

'Really?'

'Yes, and she looks like she did when we were young. I don't let on to the people here. They'd say I was imagining it.' Hope tapped the side of her head. 'She brought little Lily with her once. Bouncing about all over the place. Couldn't sit still.' She laughed at the recollection.

'We need to get you back inside now, Hope.' A care worker approached. 'It's getting cool and we don't want you catching a chill.'

Beatrice said goodbye to Hope and wished her well. As she walked back to her car, she thought over what Hope had said. Could it be Lily, bearing a resemblance to her mother, visiting with Elizabeth? Or was it a figment of Hope's imagination? A consequence of her illness? The flowers on the grave suggested Lily was in the area. Had she gone back to where she'd lived with her aunt?

The A46 passed through Middle Rasen, where Hope had lived with Lily and Andrew. Beatrice approached from the east, drove through and out the other side, before turning her car around. Her Sat Nav showed most of the housing was north of the main road. She turned in the direction of the signposted village hall and playing field, driving past a mixture of bungalows and family homes.

She had no plan of how to find Lily, if she was in Middle Rasen, and she needed one. She parked the car and used her phone to search for the village facilities.

There was a church, garage, pub and school. Beatrice

checked her watch: 3 p.m. According to the school website the children's day ended at 3.15 p.m. Elizabeth was too young for primary school, but parents there might be able to point her in the right direction. Lily had sought out a group for parents and children in Norwich and it was possible she'd have done the same here.

Beatrice started the car and drove to the school, finding a parking spot a few streets away, and walking the remaining distance. Parents and family members were starting to gather. There was one group of women who had a couple of much younger children with them. She went over, smiling to set them at their ease.

'Hello.'

The women turned towards her.

'I was wondering if you could help me, please.'

'What is it you want?' The woman regarded her with a wary expression.

'My sister is moving here soon, and wants to find a place for her daughter to mix with other children.'

'She isn't with you?'

'No. She's pregnant with her second child and isn't feeling well. I'm here to see what I can find out for her.' Rosie was being very useful in this investigation. Beatrice hoped she didn't find out.

'How old?'

'Almost two.'

The other women in the group were all listening now. 'She'll be eligible for the free hours at the nursery when she's two,' said one of the mothers, a small child pulling on her arms.

'Unless she earns too much,' said another. 'Does she work?'

'Not at the moment.'

'She might be alright then.'

'Is there a nursery nearby?'

'There's one in the village. They pick up kids here for the

after-school club.' The woman pointed across at three adults with hi-vis jackets on and who had just arrived at the school. 'You could talk to them.'

'Thank you. I will.'

Just then the children piled out of the school, distracting the parents. Beatrice left the group and stood watching. Once the nursery staff had collected all their charges, they walked away from the school, the children in pairs, holding hands. Beatrice followed at a distance, hoping she didn't appear too out of place.

Having established where the nursery was, Beatrice went back to get her car. She parked up where she had a clear view of the nursery entrance, switched on the radio and prepared for a long wait. She'd checked online and it was open until 5:30 p.m.

At 5.45 p.m. Beatrice got out of her car and stretched. The nursery had been locked up after the children had all been collected and the staff had left. She'd watched carefully, but there'd been no one who resembled Lily with a child of the right age. She couldn't realistically sit outside every day. She needed a better plan.

Chapter 40

Tuesday 9th July

It was the end of the yoga session at the gym. Beatrice had turned up, having called to arrange to attend. The hour was torture, and she was embarrassed by how difficult she'd found it, and the repeated hands-on corrections by the instructor.

After the class, the attendees – all women – collected in groups in a seating area outside the hall. Beatrice noticed Astra and discreetly positioned herself nearby.

'Nice to see you again, Astra. We missed you these last few weeks.' The remark by the forty-something, to the noticeably younger, slimmer woman, had an edge to it. The smirk accompanying it, was intended to convey a message, though Beatrice couldn't interpret it. A couple of other women stood near, pretending not to be involved, but she could tell they were paying close attention.

'I'm surprised you haven't seen me. Perhaps a visit to the opticians is called for. You can't be too careful, at your age.' Astra turned her back and strode away to the vending machine, as one of the observers stifled a snigger.

Beatrice joined Astra, forming a short queue of two. They exchanged a glance. 'It was quite a workout, wasn't it?'

'What? Oh.' Astra looked puzzled. 'I haven't seen you before, have I?'

'No. I'm new to Lincoln. I need to get in shape, so I thought I'd give yoga a try. I may have bitten off more than I can chew!'

Astra laughed in sympathy. 'Don't worry, it gets easier,

with practice.'

'I hope so. Of course, the trick is going to be surviving the practice.'

'What made you want to try yoga?'

'I was at a party and a woman there was talking about it,' said Beatrice. 'I was expecting to see her, actually.'

'Who was it?'

'Anne. I don't know her last name.'

'I know who you mean. I've met her. Her husband works with my partner.'

'Really? I only just met her at the party. It's hard making friends in a new place, when everyone else already knows one another.'

'You can live in a place for years, meet all sorts of people, and still have no real friends.' Astra's tone was dejected and her mouth dropped at the corners.

A man materialised beside them, middle-aged and nondescript, but strong. He didn't speak, merely checked his watch in an exaggerated way. Astra ignored him and bent to retrieve a bottle of water from the vending machine's slot, then stood up. 'Maybe I'll see you next week?'

'If I can still move.' Beatrice watched Astra square her shoulders, as if preparing for an ordeal, then walk away. The man took a long slow look at Beatrice, then followed.

Revived by a long, hot shower, Beatrice sat at her desk. Her body ached in places she'd never known existed before, and she doubted she'd be able to move in the morning. She'd need to speak to Astra again, hopefully break down barriers, and get information on Bugsy and maybe Malone too. Janice, Bugsy's girlfriend, sounded like a difficult character, and was in mourning, and Beatrice wasn't heartless enough to approach her yet. Besides, from what Pete said, she'd have given him any information she had about where Bugsy was going that night. Beatrice wondered if she could find a way of talking to Astra, which didn't involve going back to yoga.

Still absorbed in her thoughts, she absentmindedly answered her ringing phone. 'Hello?'

'Beatrice?'

'Yes.'

'It's Louise Prince. Can you come to my office? We need to talk.'

'What's happened?'

'The police have upgraded the charges against Michael. They're going for murder.'

'I'll be there in thirty minutes.'

Louise's receptionist placed two cups of coffee on the desktop and closed the door on leaving.

Beatrice, conscious of not wanting to get Michael into trouble with his solicitor, knew she'd have to pretend she hadn't seen the purloined papers. 'Why are they charging him with murder? Rather than manslaughter?'

'The forensic evidence shows the victim, a man called Lee Chambers, was already dead when the fire started. They contend Michael killed him, then put him in the fire, thinking it would destroy the evidence.'

'They can't believe he thought the body wouldn't be found?'

Louise stirred sugar into her coffee. 'I don't think they're worried about how weak it sounds. They've come back with evidence from a couple of motorbikes they say were involved in two earlier fires. Both bikes have Michael's fingerprints on them.'

'Did he explain how they got there?'

'He told them he likes motorbikes, and often touches bikes when he's out and about.'

Beatrice laughed.

'I know. When they told him the prints were found on the electrical wires, he returned to "no comment".'

'And the police think they can prove his connection with the earlier fires? It's the same MO, so he's responsible?'

'Something like that. But, that's for me to worry about. With a good barrister there's a lot we can attack.'

'What's his motive supposed to be?'

'They both worked for the same organisation and fell out.'

'Organisation?' Beatrice kept her eyes on Louise.

'Businesses owned by a man called Victor Malone.' The solicitor consulted a piece of paper, as if being careful to get the name right.

'I've heard of him.' Was Louise's apparent lack of awareness of the significance of Malone's name real, or excellent acting? 'What sort of work did the men do?'

'I can't get a clear answer.' Louise drained her cup. 'Michael is being uncooperative. With the police it's understandable, but he's hardly helping me put a robust defence together.'

'The police case sounds weak. Especially the motivation.'

'It's what I'm focussing on at the moment. We both know Michael isn't the brightest. There's no way he came up with a scheme to target the pubs. I was hoping you'd have an idea of who put him up to it.'

'Does it help Michael's case to know?'

'Indirectly. It's possible that whoever it was could be responsible for the body. If they knew when and where the next fire would be, they'd know the right time to dump it. It gives me another line to attack the prosecution case.'

Beatrice placed her coffee cup on the desk. 'The thing is, Louise, I have no problem with you. But Michael started a fire when he *knew* the Staines family were in there. Those girls may never recover, emotionally, from what he put them through. He may claim he'd have made sure they were safe, but I've no reason to believe him. Maybe he is responsible for killing this other man. Why should I help him?'

'I presume you still need to know if the Browns were involved?' asked Louise.

'I do.'

'Won't finding out who hired him help?'

'It might.'

'He's genuinely frightened about going to a high security prison for murder. If he didn't commit the crime, he shouldn't be jailed for it.'

'It's your job to defend him, not mine. And you'll be trying to get him off a crime we both think he committed, as well as the murder.'

Louise leaned forward. 'I'm not going to give you a lecture about the adversarial system of law we have in this country. Will you, for the sake of finding who is also culpable, tell me what you know?'

'You're appealing to my good nature?'

'Your sense of justice. Isn't the truth important to you?'

Beatrice looked steadily at her. How much did Louise really know about Michael's employer? Had he confided who he was scared of? Or had he given her the papers because he couldn't trust his solicitor?

'What are you thinking?' asked Louise.

'Honestly? Whether I can trust you.'

Louise sat back in her seat. 'I don't know how to address that. It's your call.'

'I agree he was put up to it. It's what I've been looking into, but if I share what I know, who will you repeat it to? And how does it help me?'

'I didn't have you down as a conspiracy theorist. As for helping you, unless I know what you've found out, how can I know?'

Beatrice considered her options. She could leave, saying nothing, or she could share. She had no evidence, only a suspicion about who ordered the arson attacks. And if Louise repeated everything to Malone? Would it assist or hinder her investigation? 'I can't prove anything.'

'Understood.'

'Lee Chambers, aka Bugsy, worked for Malone, who has been described to me, by several people, as dangerous. The kind of man who would be willing to act against anyone who displeased him.'

'Sounds like a TV character.' Louise laughed.

'Unfortunately, the inspiration for them comes from the real world. The people I mentioned are serious individuals. They wouldn't have said what they did without foundation.'

'You think this Malone is involved in the murder and got Michael to set the fires?' Louise frowned.

'Malone doesn't work that way. He'd have got someone else to do it for him.'

'His motivation?'

'Malone made an offer to buy the Brown's business. They turned him down.'

'You think he decided to get revenge by burning it down, one pub at a time?' Her tone showed her disbelief.

'He doesn't operate the way you or I would.'

'And the murder?'

'I don't know why Bugsy was killed. But it's more likely Malone ordered it, than Michael did it.'

Louise sat in silence, appearing to be deep in thought.

'How have you not heard of Malone?'

'I guess we're too small a firm to interest him.'

'He didn't hire you?'

'I was the duty solicitor. I drew the short straw,' said Louise. 'Perhaps I should talk to Malone?'

'I wouldn't recommend it.'

'You've spoken to him?'

Beatrice nodded. 'I thought one of his heavies was going to physically throw me out. I got the impression he'd have done whatever Malone told him to do.' She stood up. 'I'll keep investigating, and you'd best keep working on your defence.'

Chapter 41

Beatrice parked on the street, a short distance from Charles Sharpe's home. On the drive over, she'd been thinking about the brewery investigation and the need to update her employer.

'Mr Simmons, Condor Insurance.'

'Hello, it's Beatrice Styles.'

'Good afternoon, Ms Styles. You have news?'

'A little. Inconclusive, I'm afraid.'

'Please go on.'

'A Michael Burgess has been arrested and charged with the arson attacks, and murder of the man whose body was found in the Cooked Goose.'

'Goodness. Murder?'

'I'm afraid so. The man was killed, then his body placed in the building.'

'By the arsonist?'

'It's what the police are going with.'

'You do not agree?'

'I can't know for certain. I could imagine Michael inadvertently causing a death by starting a fire, but not actually setting out to kill a person. His solicitor agrees.'

'You've spoken to his defence solicitor? Isn't that rather an unorthodox approach?'

'It's an unusual case.'

'Well, it is not for me to judge your methods. As long as they are legal.' Simmons cleared his throat with a delicate cough. 'I presume you believe this man to be guilty of arson.'

'Yes.'

'And his motivation?'

'I think he was paid to do it. It's not something he would have come up with himself, or had any reason to.'

'Have you been able to ascertain whether the Browns were involved in orchestrating the fires?'

'Not with any degree of certainty, but Michael didn't seem to know them, when I spoke to him.'

'You've spoken to the arsonist too. You do seem to have unusual ways of accessing information. I am impressed.'

'Thank you.' Beatrice ploughed on with the reason for her call. 'In the circumstances, I thought I should check whether you want me to continue.'

'Do you believe there is a possibility of finding out who hired the arsonist?'

'Yes. Within the next week, I should either have found out, or I'll have exhausted every possibility.'

'Then please continue, for now. We can have another conversation in a week, to reassess. The amount of money at stake is significant. We need to be as certain as we can be that payment is legitimately due. Trying to recoup, should information come to light at a later stage, is always difficult.'

'If there are any significant developments before then, I'll let you know.'

'Thank you. Was there anything else?'

'Actually…'

'Yes?'

'The Browns are having personal difficulties.'

'Marital problems?'

'Yes.'

'That is helpful. Should we make payment, we will need to be clear about our legal obligations as to who should receive the monies.'

'Also, I found out an employee is selling waste products from the brewing process and pocketing the money.'

'That would be an issue for the Browns to deal with. I suggest you let them know.'

'Gareth does know, and has for a while. He's chosen to ignore it.'

'Interesting. I am not sure, as yet, what bearing it has on our conclusions regarding the insurance claim, I will however, keep it in mind.'

After the call, Beatrice was pleased with how it had gone. Her conscience required her to update her employer on the arrest, but she'd been concerned about being pulled off the case. She didn't want to give up, yet. There was more she could do, and she really wanted to find out who was responsible, and make them face what they'd done to the Browns, their employees, and in particular the Staines family. Michael wasn't the only one who should be punished.

She placed her mobile back in her bag, got out of the car, and walked down the street to the home of the elderly neighbour she'd spoken to previously. Today was the day her son was due to visit, and Beatrice hoped he'd kept to his routine. She wanted to question them about Lily leaving, and if they had anything useful to say about Charles Sharpe. Considering what Jules had told her about abused women, Beatrice was becoming increasingly concerned about what would happen if she found Lily. She needed to know as much as possible about their relationship, and Charles himself, in order to determine what she should do.

'I spoke to your mother previously. I'm sorry, I didn't get her name.' A man had answered Beatrice's knock.

'What were you trying to sell her?'

'Nothing. I'm a private investigator.' She handed him a business card.

The old lady appeared at the door, behind her son. 'Hello, dear. I thought I recognised your voice.'

'Hi. I'm sorry to disturb you, but you mentioned your son's visits, and I'd hoped to speak to you both.'

'Still not found her, then?'

'No.'

'Let her in, Keith. I'll put the kettle on. I don't suppose you'd say no to a cup of tea, would you?'

'That would be lovely.'

Keith stood back to let Beatrice in.

'Thank you.'

'You'd better come through to the lounge,' he said.

After a few minutes, the three of them were settled before a teapot, cups with saucers and what appeared to be homemade Victoria sponge. Gladys, as Beatrice learned she was called, insisted on cutting her a generous slice.

For the benefit of Keith, Beatrice explained who she was, and that she was trying to find Lily and her daughter.

'Who are you working for?' he asked.

She'd hoped to avoid the question but had already determined to stick to the truth, as much as possible. 'Charles Sharpe. The man across the road.' She turned to Gladys. 'The one in the sharp suit.'

'Why are you working for him?' Gladys tutted.

'He hired me. He was in a relationship with Lily, they had a child together and then she left. He wants to see his daughter.'

'You'd be better off spending your time on something else.' Keith bit into his slice of cake.

'You told me you were going to see her brother.' Gladys eyed the cake on Beatrice's plate, as if she regretted serving it.

'That's true and I've spoken to Andrew. He said he doesn't know where she is.' Beatrice turned back to Keith. 'You don't think I should find her. Why?'

'Does it matter?'

'Yes. It does. Sometimes I get hired for an investigation which seems straightforward, but once I get into it, I find things are not what they appeared to be. I may not have been told the whole truth. What I decide to do about it depends on what else I learn.'

'You wouldn't want to put an innocent person in danger?' asked Keith.

'Exactly. So, I would appreciate it, if you could tell me anything you know which might be relevant.'

'I saw them together one day,' he said. 'She had the baby in a pram, going off on a walk. He came out after her. They had an argument. It seemed heated.'

'What about?'

Keith shrugged. 'They were too far away for me to make out what they were saying. It was their body language I noticed. She looked scared, but defiant. He saw me watching. That's when he grabbed her by the arm, turned her around and pushed her towards the house. Then he got hold of the pram and pulled it inside.'

'What happened then?'

'I don't know. They all disappeared from view and someone, him I presumed, slammed the door.'

'You remember it clearly.'

Keith nodded. 'It bothered me afterwards, you know. Whether I should have done something.'

'Like what?'

'Gone over there and made sure she was OK. I couldn't get it out of my mind. When I called Mum at the weekend, and she told me the woman and baby were gone, I was relieved. I thought they'd be better off.'

'You never told me, Keith,' said Gladys.

'I didn't want you to worry, Mum, and once she'd left, it didn't seem important.'

'What you described fits with some concerns I have.'

'What are you going to do?' asked Gladys.

'I don't know, yet. But please, don't speak to Mr Sharpe.'

'We won't be speaking to him,' said Keith. 'If he comes here causing trouble, Mum, you phone the police right away. Alright?' He held his mother's hand. 'I mean it. Don't go opening the door to him. Use the peep hole, like I keep telling you to do.

There was no car in Charles' drive, but Beatrice felt obliged to knock. After all, he was paying her, and she could, in good conscience, say she'd tried. There was no reply and, whilst waiting a polite amount of time, she noticed a small black dome under the porch. She peered up at it. There was writing on the side, which was too small to read, so she reached high and took a photo with her phone. Zooming in on the writing, identified it as a 'home security' device and gave the name of a company.

Beatrice walked along the front of the house and checked down both sides, as far as she was able, given the high fences. There were similar devices on each corner. If they were cameras, they covered the whole of the front of the building. Presumably, given how security conscious this implied Charles was, there would be similar arrangements at the back.

Was this how he'd known Beatrice had been in Norwich on her previous visit? It also raised the question of where the CCTV footage of the day Lily went missing was. Had the police seen it? Beatrice doubted it. Charles couldn't have either, because if Jules had shown up on it, he would have certainly found out who she was, given her distinctive appearance.

Beatrice spent the drive home thinking about Lily, Elizabeth and Charles. Was she being over-imaginative, linking Lily with Jules and abused women? Was Keith a reliable witness? There was a possibility Lily left because of Charles, and he might be the last person who should be told where she was. Whatever, she needed to speak with her client. She parked in the next layby, and mentally braced herself for the interaction.

'Mr Sharpe. It's Beatrice Styles.'

'Yes?'

'I wanted to talk to you about the investigation.'

'And?'

The monosyllabic replies were not encouraging. 'I thought I should let you know the next stage of the investigation will be time consuming.'

'Why?'

'I need to work out where Lily might have gone, assuming she is in Lincolnshire. I don't have a lot to go on. It means it will basically be a process of elimination of possible locations. I can prioritise my search, based on the small amount of information you and Andrew have given me, but it will take time to go through all the different alternatives. Are you sure you want me to go ahead?'

'Yes.'

'I'm afraid I'll need another payment on account. I've already used up most of the deposit. I can send you an updated bill by email.'

'Do that.'

'Did Lily ever mention any particular areas in the county. Places she'd been to? Or anything she remembered about where she lived?'

'No.'

He hadn't paused to think about it. Did he not know anything? Or was he one of those bosses who issued instructions expecting others to work out how to get the results, without ever caring if the request was reasonable or possible? 'I wanted to ask you about CCTV.'

'What about it?'

'I saw you have it at your house.'

'And?'

'Do you have footage from the day Lily left?'

'No. It was switched off.'

'Who by?'

'Lily, I presume.'

'Did the police ask for it?'

'I said it was switched off. There wasn't any footage.'

'Did anyone check the images in the days before?'

'Why would they?' Charles barked the question.

'In case there was anything on it which might give a clue to where she went?'

'Like what?'

'I don't know. Could you send me the recordings from the week before?' Beatrice deliberately chose the time to include the day Keith saw the argument.

The silence went on a little too long.

'I don't have it. The files get overwritten.'

'Isn't there a back-up?'

'I don't have any recordings. Send me your report and updated costs.' The call disconnected.

Beatrice didn't believe the CCTV had been lost. Historically, tapes were reused in a systematic way for security cameras, but these days, a large capacity digital drive took up hardly any physical space. There would be no need to overwrite files for a long time after the event. Perhaps Charles knew the recordings wouldn't show him in a good light.

The detective came. Brave, but stupid. She could be dangerous. I'll have to monitor her. It was clear she has no evidence, just circumstantial pieces which amount to nothing. Could cause trouble, though. Although she doesn't know the truth, in time she could get close to it. It can't be allowed to happen. I have no objection to her personally. She's only doing what she has to, the same as I am. But she's asking inconvenient questions in inconvenient places. Someone might talk about things they shouldn't, despite me making sure they're well motivated not to. She needs warning. Gently, at first. With luck it will be enough.

Chapter 42

Wednesday 4th July

Knowing Neil was due at the brewery today, Beatrice parked in Spilsby near their office, with a good view of the car park. She'd seen Gareth in the window earlier, and kept watch for him. At 10.00 a.m., when Frankie had said Neil was due, Gareth's car appeared in the car park entrance. After he pulled out, Beatrice allowed him to get ahead before following.

Gareth crawled past the light industrial estate long enough to see Neil's van, then turned and set off west. Beatrice suspected his destination, and allowed a larger distance to develop.

At the farm, Beatrice parked in the same gateway she'd used before. Gareth's car had turned into the farmyard moments earlier. She got out of the car and looked towards the farmhouse. The hedge was high enough to conceal her vehicle, but she could easily see over. She watched as Gareth climbed out of his car. The door to the farmhouse opened, and the three collies ran out, greeting him as a familiar friend. Yasmin came out of the building. Gareth, dogs close on his heel, strode up to Yasmin and they shared a passionate kiss. Holding hands, they turned into the house. The dogs ran in, and the door closed. The silhouettes of two figures appeared upstairs moments later. One of them reached up and pulled the curtains closed.

Beatrice got back into her car, and set off, towards Spilsby. As she drove, she wondered whether or not to tell Zoe what she'd seen. It wasn't what she'd been hired to find out, but it could have a bearing on the investigation. It meant, there were secrets between the couple. Could there be more? And what if Neil knew his wife was having an affair with Gareth? Would it be motivation enough for him to take action against the business? Maybe Victor Malone had nothing to do with the fires, and it was coincidence that Bugsy and Michael worked for Malone. But why would Neil kill Bugsy? Beatrice had to follow it up, talk to Zoe, and it was better to do it now, rather than brooding on it.

At the brewery office, the secretary was sorting through boxes of papers, with piles spread over her desk and on the floor.

'That doesn't look like fun,' said Beatrice.

The young woman pushed her hair from her eyes as she stood up. 'No.' Her previous professional and courteous demeanour was gone. 'What do you want?'

'A word with Zoe.'

'She's busy.'

'She's always busy.'

The secretary regarded Beatrice for several long seconds, then shrugged. 'I'll ask.' She shoved the sheaf of papers she was holding into the top of the nearest box, and went over to the closed office door. She knocked then entered, shutting the door behind her.

Beatrice could make out indistinct murmurings. She peered at the papers on the desk, noting they appeared to relate to the accounts for the previous year. Were they under investigation by HMRC, as well as the insurance company?

'She's only got a few minutes.' The secretary was back, and she gestured at the paperwork. 'We're in the middle of something.'

Zoe stood up when Beatrice entered. 'What do you want now?' She sounded irritated.

'I need to speak to you.'

'Go on, then.'

Beatrice didn't want to add to Zoe's troubles, but she

needed answers. 'It's rather difficult.'

'I don't have a lot of time.'

'It's about Gareth.' Beatrice looked Zoe in the eyes. 'Did you know Robert has been selling brewery waste for cash, and pocketing it?'

Zoe's eyebrows raised a few millimetres. 'No. That's Gareth's area. You'd need to talk to him. It can't be much money, though. Surely?'

'Not a lot. I've tried speaking to Gareth about it. He said he'd look into it.'

'Sounds reasonable.'

'He said the same to Frankie. Months ago.'

Zoe frowned.

'I'm interested in why Gareth hasn't done anything.'

'You have a theory?'

'The man Robert sells the waste to is called Neil.' Beatrice saw Zoe sit more upright. 'Neil goes to the brewery regularly, to talk and drink beer with Robert. That's when he hands over the cash. He's normally there for a couple of hours, at least.'

Zoe strode to the window. Her shoulders were tense, her back rigid. 'Good grief, Beatrice. Just say what you want to.'

'I believe Gareth may be involved with Neil's wife, and it's why he won't tackle Robert. He doesn't want the current arrangement to stop.'

Zoe remained staring out of the window, motionless. After a long minute, she turned back to Beatrice, running her hands across her face. 'Why did you have to get involved?' She exuded weariness.

'You knew?' It was not the response she'd expected. Anger or disbelief, maybe, but not this.

'Of course. I know Gareth. I wish you had left it alone.'

'I'm sorry, I thought I was doing the right thing by telling you.'

'The expression "the road to hell is paved with good intentions" springs to mind. Oh well, it's not your fault. Gareth is responsible for his own choices. I was hoping we'd be able to sell the business, salvage something, then go our separate ways.'

'You've got a buyer?'

'Victor Malone is still interested. At a much lower price than his previous offer, of course.'

'You've talked to him? Recently, I mean?'

'Yes. I planned to present Gareth with a choice: sell and pay off our debts, or wait a few more weeks, until we're bankrupt and lose the house. I was hoping he'd agree and sign the papers this week.'

'You still can, can't you? Gareth isn't aware we know.'

'So, if he thinks everything is carrying on as usual, I might be able to get it done without arguments? I can confront Gareth about the affair in my own time?'

'As far as I'm concerned you can. There are rumours circulating about Gareth, but I don't think he's been connected with Yasmin yet.'

'Hopefully I'll have enough time to get the sale papers signed. We can deal with the separation and divorce, once the business is taken care of.'

'Zoe, do you know Neil?'

'A little.'

'Do you think he knows about the affair? You did.'

Zoe considered the question. 'I don't believe so, because he'd have punched Gareth and thrown Yasmin out. Why do you ask?'

'He might want revenge against Gareth.'

'By destroying our pubs?' Zoe shook her head. 'He's not like that.'

'The only other person I've identified who might have a grudge against you both, is Victor Malone.'

'Why would he?'

'Because you turned down his offer to buy the brewery.'

'That's not a good enough reason. Why would he bother?'

'Well, he's getting the brewery now, isn't he?'

'I can't believe it's him.'

'I can't find any other suspects.'

Zoe's eyes widened. 'Do the insurance company think we were involved? We need the payout to make Malone's offer work. Otherwise, we'll lose everything.' Zoe's voice rose in pitch.

'I've told them I don't think you were, but without evidence of someone else being guilty, I can't prove it.'

'You're going to keep trying though, aren't you?'

'As long as they let me.'

'Please do whatever you can. We need them to pay out.' Zoe slumped in a chair, dejected.

'I'll do my best.'

Zoe nodded. Silent.

Beatrice left the office closing the door gently behind her. The secretary glanced at her, then returned to sorting the papers, presumably to prepare them for Malone's lawyers. It seemed like he was going to get what he wanted after all.

Chapter 43

Beatrice made a detour to Middle Rasen. She didn't want to add to Zoe's troubles, but the possibility of Neil holding a grudge against Gareth had to be investigated. Although certain Zoe had nothing to do with the fires, she was less sure about Gareth, given the evidence of his duplicitous and selfish nature, but she doubted even he would want everything they'd built in the business to be destroyed.

In Middle Rasen, she parked outside the nursery and made a call to the office number she'd found online. She explained she was in the area and wanted to see about a nursery place for a nearly two-year-old. Could she look around? The person who answered the phone said she could spare quarter of an hour.

Inside, Beatrice repeated the story about her sister needing a place, to a welcoming middle-aged woman called Heather. She was given a leaflet on the free places scheme and shown around. Beatrice feigned interest in the children and their activities, but she found the chaotic, noisy atmosphere disturbing. In the room allocated to Elizabeth's age group she paid closer attention.

There were four members of staff and fifteen children. Heather explained that every child was involved in a structured activity, led by an adult. Beatrice kept watch for anyone who might be Elizabeth. She had no idea what the child looked like. One girl with blonde hair was sitting with a group of other children drawing, or rather scribbling, on pieces of paper. Beatrice drew near.

The woman supervising at the table looked up and

nodded, before turning her attention back to the children. 'It's lovely Jonathon. Would you like to try another colour?' She held out a red crayon. The boy sat before a page covered with green scribbles. He squinted at the crayon, shook his head, then continued covering the paper in green.

'How about you, Lizzie? Would you like the red crayon?' The blonde girl gave a small nod and took it. Beatrice noticed her name.

'Is there anything else I can show you?' asked Heather.

'No, thanks. I think I've enough to tell my sister about. The children seem happy.'

'Oh, yes. There's always plenty for them to do. When the weather's good, we take them outside. There's a lot of variety.'

'How does my sister apply for the waiting list, if she decides to go ahead?'

'Get her to call and I'll talk her through the process. It's quite straightforward.'

Outside, Beatrice checked her watch. There was an hour until the nursery closed. She had nowhere else to be, so she waited in her car.

At 5 p.m. her patience was rewarded. A woman with startling red hair approached the nursery. A short time later, she came out with Lizzie. The pair ambled away, chatting. Beatrice debated how to follow. She hadn't seen the woman get out of a car, but maybe she'd parked out of sight. Gambling on her travelling by foot, Beatrice left her car and followed at a good distance. Ten minutes later, she watched Lizzie and her mother enter a small house. She continued walking and, using the map on her phone to guide her, circled back to her car without having to go past it again.

Beatrice checked the photos of Lily she had on her phone, taken from the ones Charles had given her. There was a superficial resemblance between the woman and Lily, but the red hair made such a difference. It was a real red too, not ginger or strawberry blonde, but a bright, artificial red. Beatrice couldn't help but think of Jules and her changes of hair colour. An effective way to distract from a person's features. Had Jules suggested it to Lily? She needed time to think things through. Her next course of action could alter the lives of the woman and child.

Back home, she spent time writing up notes from the last few days, and sending Rosie the details for adding expenses to her invoices. She then began to plan out an evening for her and James, thinking it was time she cooked for him.

'Beatrice? Can we talk?' James stood in the doorway to her office.

She'd heard him enter the house earlier, but been focused on her work. Vaguely aware of the noise of him moving around the house and in his room, she assumed he'd things to do, so left him to it. Beatrice thought she'd heard him go outside to his car several times too. She put down the lid of the laptop. 'Sure, come in.'

'Actually, can you come downstairs, please? This isn't a conversation I want to have whilst sitting on the floor.' He turned away and Beatrice heard his footsteps on the stairs. Concerned by his solemn demeanour she followed.

In the living room James was sitting on the sofa, leaning forward, elbows on his knees, head in his hands.

'Are you OK?' asked Beatrice.

He looked up. 'Will you sit down?' He patted the seat next to him.

'This is serious.' The joke fell flat in the tense atmosphere. She sat down beside him.

James turned sideways in his seat to face her. 'I thought it was time one of us was brave enough to start the conversation we've been avoiding.'

Beatrice sighed and turned towards him. 'You're breaking up with me?'

'It's probably more accurate to say we're breaking up with each other, don't you think?' His mouth twitched in the semblance of a smile and he reached for her hand. 'I like you,' he said. 'A lot. But we want different things in life, and as much as I've really enjoyed our short time together, we have to face the truth.'

'Which is what exactly?'

'It isn't going to go the distance, is it? We get on, but we're not in love. Are we?'

'Sorry,' said Beatrice.

'Don't be. It's better if neither of us gets too badly hurt.' He inhaled a deep breath and expelled it slowly before continuing. 'The thing is, I want a family. Children. All the stuff I know you don't want.'

'I never hid how I felt.'

'I know. And honestly, when we met, I wasn't sure if it was something I'd ever be interested in. But it's become clear to me that I want to be a dad, have a wife, go on family holidays: all the conventional stuff. If we'd been in love, maybe I'd have been happy with the two of us. But… Well, here we are.' He squeezed her hand. 'I'm really sorry, Beatrice. You know as well as I do, this is right for both of us.'

Beatrice looked into his bright blue eyes, and saw genuine concern. She nodded her head. 'You're right. We don't love each other, but we could love other people, and should have the chance to find out if it's possible. Thanks for not thinking you could change my mind about having children. I'm sorry it hasn't worked out differently though.'

'I've found somewhere else to stay,' said James.

'You don't have to leave.'

'I know. We'd have managed. But I do have some feelings for you, you know.' James removed his hand from hers. 'It's better this way.'

He stood up and so did Beatrice. Tears were welling in her eyes, and she blinked them back. James held out his arms and she stepped into his embrace, holding him tightly, breathing in the scent of him, and enjoying the warmth of his body for the last time. She noticed moisture on her cheek and looked at James. Whether they were his tears or hers, she wasn't certain. They kissed tenderly, then, as if by mutual agreement, their arms dropped, and James walked away. At the front door he stopped and turned back. 'You'll take care, won't you?'

'Same as always.'

'That's what I'm worried about.' James opened the front door and left, closing it gently behind him.

Chapter 44

Thursday 5th July

After a disturbed night, her mind replaying her relationship with James, Beatrice had spent most of the day ignoring the demands of work. Finally, in the afternoon she remembered the need to buy cat litter and walked into town. She still hadn't bought it, when she spotted Astra on the High Street, and trailed her, at a discrete distance.

Judging from the number of bags her 'minder' was carrying, Astra was having a successful shopping trip. Beatrice followed her into a designer store, keeping out of her line of sight. When the younger woman had taken a bundle of clothes to the changing rooms to try on, Beatrice had, without thinking, grabbed a couple of items and followed into the one place her male companion wouldn't be allowed.

'Hello. You're Anne's yoga friend, aren't you?' Astra handed her clothes selection to the assistant, who hung them up in a cubicle.

'Yes, I was there on Monday.'

'Have you recovered from your ordeal?'

'Just about. Not sure I'll be going back, though.'

'I wouldn't have thought this was your kind of shop.' Astra looked down at the bundle of fabric in Beatrice's arms. 'And I don't think those are your kind of clothes.'

Beatrice examined the pink, frilly items in her arms. 'I think you're right.'

'Who are you?' Astra placed her hands on her hips. The assistant stared at them. Astra glared at her until she left.

Beatrice stepped close to Astra, keeping her voice low as she spoke. 'My name is Beatrice. I'm a private investigator.'

'This is about Victor, isn't it?' Astra's stance had become tense, her lips pursed.

'Not directly. I want to talk to you about Lee Chambers.'

'I don't know who that is.'

'You know him as Bugsy.'

Beatrice saw Astra's eyes narrow, then her face returned to an impassive state. 'Sorry, don't know him.'

'He works for Victor.'

'So what?'

'I say works, but he doesn't work for Victor anymore, because he's dead.'

Astra became still, but didn't speak. She waited for Beatrice to continue.

'Bugsy used to be one of your minders. Took you places, like yoga.'

'Was he? I don't remember. What's it got to do with you?'

'I'm investigating the Wild Geese Brewery fires. Bugsy's body was found in one of the pubs.'

Astra's eyebrows raised a little, then she frowned. 'What do you want?'

'Did Bugsy do something to upset Victor?'

'It's none of my business. Anyone who works for Victor knows what his expectations are.'

'And there will be consequences if they don't meet his expectations?'

Astra shrugged.

'Who would know if Victor had an issue with Bugsy? Jackson?'

'What do you know about Jackson?' Astra sat on the chair in the changing cubicle.

'I've met him. I got the impression he'd do anything Victor asked him to do.'

'You've seen Victor too?'

Beatrice nodded.

'That was brave.' Astra's lips formed a small, brief smile. 'Foolish, but brave.'

'How did you become involved with Victor?'

Astra exhaled slowly. 'I'm not sure I can explain it. He was charming, interesting, fun to be with. I was already in too deep, by the time I found out what kind of man he is.'

'Why do you stay with him, when you know he's dangerous?'

'I think you've answered your own question.'

'He'd hurt you?'

'It's a risk I'd only get to take once.'

'You can't come in here. Women only.' The loud voice of the assistant rang out.

'We've got to go.' Astra's minder had had enough waiting and he barged in. His eyes darted between the two women, suspicious. 'Who the hell are you?'

Beatrice remained silent.

Astra stood and ran a hand down the red silk dress she'd planned to try on. 'Shame. I rather liked this one.'

The minder grabbed Astra roughly by the arms. 'Stay away, if you know what's good for you.' He dragged Astra from the changing room.

Beatrice left the shop and started walking at a slow pace back up Steep Hill towards home.

She'd not managed to get any information about Bugsy out of Astra. No one in Malone's circle was going to talk, but whoever put the body in the pub cellar, must have known there was going to be fire that night. They couldn't have followed Michael, because there wouldn't have been time to dump the corpse. They must have known in advance.

The fact the fire followed so soon after the previous one, implied a hurry, to destroy the body, perhaps. Michael must have been told when to do it, and that meant if she could find out who had ordered the fires, it would lead her to the killer. She had to talk to Michael again. He was the one person who could tell her something. Perhaps his solicitor could arrange another meeting, and she could try again to persuade him it was in his interests to give up the other person.

Halfway up Steep Hill, her phone rang.

'Hi, Beatrice. It's Louise Prince.'

Though walking slowly, Beatrice was out of breath and glad of the interruption. 'I was just thinking about you.'

'I'm not sure that's a good thing. I don't have long, but wanted to let you know Michael is in hospital.'

'What happened?'

'The other inmates is what happened. But no one is talking. Not even Michael.'

Had whoever instructed Michael found out he'd given her copies of the evidence from the case against him? Had he been attacked as punishment? Or a warning? Beatrice had pushed him hard, thinking he was overreacting, but it appeared his fears about speaking out were well founded. There was no way he'd talk to her now. 'Will he be alright?'

'It was a thorough beating, and he'll take a long time to recover, but the doctors say his injuries aren't life threatening.'

'That's good news. Will he be safe when he gets back to prison?'

'The prison officers will do what they can, but there's no guarantees.'

'I'd been hoping to speak to him again, but I assume it can't happen now.'

'I'm afraid Michael isn't capable of speaking, and when he recovers, I doubt he'll want to.'

'Thanks for letting me know.'

'Have you found out anything to help his case?'

'Not yet. Sorry.'

Beatrice continued walking up the hill, her mind swirling with too many things to resolve. In the arson and murder case, she still wasn't able to confirm whether the Browns had been involved. It appeared Michael didn't have any dealings with either of them, but it didn't mean they weren't the orchestrators. She suspected Zoe's gut instinct about Neil was correct, he was more likely to take direct action against Gareth, and had no known connection or reason for killing Bugsy. Was Victor Malone involved? Had he ordered the fires and the murder? How could she find out?

She was also worried about Lily. If she was the woman in Middle Rasen, then Beatrice had done what she'd been hired for, but what to do with the information? Would telling Charles put Lily and Elizabeth in danger? It was a big risk.

Her phone rang. This time, it was Vanessa. Keen to hear positive news, she swiped to answer. 'I'm glad you've called.'

'Ms Styles. This is Sergeant Holmes. I'm calling regarding your official complaint about Simon Atkinson.'

'Vanessa? Are you OK?' It was the right voice, but the words were stilted and formal.

'As agreed previously, I have discussed the substance of your complaint with Mr Atkinson. As a result, I have to let you know we have no further interest in the matter, and consider the complaint closed.'

'I don't understand? What's happening, Vanessa? What did you find out?'

'I can't go into details about confidential matters.'

'But I'm no further forward than I was before.'

The silence stretched.

'Come on Vanessa, you know me. Surely you can give me something?'

'I've told you what I can. He isn't doing anything he shouldn't be. I have to go. I'm really sorry.' Vanessa hung up.

Beatrice stared at her phone, bewildered. Vanessa had behaved so differently, nothing like her normal self. She'd said everything was above board with the solicitor, and Beatrice didn't think she'd lie about it, but to be so abrupt and unfriendly didn't reflect the woman she knew in the past or had seen on their night out together. She selected Vanessa number in her contacts and pressed 'call'. The phone rang twice before cutting out. Vanessa didn't want to speak to her again.

In the house, Beatrice sat for a while, with the cat on her lap, trying not to think about James. Her cases had stalled and she needed a mental break from thinking about them. The cat's purring was soothing, as she stroked the animal's fur.

'I guess it's you and me now.'

The house seemed emptier than usual, though she reasoned it was more to do with her state of mind and the knowledge James wouldn't be coming home that night. Or again. She missed him, and although they often spent the night in their own rooms, for practical reasons, her bed had felt lonely last night.

'I should do something. Keep busy,' she said to the disinterested cat, who appeared to believe stroking her was sufficient activity. Beatrice picked the animal up, to a meow of protest, and set her on the floor. 'I'm going out.' A walk usually helped her clear her mind, so she decided to pick up a bottle of wine, a takeaway, and watch mindless TV.

Chapter 45

Beatrice had spent a couple of hours wandering through the lower part of Lincoln. She couldn't remember where she'd been, but when she was passing her favourite Indian takeaway, it reminded her of her earlier plan to buy food. She went inside to place an order. Whilst it was being cooked, she had plenty of time to buy wine.

The short cut through the alley was one she'd taken several times, and had no qualms about using. Even the sudden appearance of a figure at the far end didn't cause her to hesitate. She moved to one side as he came near, to allow him to pass. He stopped in front of her instead. She stopped too. Wary now, she started to turn, to go back the way she'd come, when there was the pressure of hands on her lower back. They shoved her hard into the brick wall of the alley. Her head made a dull thud, as it hit the hard surface. Her breath was forced from her lungs.

She was held in place by strong arms, and a large man's body pressed against her back, the cold wall against her front. Beatrice filled her lungs, ready to scream, but before she could, a rough hand came from behind and clamped over her mouth. The only sound which came out was too muffled for anyone beyond a few feet to hear.

The man's other hand wrapped around her waist and turned her to face a second, smaller man. Beatrice's handbag fell to the floor. The short man stepped close to her and she could smell his body odour. He grinned, enjoying the fear she was certain was reflected in her eyes.

'Now, you'd better listen.' His voice was quiet, but clear.

'You need to stop poking around in things that are no business of yours. Otherwise, we're going to come back again. And you'll like it even less next time. We'll enjoy it though, won't we.' He glanced at his companion.

'Oh, yes.' The menacing voice spoke directly into her ear. 'Too right.'

'Hey, you!' A voice echoed down the alley, startling the two men.

'Piss off,' growled the largest of Beatrice's tormentors. 'This is nothing to do with you.'

'I've called the police.'

The man behind Beatrice squeezed her more tightly before speaking again. 'Don't you forget what we said. Or else.' He then let her go and shoved her against the alley wall once more. On instinct she raised her arms to cushion the blow, scraping her bare forearms on the rough surface and she fell to the floor, bruised and dazed.

She heard the two men run down the alley, quickly disappearing from sight.

'Are you alright, love?'

Beatrice looked up. The familiar, unkempt face of homeless Trevor swam before her eyes. She struggled, trying to get up, then his hands were on her shoulders, gently pushing her back down.

'You'd best stay there a minute. Looks like you've had quite a bang.'

The police arrived and questioned Beatrice and Trevor. There were no other witnesses. Remembering her paid-for takeaway, she told Trevor to collect and enjoy it. The uniformed officers then drove her home. A WPC stayed with Beatrice, waiting for someone from CID to take her statement.

Beatrice was relieved when Susan arrived. The DC paused when she saw Beatrice, who realised she must have looked in a sorry state.

Susan sat down with her notebook. 'I've been given an idea

of what happened, so I'll keep this brief.'

'Thank you.'

They went through the events of the evening, but it had happened fast and there wasn't much Beatrice could tell her.

'They told me to stop asking questions.'

'About what?'

'I'm sure you can work that out.' In her peripheral vision, Beatrice could see the WPC's head moving as she glanced back and forth between the two of them, not understanding.

Susan nodded. 'They threatened you?'

'Not in a clear way, but they said they'd be back, if I didn't do as they said.'

'Could you identify them?'

'No. It was too dark.'

'What about their voices? Any accents? Distinctive words or phrases?'

'I'm sorry, I can't remember exactly what they said, just the sense of it.'

'OK.' Susan closed her notebook. 'There's not a lot to go on, but we'll check CCTV. It might give us more witnesses, if nothing else.' Susan peered at Beatrice's head. 'You need to go to hospital to get checked out. You could have concussion. Shall I call James?'

'No.'

Susan's gaze was intense and Beatrice turned away.

'I'll take you, but I'll have to go to the station afterwards.'

'Thanks.'

Because the WPC was with them in the car, Susan couldn't quiz Beatrice about James, much to her relief. They left her at A&E, Susan's expression concerned as she drove off.

Having been seen quickly at the hospital, Beatrice called Rosie. 'Hi, it's me.'

'It's late. Everything OK?'

'I was wondering if you could pick me up from hospital…'

A man's voice sounded in the background.

'What were you saying?' asked Rosie.

'Can you pick me up…'

'I'm really sorry. I've got stuff going on here. Let's speak tomorrow.' Rosie ended the call.

Beatrice had been hoping her sister would invite her to stay in Sudbrooke overnight, but Rosie had other things on her mind. In the end Beatrice called a taxi. The driver, a middle-aged man, had been kind, walking her to her house and waiting until she was inside with the door closed. She'd been told to stay off alcohol and, having lost her appetite, she locked up the house and went to bed.

Chapter 46

Friday 6th July

After a night of broken sleep, Beatrice finally forced herself out of bed in the late afternoon. Her head ached and she was exhausted, but her hunger needed assuaging. The cat had joined her sometime in the night, and Beatrice had appreciated the company. Now she left her sleeping, curled up on the bed.

In the kitchen, she'd finished making coffee when there was a banging at the door. She opened it to be confronted with the unshaven, scowling face of DS Fisher.

'What do you want?' asked Beatrice, choosing to leave him on the doorstep.

'We've had a complaint.' Fisher glared at her. 'About you.' He peered up at her bruised face, frowning.

Beatrice knew it looked bad. 'What law do you imagine I've broken this time?'

'You've been harassing Victor Malone.'

'How have I harassed him, exactly?' Beatrice leaned against the doorframe.

'You know.'

'No. I really don't.' Beatrice dismissed the fleeting thought of making a complaint about Malone and his threatening behaviour. Fisher was the last police officer to take any accusation from her seriously.

'You've been asking questions about things which are nothing to do with you. Being nosey.'

'Is it a crime, now? Asking questions?'

'You need to leave the investigating to the police. Keep out of our business.'

'Or?'

'I'll arrest you for obstruction.'

'How am I stopping you doing your work? How am I obstructing you or any other police officer? What's stopping you from questioning Victor Malone?'

'You've got no evidence he had anything to do with the fires, or the murder,' Fisher growled. 'You can't go around accusing people of committing crimes and expect them to put up with it.'

'I didn't accuse him of anything. I pointed out a few coincidences and asked him about them. I take it you've not asked him any questions at all? What are you hoping for? That "evidence" will somehow drop into your lap? Isn't it your job to go out and look for it?'

'Don't tell me how to do my job. You've no idea about police work.'

'Not much. Doesn't mean I don't know about investigations. The victim worked for him. Was last seen going to see him. You can't be unaware of the reputation Malone has. The chances are, Bugsy did something to upset him and was got rid of. Who else would want to kill him? And what about Michael Burgess? He worked for Malone too. Another coincidence?'

'If *you* know anything about his reputation, you'll stay well away from Malone and anyone connected to him.'

'Oh, I see. This is about Astra, isn't it? I went to Malone by appointment. As for Astra, well I happened to bump into her…'

'Bump into? Really?' Fisher curled his top lip.

Beatrice ignored the remark. 'Since I knew who she was connected to, I thought I'd take the opportunity to ask about Bugsy.'

'What did she tell you?'

'Why do you want to know? For your policework, or so you can report back to Malone? A friend of yours, is he?'

Fisher turned red-faced and stepped up close to Beatrice. He spoke through gritted teeth. 'Keep away from him and anyone connected to him. You've been warned.' His eyes narrowed, then he made an abrupt turn and left.

Beatrice watched him stalk away, then closed the door, wondering who had sent him.

Back inside, she made herself toast and fresh coffee. She was about to sit at the dining table when there was another knocking on the door. She hoped Fisher wasn't back for round two.

'Hello?' Beatrice opened the door to a vaguely familiar elderly couple.

'Joan and Fred,' said the woman, to Beatrice's blank look. 'You bought the house off us.'

'Goodness, yes.' She stood back. 'Come in, please.'

As the couple entered the house, they both looked at Beatrice's head wound, turning their eyes away again quickly.

'How are you? Settling into your bungalow?'

'Oh, yes,' said Fred. 'It's lovely.'

'And no stairs to keep running up and down,' added Joan. 'We should have done it years ago.'

'Would you like to sit down?'

'Actually, we can't stop,' said Joan.

Beatrice waited for an explanation. She saw Joan tap Fred's leg with her foot.

'The thing is,' he looked at his wife. 'Joan here misses Tabitha.'

A dim memory of her cat's name surfaced. But it wasn't *her* cat, really.

'We've come to collect her,' said Joan. 'We'll keep her in the bungalow for longer this time. Fred let her out too soon, she hadn't adjusted to it being her new home.'

'You've come for the cat?' Beatrice swallowed.

'I'm afraid so,' said Fred. 'Is she in?'

'She's upstairs.' Beatrice hesitated. 'I suppose I'd better go get her.'

'I'll fetch the carrier from the car,' said Fred.

'We'll take her home, and she won't bother you again.' Joan spoke with certainty.

Beatrice shut the door behind the couple. The cat hadn't seemed pleased to see them, and as the flap to the carrier had been closed, putting her little face behind bars, the sensation of sadness had been almost overwhelming. Had she imagined the look of gloom on the animal's face? She went to the dining room and spent several moments staring at the now-cold toast and coffee. Leaving them, she turned away and went back upstairs to bed.

Chapter 47

Saturday 7th July

Beatrice, face down on her bed, opened her eyes. The light from the window, curtains undrawn, was piercing. She pulled herself upright, groaning at the pain from the bruises on her shoulder, arms and most significantly, her head. They hurt worse than on the previous day.

She staggered to the bathroom and looked at herself in the mirror. The pale skin of her face was marred by a pool of purple spreading across her forehead, punctuated with thin red streaks, where the alley wall had grazed her skin. She straightened her ponytail and splashed water on her face.

In the living room Beatrice bent to retrieve the post from the floor behind the front door. The motion made her dizzy and she grabbed at the wall to steady herself. Once her balance returned, she headed to the kitchen, dropping the post on the dining room table as she passed.

Setting the coffee machine to work, Beatrice rummaged in the kitchen drawer until she pulled out a packet of paracetamol. She washed two down with water. Adding a splash of milk to her coffee, she took a sip then reached, without thinking, for the bag of cat food. Her hand stopped mid-motion and her shoulders drooped. Taking out a packet of biscuits she picked up her drink and went back into the living room. Flopping on the sofa, she switched on the TV.

After staring blankly at the moving images for a while, Beatrice was pulled out of her trance by her mobile buzzing. It was Susan. She left it, in no mood to speak with anyone. A short time passed before her mobile buzzed again. A voicemail. She played it.

'Hi Bea, it's me. Just calling to check how you're doing. I've got the day off today. How about I come to yours and you can feed me?' Beatrice heard a light, forced chuckle. 'No news on the men who attacked you. Not yet anyway. We'll keep trying.'

There was a pause.

'Give me a call when you get this. Please.'

Beatrice deleted the message and put the phone back on the table.

The incessant banging interrupted a deep sleep. The paracetamol had done its job, and Beatrice's head was marginally less painful. The banging continued. It was the front door. She threw off the duvet and made her way downstairs. At the bottom, she stopped and peered around the doorway into the living room. The flap to the letterbox opened and she could see movement through the slit.

'Beatrice, I know you're in there.'

Rosie.

'Come on, open up. Susan told me you'd been badly hurt. Why didn't you tell me? I thought it was just a scratch. I would have come to the hospital.'

A pause.

'Beatrice!'

The flap closed and she saw movement at the window, obscured by the net curtain she'd put up for privacy. Rosie was cupping her hands around her eyes, pressing her face to the glass. Beatrice remained still, and her sister left.

Her mobile buzzed. She waited until she'd seen Rosie's car pass on the road, then went to check the text.

I know you're in there. You can't hide forever. Call me. Rosie xxx

Beatrice deleted the message, saw she had a voicemail and played it.

'It's Charles Sharpe. I want an update. I'm paying you a lot of money and I expect results. I want to know what's happening.'

Hungry, she took the phone into the kitchen and placed an order for a curry to be delivered. Once done, she collected a glass and bottle of wine. Back in the living room, she closed the curtains on the daylight, and switched the TV on.

Chapter 48

Sunday 8th July

Mindless films had kept her entertained and distracted until the early hours. Beatrice had a vague memory of it being about 3 a.m. when she'd finally dragged herself off to bed. She glanced at her watch: 2 p.m. A gentle stretch revealed some pain, but not as much as before. She was beginning to recover from her ordeal. Physically at least. Her headache had more to do with too much wine, than the attack.

Down in the kitchen she made a large coffee and had another dose of paracetamol. Perhaps it hadn't been a good idea to drink so much, on top of the tablets yesterday and the possible concussion. The bag of cat food was still on the kitchen work surface. She grabbed it and shoved it into a cupboard, out of sight. Hesitating a moment, she put the cat's food bowl in too. Unwashed. She'd deal with it another time.

Beatrice sat in front of her laptop, but couldn't bring herself to open it. What was the point? Yes, OK, she'd found Lily. Or at least thought she had, but didn't know what to do about it. Charles Sharpe was, in her mind, rapidly turning from the over-smooth businessman into a potential danger to the woman and child.

As for the arson and murder, she was nowhere. She suspected Malone, but had no proof and couldn't see how to get any. Michael could have provided evidence, but there was no way he would now. Malone had him terrified, with good reason.

Her mum was still missing, her dad still dead. Vanessa, who she'd thought was on her side, had cut her off. What else could she do? Rosie was having a hard time, and she didn't know how to help her either.

The flow of gloomy thoughts was interrupted by a knock at the front door, preventing her getting onto James and the cat, and how alone she was. Beatrice went through to the bedroom at the front of the house and peered out of the window. It was Susan. With a pang of guilt at ignoring her, she watched her friend walk away.

Beatrice stood in the doorway to her office and realised she'd wouldn't achieve anything today. In the living room, she picked up her discarded mobile. There were several unread texts and voicemails. She ignored them and ordered another delivery of food and wine.

Chapter 49

Monday 9th July

Beatrice stared at the detritus in the living room. Takeaway containers and empty wine bottles. The sight disgusted her. The last time she'd done something like this was after her father had died, her mother had disappeared, and the police had told her they were going to stop searching. Somehow, she'd managed to get herself out of that slump, but she wasn't sure she wanted to this time. She'd been threatened and hurt, her investigations had stalled, her relationship with James was over, and even the cat was gone.

At the dining room table, Beatrice turned her mobile over in her hands. Had she switched it off, or had it run out of charge? Was there any point putting it back on? Rosie would be worried. Maybe she should send a text, let her know she was still alive. Unlike their father. And maybe their mother. Perhaps she was dead too, and there was no chance she'd ever see her again. Tears splashed onto Beatrice's phone and hands. Using the sleeve of her dressing gown, she wiped her face, wincing at the still-tender spot on her forehead. It wasn't fair to Rosie to ignore her.

Beatrice pressed the phone's on-button. Nothing happened. Her mind was sluggish, and it took a long moment to realise she needed to take it to her office.

Sitting at her desk, she set the phone charging. Out of habit, she started up the laptop. Her email system opened automatically, and there was a message from Rosie, headed: ANSWER YOUR PHONE!!!! Beatrice ignored the email and opened up a web browser instead.

She wasn't cut out to be an investigator. It was a mad idea she'd got hooked on, just because she'd been good at her old job, and it was the only thing she knew how to do. She searched online for local jobs and selected a few at random to check the details. She was in the process of considering a position as a checkout operator, when her phone beeped. It had enough charge and was restarting. Once the operating system had loaded and it had connected to the network, the mobile started buzzing, the vibrations making an unpleasant noise on the desktop.

Beatrice picked up the handset. There were twenty texts, from a combination of Rosie, Susan, and even one from James. She checked the latter first.

Hi. I heard from Rosie you've had a bad experience. I'm worried about you. I know we're not together anymore, but if there's anything I can do, please tell me. Take care. xx

The message was well intentioned, and it brought a lump to her throat to know James cared enough to send it, but if she was going to get over their break-up, it was best to keep him out of her life. She typed a quick reply.

Thanks. I'm OK. I've had a few quiet days. Take care.

Susan's multiple messages were brief and to the point, asking if she needed anything, to call as soon as she could, and saying she was concerned about her. Beatrice was touched by her persistence. She sent a text reply, similar to the one she'd sent James, with the added note that she'd call later in the day.

The texts from Rosie consisted of instructions to answer her phone and answer the door. There was also a voicemail message from her.

'I know you're in there. There's even more rubbish in the living room than yesterday, so you're still eating. And drinking too, from the looks of it. It's silly, hiding yourself away like this. Susan told me what happened. She's been worried about you, too.

'I know those men scared you, but maybe it's for the best.

It isn't the first time this business of yours has got you into trouble. It's too dangerous, Beatrice. Why not try something else? You've given it a fair shot. There's no shame in acknowledging it hasn't worked. You're good with numbers. Why don't you become an accountant? Like Mum and Dad. You wouldn't have to work all hours of the day and night, then. Use this as a chance to rethink what you're doing. Make a fresh start.

'Anyway, give me a call, please. Let me know you're alright.'

Beatrice played the message again. And again. And again. Each time she heard it, her anger intensified.

Refreshed by a shower, Beatrice cleared the rubbish from the living room. As she worked, she replayed her sister's voicemail in her head. How dare Rosie tell her what to do? She shoved a pizza box into the rubbish bag. Like she couldn't make her own decisions. What did Rosie know about accountancy or investigations? Nothing. That's what.

She picked the dirty cutlery from the empty Chinese containers, throwing the cartons into the plastic sack. Rosie had been critical from day one. Acting like she knew it wouldn't work. It was like that when they were kids. Rosie always thought she knew best, telling her what to do, knocking down any idea Beatrice was excited about.

I should never have come to Lincoln, she thought. Rosie was never going to resist interfering. Beatrice paused her tidying and stood up straight in the middle of the lounge, looking at the nearly full rubbish bag and empty wine bottles, with a sense of shame. She sat on the sofa and forced herself to take deep breaths for a few moments. She let go of the rubbish bag she was still gripping. She wasn't being fair on her sister. It was Rosie's way of showing she cared, and after all, she and the girls were the only family she had left now. It was no good getting mad. Her own decisions had led her to this point, not Rosie's.

Now it was time for another decision. Should she take all the recent difficulties as a sign it was time to stop investigating, maybe even move again? Admit it hadn't worked? Give up on her cases? On her mum? Beatrice had been scared by the threats, almost certain to have come from Victor Malone, but was she going to let it dictate what she would do? If she walked away, she'd feel like a coward. Bugsy hadn't deserved to be killed. His murderer should have to face consequences.

And Lily? Beatrice was now convinced Lily had good reasons to get away from Charles. But she realised he wouldn't give up looking for her, and she didn't want to leave Lily to whoever Charles sent next. There was more going on there than she'd been told by her client, and her concern for Lily made her want to see it out.

As for her mother, she couldn't give up until she'd been found, or until Beatrice knew what had happened to her, however upsetting it might be.

Beatrice went back upstairs to her study and typed out a text: *Sorry I've been out of touch. I needed time to myself, to get my head together. Thanks for the advice on a career change, but I've decided to stick with this one. Will come to see you and the girls soon. xxx*

Chapter 50

In her office, Beatrice reread her to-do list and ticked off several items. Contrary to its intended effect, Rosie's telephone message had reinvigorated her, and made her determined no one else would dictate how she lived her life. If it was going to be a disaster, then at least it would be a disaster of her own making.

Her next item was the search for Lily Taylor. Andrew had said the previous investigator was an ex-police detective, based in Norwich. What she didn't know was whether he'd failed to find Lily, or if he been successful and developed the same concerns she had? There weren't many PIs in Norwich, her internet search producing only half a dozen. She went through each in turn. There was one large firm, but the rest were sole operators.

She researched each of the investigators as much as she could and found only one who claimed to be ex-police. His name was Joseph Fine. He'd had a couple of name checks in newspaper reports and the online reviews for his services were glowing. He seemed to know what he was doing. She rang, getting an answering service. She left a message asking for a face-to-face meeting, for help finding a missing woman and child. It was the truth, but not the whole truth. She left her mobile number and stressed she needed to speak to someone as soon as possible.

Refreshed by sandwiches and a pot of tea, Beatrice returned to her office. Vanessa's phone call kept scratching at the back of her mind. The policewoman had been so out of character in their last conversation, she could have been a complete stranger.

Thinking about it logically, Vanessa had voluntarily agreed to help find out what the solicitor was up to, keen to put Beatrice's mind at rest. She had line manager approval, so there couldn't have been an issue with her using police resources inappropriately, and after all, there was the possibility a crime had been committed. Plus, although the police weren't proactively searching for her mother, the case was dormant, rather than closed, or so she'd understood. So, Vanessa suddenly acting the way she did must have been to do with what she found. She must have discovered something she couldn't tell Beatrice about. How was it connected to the solicitor? Was her mother dead? Had they found her body, but couldn't tell her family? Wouldn't they have an obligation to notify them? It couldn't be that. However, she wasn't going to get any more out of Vanessa. Beatrice had to find another approach to finding her mum.

Beatrice checked the letter over before printing it off. She signed the bottom, slipped it into the envelope she'd already addressed, then sealed it shut, and added it to the small pile. Now a route through Vanessa wasn't possible, the only thing she had to go on was the solicitor claiming to represent her mother, which dictated how she could act. She'd written letters to as many people and organisations as possible, including the Law Society, Solicitor's Regulator, Law Ombudsman and her MP. She'd sent electronic copies via email, but decided to post paper duplicates by recorded delivery, so there could be no doubt the letters had been received.

With no other obvious course of action, Beatrice was determined to make a nuisance of herself until someone, anyone, told her what was going on. Each letter outlined the facts of her mother's disappearance and the subsequent actions of her solicitor. Beatrice had been careful to use unemotional language and had included an outline of the research she'd done into the legalities. She wanted the recipients to take her seriously, and to understand she wasn't going to back down. She'd give them time to reply, but, as her letters made clear, her next step was to go to the press. Pete Evans owed her. She'd be able to convince him to do a story. He'd need an angle, maybe 'what were the police hiding?'. As long as it made a big enough splash to create waves, at this point Beatrice didn't care what she had to do.

Having left the fires and murder until last, Beatrice considered her next steps. She'd had an idea earlier in the day, but it could be considered rash, and she'd needed time to think it over. It was probably foolish, provoking a dangerous man, but she couldn't leave things as they were.

She selected the phone number from her contacts list and pressed call. It was answered within a few rings.

'Malone Holdings.'

Beatrice recognised the voice as belonging to Victor's secretary. 'I'd like to speak to Mr Malone, please.'

'That won't be possible.'

'My name is Beatrice Styles. I need to talk to him.'

The sound emanating from the phone changed. Beatrice recognised what had been done. 'You've put me on speakerphone. Is Mr Malone there?'

'No. He's not.' The new voice was a deep rumbling.

Jackson, Beatrice concluded.

'What do you want?'

'I had some visitors the other night. Friends of yours, were they?'

There was a silence from the other end.

'Were you too much of a coward to do it yourself? You couldn't look me in the eye whilst threatening me?'

'You should be careful what you say.'

'Or what? Your friends will come visit again? I don't give in to threats. Trying to scare me off has had the opposite effect. I might have been willing to give up for lack of evidence, but you came after me, tried to make me feel unsafe, but I won't give in to bullies.' Beatrice took a steadying breath. 'I know Malone is buying the Wild Geese brewery. At a knock down price. Much less than he'd have paid for it before the fires. I know Bugsy and Michael both worked for him.'

'So what? It's evidence of nothing,' said Jackson.

'No. But now I know exactly where I'm looking, and I'm not going away. You can tell Malone that I am going to dig into his life, and his businesses. I'm going to keep digging until I find something to make whoever did this pay for it, and I'm going to make a lot of noise in the process. He may have influence, and his lackeys planted in all sorts of places, but if something happens to me, I'll make sure everyone is looking at him for it.'

'Anything else?' Jackson's voice was calm and matter of fact, having lost its earlier air of aggression.

'No. I've said what I wanted to.'

'Thank you for calling.' The line went dead.

Why wasn't Jackson angry? What did it mean? Beatrice's gaze landed on the pile of letters she'd prepared earlier. There was still time to get them into the post, then she'd have achieved everything she'd planned. She picked up her bag, phone and the letters, and set out at a brisk pace.

They funked it. I should've known not to trust anyone else. She'd have recognised me though. I'd have never let it get into the position where she could testify against me, but it's all drawing too much attention to things which need to remain unnoticed. I should have disposed of her, before it got to this point, but there is something about her I admire. I've got limited options now: the truth, the partial truth or to run. Running would only be a temporary solution. The whole truth and nothing but the truth? Well, it isn't really an option either. Any hint of that and I'm done for. Looks like I'll be leaving for a while. Shame it won't be somewhere nicer to stay.

Chapter 51

Tuesday 9th July

Beatrice handed Susan a mug of tea. 'Shall we go into the front room?'

The DC, rooted to the spot, looked down at her drink, then back up at Beatrice.

Beatrice reached into a cupboard, pulled out a packet of biscuits and handed them over. Susan's face brightened and she led the way into the lounge, choosing the armchair with its footstool. Without it, her feet would dangle in the air. She placed the mug on the side table, made herself comfortable, then got to work opening the biscuits.

'I assume this isn't a social call?'

Susan shook her head; her mouth occupied with chewing.

Beatrice settled on the sofa and left Susan to talk in her own time.

Once she'd polished off a couple of biscuits, and drunk most of her tea, Susan appeared happier. 'Thanks. I've been up since five and haven't had time to stop.'

'Out with it, then.'

'In a minute. First, how are you doing?'

'Surviving.'

Susan nodded. 'It's tough, a break-up. And on top of everything else…'

'I'll be OK.'

'I know you will. And if you need a shoulder to cry on, well, I've got a step ladder I could bring.'

Beatrice chuckled.

'If not, I'm always available for a drink or a meal. Shifts allowing.'

'Thanks. I'll take you up on the offer at some point, but I'm keeping busy for now.'

'It helps.' Susan put down her mug. 'Right. To business. We've found the person responsible for the death at the Cooked Goose.'

'Who?'

'Guy by the name of Jonny Jackson.'

'There was a man at Malone's place called Jackson. We were never formally introduced. He's about six foot eight and three foot wide. Big muscles. Is it the same one?'

Susan nodded. 'We had four PCs watching him when he came in. Scary bugger.'

'I agree.'

Susan paused. 'Sounds like there's a story there.'

'Another time,' said Beatrice. 'How did you find out it was him?'

'He confessed.'

Beatrice was stunned. 'Seriously? Why would he?'

'Because he did it.'

'I'm not arguing about that, for now. But why confess? There wasn't much chance of him being caught. I had nothing on him, or anyone for that matter. I've got lots of circumstantial evidence, all pointing towards Malone, but nothing which would make for a court case. What evidence do you have?'

'You know I can't tell you.'

Beatrice regarded her friend, who, whenever possible was open and honest with her. Now, under scrutiny, she shifted in her seat and was refusing to make eye contact. 'There isn't anything, is there?'

Susan shrugged.

'So there really is no reason why he'd confess. I presume he already has a record?'

'Yes. Assault being the most serious up to this point.'

'Then he's pretty certain to be put away, even if he only fesses to manslaughter. Is that what he's claiming?'

'He is. Says it was self-defence. Bugsy attacked him.'

Beatrice laughed. 'You've got to be joking? With the size of Jackson? The victim, I would remind you, was a small man. He would have had to have been a complete idiot with a death wish to try it on with Jackson.'

'It's hard to believe, but, if we push for murder, he'll plead "not guilty", and it could take a couple years for the case to be heard, with the current court backlog. He might, with Malone bank-rolling a high-end criminal barrister, get bail and be out causing more damage before then. If we all agree to manslaughter, he gets locked up straightaway. Isn't the certainty of him being inside now better than a mere possibility of a longer sentence in the future?'

There was sense in what Susan was saying, but Beatrice didn't think it was how the justice system should work. Her mind turned back to the idea of Jackson confessing. It didn't make sense.

'What are you thinking?' Susan interrupted.

'I can only come up with two reasons Jackson would confess. Firstly, because he was about to be arrested, and wanted to help mitigate his sentence. And we both know that wasn't going to happen.'

'Secondly?'

'He does what Malone tells him, so I think that's what happened. Malone told him to admit to it, or at least to take the fall for someone else.'

'But why? He's much more use to Malone outside jail. From what we know he's Malone's right-hand man. He can't do much from inside.'

'True. But what if Malone thought there was too much attention coming his way?'

'Where from?'

'Well, not your lot, obviously.'

Susan frowned.

'I know it's not your fault, but the police have been keeping away, despite the connections in the case.'

'You think he was feeling pressured by you?'

'It could be.'

Susan tilted her head and raised her eyebrows.

'I'm not saying I had anything concrete on him, or ever would have. He'd have known I couldn't make a credible case against him.'

'So why would he be bothered about you asking annoying questions?' Susan grinned. '*I'm* not saying your questions are annoying, it's what he'd think.'

'Mmm.' Beatrice gave her friend the side-eye. 'What if Malone's got something going on right now, or happening soon? Something he needs to keep the police well away from.'

'Like what?'

Beatrice shrugged. 'I don't know. Isn't it supposed to be your area of expertise? Maybe a drug shipment arriving, or a lorryload of illegal immigrants. It could even be legitimate, but he thinks the untoward attention will scare off the other party.'

Susan sighed. 'You could be right. But we have a confession and we're accepting it.'

'Why aren't the police using this chance to dig into Malone? At least asking questions about what he's up to?'

'We're not stupid, Beatrice. We have looked into it. To a point. Jackson gave us full details though. He knows things about the body and what happened to it after death, that were never reported on. We're certain he was involved.'

Beatrice leant forward, placed her elbows on her knees and rested her chin in her hands. 'What does he say about the fires?'

'That it was his idea to burn down the pubs and he paid Michael to do it. Told him which ones to do and when.'

'Did he say why?'

'Gareth Brown had upset him.'

'How?'

'He won't tell. Says it's personal.'

'Really? More like Malone told him to do it, so he could devalue the business and create enough trouble so the Browns would sell to him at a knock-down price.'

'We've no evidence of that and unless Jackson tells us otherwise, we're not going to get any. I'm sorry Beatrice. You're going to have to accept the case is done. You can report back to the insurers and say it's over.'

'I guess.' Beatrice realised she'd lost sight of what she'd been hired for. So involved in trying to figure out the murder, she'd forgotten she was only being paid to find out about the involvement of the owners. 'From what you've told me, I assume it's safe to say the Browns weren't involved in the fires and weren't trying to defraud their insurers?'

'It seems that way, so they'll have to cough up, won't they.'

'Maybe?'

'Do they have a reason not to?'

'Gareth was aware an employee was stealing from the company and didn't do anything about it. Only small amounts, but I expect the insurance company will use it to argue over what they're prepared to pay out.'

'The Browns have had really bad luck, haven't they. Why didn't Gareth take action?'

'Because he was up to no good himself. With someone else's wife.'

'Good grief! Who?' Susan put her palms up. 'No, don't tell me. I don't need to know. Does his wife know?'

'Yes. She's trying to get the business sold, then will ask for a divorce.'

'I'm surprised they've got a buyer, with the fires.'

'It's Victor Malone.'

Susan stared at her, open-mouthed.

'Of course he's getting it at a much cheaper price now, than he offered before.'

'You mean he'd actually made an offer previously? It wasn't just vague interest?'

'Yes. The Browns turned him down. They had a good,

thriving business, then these mysterious fires happened, devaluing what they had. Now they want to get out, or at least Zoe does. Coincidence, isn't it?' Beatrice raised her eyebrows. 'How lucky for Malone. He can get what he wanted all along at a cheap price.'

'You think he got Jackson to sort it?'

'Yes. There's no proof though and I don't suppose there ever will be.'

'Well, Jackson isn't going to give us anything against Malone and I don't see where else any proof would come from.'

'No. Malone would make sure he kept his hands clean. Anyway, are you allowed to talk to me about this? Isn't Jackson's arrest confidential?'

'I got permission.' Susan paused. 'Actually, I was told to.'

'Who by?'

'Inspector Mayweather.'

'Why?'

'She thinks it will stop you asking questions where you might cause yourself and us problems.'

'You mean she wants me to stay away from Victor Malone and his cronies?'

'No comment.'

Chapter 52

Wednesday 10th July

Beatrice picked up her mobile. The call was from an unknown number.

'I can't talk freely. You know who this is?' The gruff, deep voice sounded muffled.

'Jackson.' She was surprised to hear from him.

'You know where I am?'

'Lincoln prison.'

'I need to talk to you, when we can't be overheard. I could be moved any time. Can you come to see me tomorrow?'

'Will they let me?' Did she even want to?

'You're on my approved visitor's list. I pulled some strings, and booked you in for ten tomorrow morning. You'll need to bring photo ID.'

'Why should I bother? The case is solved.'

'It'll be worth it, trust me.'

Beatrice thought Jackson had lied to the police. Would he tell her the truth? 'So you say.'

'You'll come.' He hung up.

She stared at her phone. What did Jackson want? Her eyes lighted on the clock and she jumped upright. She had an appointment and a long drive ahead.

Joseph Fine's Norwich office was through a large stone archway. A sign above it advertised Fine's self-storage. A smaller, more discreet plaque, inside the arch, pointed the way to Fine Investigations. The man she'd come to meet was clearly a multi-tasker. She briefly considered whether she needed a similar name for her own business. Stylish Investigations or Investigate in Style maybe? No. Neither suited her.

In the courtyard there was room for several vehicles, but two of the spaces were taken up by a portacabin. The laminated sign stuck in the window read 'Office'. Beatrice knocked and heard a muffled, incomprehensible response from within. She opened the door and popped her head into the room. A tall, thin man, around sixty, stood and came around from behind his desk, hand outstretched.

'You must be Ms Styles.'

'Beatrice, please.' They shook hands.

'Joseph.' He returned back behind the desk, lowered himself into his chair and adopted a serious expression. 'Please, take a seat.'

Beatrice settled into the chair indicated. She was uncomfortable. Not because of the chair itself, but because when she'd called to arrange the appointment, she hadn't been completely honest.

Joseph rested his forearms on the desktop. 'Why don't you tell me about who you are looking for, and why?'

'Right.' Beatrice looked directly at Joseph. 'The thing is…' She paused, then continued. 'What I didn't tell you on the phone, is I'm a private investigator too.'

Joseph's eyes narrowed and he sat back. 'You didn't think professional courtesy meant you should have been honest?' There was an edge to his voice.

'I'm sorry, but I didn't know if you'd agree to see me.'

'That's my decision to make. I could have been using this time to see a real client.'

'I understand, but in mitigation, I have told you now, straight away. I could have come in here and tried to find out what I want to know using deception. I prefer to be straight with people, which is why I came clean.'

Joseph appeared to consider her words.

'I'm relatively new, as a private investigator. I've not had any dealings with other PIs. I'm sorry if I've offended you, but surely you can understand, in our line of work, we can't always tell the whole truth.'

'What do you want to know?' He raised a hand to make her wait before speaking. 'I'm not saying I can, or will help you, but I will give you ten minutes to persuade me.'

'Thank you.' Beatrice gathered her thoughts for a moment, then began to explain. 'I believe a year ago you were hired by a man called Charles Sharpe, to find Lily Taylor and her daughter, Elizabeth.'

'Go on.'

'Recently, Charles came to me and asked me to do the same job. Well, I think I know where she is.'

Joseph leaned forward. 'You've found her?'

'Yes. I haven't approached her. Or told Charles.'

'I don't believe you've found her.' He spoke without conviction and a deep frown created wrinkles along his brow.

'She's in Middle Rasen, Lincolnshire.'

Joseph took out his mobile phone. 'How did you find her?' The words came out quietly.

'Does it matter?'

'It might.' Joseph looked directly at Beatrice. 'Why did you come to see me, if you know where she is?'

'My next move should be to go to Charles and tell him I've done the job I was hired for.'

'My question about why you've come still stands.'

'As I said, I'm new to this kind of investigation but after a relatively short period of time, I was able to find the village where she was living.'

'Your point?'

'I researched you. You've been in the press a few times over the years. Even helped the police in a couple of high-profile investigations.' Beatrice regarded him steadily.

Joseph shrugged.

'The thing is, I can't believe you didn't track her down.

With all your experience you should have easily been able to do what I've done.'

'If I did, why wouldn't I have told my client? It's what I was paid to do. As it was, he refused to settle my whole bill.'

Beatrice thought about the deposit she'd received from Charles. She'd pretty much used it up. She'd asked for more, but hadn't checked whether he'd paid up. That was worth doing, before she spoke to him again.

Joseph had been watching her during the silence, turning his mobile phone over and over in his hands. She could sense he was appraising her. His words had been carefully chosen and he hadn't denied he'd found Lily. Beatrice thought he was being strictly honest with her. She'd have to trust him with her concerns. Maybe he was exactly the right person to advise her. 'Lily had help to leave Charles and I believe she had good reasons for wanting to get away and not be found.'

'It's not unheard of.'

'Charles said he wanted to establish paternity for Elizabeth, and go through the courts to gain access to his daughter. It all sounded reasonable, the way he said it.'

'But?' Joseph prompted.

'But I don't know if I can trust him. If that's his real motive.'

Joseph's shoulders lowered as he relaxed a little and he placed the mobile on the desk. 'What's made you doubt it?'

'I met a woman, Jules. She's involved with the community centre in town. You probably know her.'

Joseph nodded his head in acknowledgement. The first concession that Beatrice was on the right track.

'She told me things about the lengths some men will go to, when they see a woman as their property. I'd been aware such things went on in the world, but never come across anything like it myself.'

'Until now?'

Beatrice nodded. 'Until now.' The mood had shifted, and they were now talking as professionals about a difficult moral issue, but she struggled to find the right words to explain. 'You see, Charles is so… plausible. Believable. I've found no evidence of him ever having harmed or threatened Lily or Elizabeth, only one eyewitness who saw them arguing. Anyway, it doesn't feel right anymore. Maybe I'm letting the things Jules told me get to me. She even had me worried about my own sister.' She examined Joseph, hoping for something from him, anything which could help her see her way through the muddle in her brain.

'Most men wouldn't hit a woman.'

'Jules talked about other ways of being abusive. Non-violent ways.'

'There has to be give and take in every relationship. Disagreement doesn't mean someone is being abusive.'

Was he playing devil's advocate? 'I realise I'm probably letting my imagination run wild with regards to my sister, at least. As for Lily. Well, I'm at a loss.'

'You don't know what to do?'

'No. I hoped by coming here, talking to you, things might become clearer.'

'There is such a thing as client confidentiality.'

'You won't help me?'

'Can't.' Joseph paused. 'Though, as one professional to another, I'd like to commend your investigation skills. And you appear to be developing good instincts.'

Beatrice sighed. It was the best confirmation of her fears she was going to get. 'Thank you. Now I have to decide what to do.' She stood, ready to leave.

'You work completely alone?' asked Joseph.

'Yes. I'm kind of making it up as I go along.'

'Successfully it seems.' He smiled. 'There are lots of difficulties that arise when doing this kind of work alone. It can be helpful to have someone in the same situation, to talk things through with.'

'It does seem I still have a lot to learn.'

'Were you followed here today?'

Beatrice was surprised by the sudden change of direction, and the question itself. 'No,' she managed. 'I don't think so. No one knew I was coming.'

Joseph stood in thought for several seconds. 'Right,' he said. He grabbed a piece of paper, wrote on it and handed it to Beatrice.

It was the name of a pub and an address. She looked at him, seeking an explanation.

'Kill some time in Norwich for a couple of hours. Make it seem like you're searching for clues, but getting nowhere.' He pointed at the paper. 'Meet me there in three hours. If you think you're being followed, park up and send me a text. We'll try again another day. If you're certain it's all clear, go into the pub and say you're there to see George. You'll be taken into a back room. I'll be waiting for you.'

'Is all this really necessary? It seems rather elaborate.'

'We have to be careful,' he said. 'There could be lives at stake.'

Chapter 53

Feeling self-conscious, Beatrice did as Joseph had told her. She spent time wandering in and out of shops, especially any related to young children and babies, as if she were questioning people about Lily. In fact, she didn't speak to anyone, unless it was unavoidable. The time dragged. When she went back to her car, she was careful to check and see who else was nearby. There were only a few people in the car park. No one she thought could be following her.

She set the Sat Nav for the pub and deliberately made a few wrong turns on the way. She spent ten minutes in a layby to allow cars behind her to pass, using the time to work on the glimmer of an idea which had begun to form. A possible way to misdirect Charles and provide Lily with security, if it was what she decided was needed after meeting with Joseph.

By the time she reached the pub, she was tense and paranoid. She spent another five minutes waiting to see if anyone else arrived, but no one did, so she went inside. The landlord didn't seem surprised by her request to speak to George. He gave a slight nod, came out from behind the bar and led her into a small room, furnished with a table and two chairs. Joseph Fine was already seated.

'Drinks?' The landlord finally spoke.

'White coffee, please,' said Joseph.

'Make it two.' Beatrice sat down on the empty chair, as the landlord left.

'Everything OK?'

'Yes. Though I'm pretty wound up at this point.'

'So, you're the one who went and talked to Andrew?'

'How did you know?'

'He called after you saw him. To let me know Charles was searching for Lily again.'

'To warn you?'

Joseph shrugged. 'How did Charles know Lily had gone back to Lincolnshire?'

'I'm not sure he did, for certain. He said she'd talked fondly of her childhood there. Maybe he decided it was worth trying, assuming Lily wanted to give her daughter the same childhood she'd had.' Beatrice paused. 'Well, aspects of it. I take it you know what happened to her parents?'

'A terrible accident.'

'I spoke to Lily's aunt. The one who looked after them. She's got dementia and believes she's been visited by Grace, Lily's mum. I think it's actually Lily. It was risky, if she didn't want to be found.'

'It's hard to completely let your family go, though.'

Was that a meaningful look in his eyes? Had he researched her too? Did he know about her mum?

The landlord brought their drinks then left them alone again.

'Did Jules tell you what happened to her?' asked Joseph.

'No. She hinted that there had been something in her past, but didn't go into specifics.'

'Well, let me tell you. Maybe you'll realise the kind of man you might be dealing with. Perhaps you'll think carefully about what you do next.'

'I'm listening.'

'Jules was in a relationship with a slightly older man. She was young, mid-twenties. She was in love. It was all sweetness and romance. Things progressed quickly, they moved in together and she soon found out she was pregnant. It's when his controlling behaviour became more obvious. Before then, he was subtle. Telling her, through *suggestions* and *advice*, who she should be friends with, what she should wear. Jules was seeing less and less of her parents. He encouraged her to think they were against their relationship, that they thought she was incapable of making decisions about her own life.'

'And after she became pregnant?'

'He took over. Told her it was his baby and she'd better do as he said. He began hitting her, places it wouldn't hurt the baby. He told her it was for her own good.' Joseph sighed. 'Did you know some of the most dangerous times for an abused woman are when she's pregnant or when she's planning to leave?'

'No, I didn't.'

'Neither did I, until I was asked to find Lily. Like you I tracked Jules down at the community centre. By the way, I'm impressed you managed it, so long after the event.'

'A combination of legwork and luck.'

'Sometimes it's what we have to rely on. Anyway, I didn't get much out of her, but I liked her. I did some research. The information is out there if you go looking for it, and I had local contacts who had an idea of what she was doing. That's when I learnt how obsessed and dangerous some men can become. I went back and talked to her again. I came clean about who I was, said I'd like to help, but I needed to know I was doing the right thing. I asked her to tell me what I was protecting Lily from.'

'What did she say?'

'That Charles had been doing all the controlling behaviour I described to you, and he'd recently started getting physical.'

'He was hitting her?'

'And worse.' Joseph cleared his throat. 'Jules wanted me to tell Charles I hadn't found anything. That Lily had vanished without a trace. Of course, I agreed.'

'What happened to Jules?'

'In her case, she was both pregnant and preparing to leave. Only she wasn't careful enough to cover her tracks.'

'He found out?'

'Yes. Before she'd had a chance to get away. A day earlier and maybe she'd have been OK.'

'What did he do?' Beatrice was compelled to ask.

'He beat the living daylights out of her. Only this time he didn't worry about the baby.'

'She lost it?'

He nodded. 'And he got away with it.'

'Surely he should have been prosecuted?'

'Insufficient evidence and Jules wouldn't give a witness statement. He told the doctors, and later the police, that she fell down the stairs. The hospital staff didn't believe him. They've seen that kind of accident, and beatings too. They've enough experience to know how to tell the difference. It was the medical staff who called in the police. Not Jules. She refused to contradict his story.'

'Why?'

'Would you want to? After you'd lost your baby? Knowing he'd do exactly the same thing to you again if he got the chance? When she was well enough to leave hospital, a nurse helped her get far away.'

'So that's why she helped Lily? Her past experience and because another woman helped her?'

'I imagine so.'

'And you think Charles Sharpe is like that?'

'All I know is what Lily told Jules. She could have been lying, but I reckon Jules would have known.'

There was a silence while each contemplated the experiences of both Jules and Lily. How many more women were in the same situation, wondered Beatrice.

'Will you tell Charles you've found nothing?' asked Joseph.

'He'll just hire someone else. I don't think he's going to let it go.'

'Then how do we stop him trying to find her?'

Beatrice drained the last of her, now cold coffee. 'He'll only give up, if he gets another poor woman in his clutches. It's Elizabeth he'll keep going for.'

'So, we need to do something to throw him off track, and give him a reason to stop,' said Joseph.

'Or at least reduce his motivation.'

'You have an idea?' Joseph looked eager.

'Actually, I do. But…'

'What?'

'We'll need Andrew and Jules to help. They're not going to trust me, but they'll trust you.'

'I'm in. What's your plan?'

Beatrice described her idea. It wasn't guaranteed to be successful, but it was worth trying. 'You see the main flaw though?'

'I think so,' said Joseph. 'How did Andrew, who was in France when she left, let Lily know his London address, if he didn't have a way of contacting her?'

'Do you think Charles will realise?'

'We'll have to hope he doesn't.' Beatrice ran her fingers through her hair. 'If he doesn't fall for it, then Lily isn't safe where she is.'

Joseph sighed. 'She's going to have to move again, then.'

'I'm afraid so. Somewhere much further away from Lincolnshire and Norfolk. A place Charles isn't likely to go.'

Joseph nodded. 'I'll talk to Jules about moving Lily and getting what we need from her.'

'Ask her to send it to me.'

'Shouldn't it go straight to Andrew?'

'No. If Charles is having me followed, I need to convince him I've found it in Andrew's flat and be able to prove I was there in London.'

'So, we have a plan,' said Joseph. 'Let's hope it works.'

Chapter 54

Thursday 11th July

The procedures at Lincoln prison were intimidating. Purposefully so, Beatrice concluded. The cold austere décor, the ritual of emptying pockets, photo ID checks, signing in, and an intrusive search. The clang of heavy metal doors and substantial locks echoed as she was led to her destination. It all combined to create a nervousness which increased the longer she was in the building.

After following the dour prison officer, she was shown into a small room, not the main visitor area.

'I'll be right outside.' The officer closed the door with a loud bang.

Jackson, who looked larger than before, in the confines of the small space, was seated at a metal table, its legs screwed into the concrete floor. His hands were bound by metal cuffs, a chain linked to them, restraining the movement of his arms.

Beatrice sat opposite, pulling the chair away from the table.

Jackson noticed and grinned at her. 'Don't worry. You're quite safe.'

Beatrice eyed the cuffs and chain.

He raised his hands a short distance off the surface of the desk. 'Not because of these. I've no reason to harm you. Even if it was your nosing around that got me here.'

'You confessed.'

'Only because I had to.'

'Why?'

Jackson laughed. 'Still asking questions.'

Beatrice shifted in her seat. 'Why did you want to see me? And how did you arrange this? Us meeting alone, without your lawyer? I can't imagine Victor Malone would approve.'

'Victor knows I'd never send heat his way. As for the private meeting: well, I have influence in the right places.'

No doubt through his association with Malone. 'So why am I here?'

'You don't get much intelligent conversation inside.'

'You're wasting my time.' Beatrice rose from her seat.

'Sit down.'

'Why?'

'Because listening to what I have to say is the only chance you have of finding out what really happened.'

'You're admitting what you told the police wasn't true?'

'Not completely true. But they don't need to know that.'

Beatrice returned to her seat, intrigued by the large man. Not only because he could give her information no one else could, but because she hadn't expected him to be so articulate. She'd assumed he was a mindless thug. 'I'm waiting.'

'Seems to me, you're the kind of woman who wants to know the truth, no matter what it takes to find it.'

Beatrice wasn't comfortable with the implication she'd have no limits, but she allowed him to continue.

'In fact, I'm the only one who can give it to you. But in exchange, you have to do something for me.'

'I can't get you out of here.'

Jackson shook his head, dismissing the notion. 'I want you to help Astra.'

Beatrice relaxed, though she was still wary. 'Astra was planning on leaving Victor, wasn't she?'

'How do you know?'

'Let's say I've recently acquired knowledge of what can happen to women who've tried to leave abusive men.'

Beatrice saw Jackson wince at the term. 'What? You can't pretend he loves her, or her him. He treats her like an object: something pretty to hang on his arm and worse when they're alone. You can't seriously expect me to believe you don't know how things are, that you haven't seen what he's like.'

Jackson stared at his huge hands which were splayed in front of him on the table. Beatrice was glad of the handcuffs and chain as she saw the muscles in his shoulders tense. He paused, then relaxed. 'Can you help her?'

'Astra?'

He nodded.

'Do you mean get her away from him?'

'Yes.'

'Unfortunately, I've found out how hard it is to really disappear.' Beatrice sighed. 'Malone has the resources and obsessiveness to make it almost certain she'd be found.'

'Unless he's got other things to worry about.'

'The police?'

'You don't think fast, but you get there in the end.'

'Thanks!'

'I meant it as a compliment.'

Beatrice raised her eyebrows, causing a fleeting smile to cross his face.

'I can't do anything from in here,' Jackson continued. 'Malone would find out about it. I'm taking a risk speaking to you at all.'

'Then why do it?'

'To help Astra.'

'She's important to you?' Beatrice regarded Jackson, who wouldn't meet her gaze. His motivation was personal. It was the only explanation. 'You could have helped her yourself, any time in the last few years. Why now?'

'Malone.'

'I saw from the visitor's book he came to visit yesterday.'

'Yes.'

'What did he want?'

'To make sure I understood how things were.'

'Which is?'

Jackson shook his head. 'Not yet.'

Beatrice's interest prickled at the possibility he might eventually tell her the truth about the murder and the fires. 'When?'

'Find a way to help Astra, then we'll talk.'

'You still haven't explained why now. For Astra.'

'Something Malone said. He's losing interest. Got his eye on another woman. A replacement.'

Beatrice sat back. 'And Astra becomes expendable?'

Jackson nodded.

'There's no chance he'll let her leave?'

'She seen too much. Probably doesn't even realise how big a threat to him she is.'

Beatrice thought about what Jackson said. Did Astra know enough about Malone's activities to be useful to the police? Could they help her to disappear more effectively than Lily and countless other unfortunate women had been able to? 'If I can help her, you'll tell me the truth about what happened?'

Jackson nodded. 'It won't be any use as evidence though. The police are happy the arson and murder are closed.'

'I know. But it's not the complete answer.'

'I've confessed. So has Michael, to setting the fires. I'll be sentenced quickly and put in maximum security. They won't want to open it again and it's not in my interests for them to do it.'

'Did the Brown's have anything to do with the fires?'

'No.'

'Good.' Beatrice stood up. 'You do realise, I'll try to help Astra anyway? Even without your information, I'd rather she wasn't under the power of Malone.'

'I know.' Jackson smiled, genuinely this time. 'But you deserve something, for all your hard work. I don't hold you completely responsible for me being in here, but you played a significant part. I admire you for it. The police have tried for years, and you turned my life over in weeks.'

'Don't you think the reason you're here is down to you?'

'I'm not an idiot. I know I've done things I shouldn't have.'

'Perhaps you should have chosen a different way of life?'

'What makes you think I had any choice? Guard!'

The door opened and the prison officer tilted his head in a query.

'We're done here.' Jackson looked at Beatrice. 'For now.'

She nodded and left the room, her mind so occupied she barely registered the return journey through the prison.

Outside, Beatrice called Percival Simmons.

'Ms Styles, what can I do for you?'

'There's been progress on the case.'

'Excellent news.'

'I've been able to confirm the Browns didn't have anything to do with arranging the fires at their pubs.'

'How can you be certain?'

'I'll send you a detailed report with my final bill, but I've just left Lincoln prison. I've spoken to the man who paid Michael Burgess to start the fires. He's in prison for it and killing the man whose body was found in the Cooked Goose. The plan was to devalue the business and get back at the Browns for refusing to sell earlier in the year.'

'Goodness me. It all sounds rather complicated.'

'It is, but at least we know for sure.'

'Well, thank you very much. I'm pleased we have a solution.'

'So am I. I hope you'll consider me again in the future, should anything suitable come up?'

'Absolutely. I look forward to receiving your report and account, which I shall arrange prompt payment of.'

'Thank you.'

Chapter 55

Friday 12th July

'What are you doing here?' The aggressive, demanding voice of Sergeant Fisher was unmistakeable.

Beatrice finished signing the police station's visitor book and slipped the lanyard with its pass over her head. She then turned to face Fisher, who had flushed a light shade of red by this time. 'I've an appointment.'

'Who with?'

'None of your business.' Beatrice walked to the waiting area and sat down.

Fisher called out across the space. 'If you've come to see your little friend, she's not here. I've sent her out to do real police work.'

Beatrice didn't respond.

Whilst the sergeant was talking to the receptionist, presumably trying to find out who she was seeing, a woman came out of the secured door and approached Beatrice.

'Ms Styles?'

Beatrice nodded.

'Inspector Mayweather can see you now. This way, please.'

She could almost feel the glare she was sure Fisher directed at her, as he registered who she was seeing. She hoped it had him worried.

'Ms Styles. It's been a while. Please, sit.' Inspector Mayweather indicated a seat opposite her.

As she sat, Beatrice felt her face flush. The last time they'd seen one another, the Inspector had seen her become distressed after interviewing a murder suspect. 'I've come to talk about Victor Malone.'

'I believe Sergeant Fisher has already spoken to you, and asked you to stay away from him. Which you've ignored.'

'I didn't approach him again, directly.'

'You made waves, though. It's caused us a few problems.'

'We both know Malone is a criminal. He should be locked up, instead he seems to do whatever he wants. He treats other people as his toys to be played with, and…'

'Ms Styles.' Mayweather raised her hand. 'If I could put someone, who is like you describe, into prison, I would. We have to follow the process of the law.'

'But as long as he's prepared to do whatever it takes to intimidate, or get rid of witnesses, he's never going to be held to account.' Beatrice sighed. 'Like the recent fires and the dead man. Malone was responsible. He didn't light the matches and he didn't lay a finger on Bugsy, but he was responsible all the same. Shouldn't the police at least be making his life difficult?'

'We do what we can, within the law.'

'It's not enough.'

'What makes you think you know anything about what we are or aren't doing?'

'He's been here for years, flouting the law. Whatever it is you're doing isn't working.'

'You have a magic wand?'

'No. But I may have a way for you to get the evidence you need on what he's been doing.'

Mayweather leaned forward. 'Go on.'

'I'm not simply handing this over to you.'

'What do you want?'

'I want to talk to someone who is looking at Malone's activities. There must be a team investigating organised crime and investigating him in particular.'

'What makes you think that?'

'You're ignoring all the petty things he's doing, which he'd never do time for. I figure you're waiting for something big. Well, maybe I can help.'

'If you have evidence you need to turn it over to us.'

'I don't have any. But, like I said, I may have a way for you to get some.'

'And you're not going to tell me?'

'No.'

'Perhaps I can work it out. After all, you came across Malone in respect of the arson and the dead man you mentioned earlier. Presumably you think you've found someone in his organisation you think will talk. I know you've been to see Jackson. There's no way he'd turn on Malone. Not with their history.'

'What history?'

'So, you don't know everything.'

'Put me in touch with the lead investigator, if you're serious about getting Malone. This might be your only chance, since you seem to be waiting for evidence to fall in your laps.' Beatrice stood up. 'You know how to contact me.'

The lunchtime train journey to London had been uneventful, which Beatrice was grateful for. She'd checked her bank balance before leaving, and Charles Sharpe had paid her what she'd requested, so even if he refused to pay the rest of the bill, as he had done with Joseph, she wouldn't be too much out of pocket. She hoped Andrew had kept his end up and taken the day off work. Joseph had spoken to him and Jules, and she had Jules' contribution to the scheme in her bag. She hoped their plans would work and Charles would be satisfied, and willing to leave Lily and Elizabeth alone.

At Andrew's flat she was relieved when the door lock clicked in response to her pressing his bell. She made her way inside and found him waiting for her at his open door. They moved into the flat and sat in the small living area.

'You realise he may come after you?' said Beatrice.

'Why?'

'He'll be angry you've kept this letter from him.' She gestured at the notepaper in Andrew's hands. She'd given it to him to put his fingerprints on it. She didn't know the lengths Charles would go to, but if he did have it tested, he'd find it was Lily's handwriting and it would have Lily's, Andrew's and Beatrice's fingerprints on it. All consistent with the story she was going to tell him.

'So, I'll have to move as well.'

'I'm afraid so.' Beatrice handed him a slip of paper. 'This is the number of the woman who helped Lily. I'll need you to memorise it, then destroy it. Charles can't find this link to her. You understand?'

'Who is she?'

'Another woman with an unhappy past,' said Beatrice. 'Give it a few months, then ring. Hopefully by then Charles will have tried the address on the letter and drawn a blank, or, even better, he may have given up completely, if he accepts Elizabeth isn't his.'

'He is her father though. Lily wasn't the type to string along several men.'

'Yes. But Elizabeth was born prematurely. Combined with the letter it might set him thinking. It adds credence to the idea Lily was already pregnant when she met him, assuming he didn't get involved much in the pre-natal visits.'

'From what Lily said he left her to it. He wasn't interested in all the stuff surrounding the pregnancy, only the outcome.' Andrew gazed around his flat.

'You'll be sorry to leave?'

'Not at all,' he said. 'I'd been thinking about going back to France anyway. My life was much better there. This gives me another reason.'

'Go somewhere else first, to create another blind alley for Charles. Maybe Spain on holiday, for example?'

Andrew nodded. 'A good idea. Southern Spain, I think.'

Beatrice grinned. The false address for Lily they'd used was in the south of Spain.

'Thank you.'

'What for?'

'Doing the right thing.'

'If I'd know where this would lead, I'd have never taken the job on.'

'But then maybe someone else would have done, and having found Lily, told Charles, without warning her. Instead of trying to help.'

Beatrice had sent a text to Vanessa, saying she'd be in the coffee shop at Kings Cross. But it wasn't Vanessa who turned up. It was Jan, her girlfriend.

'I can't stay long,' said the younger woman. 'In case someone who knows me sees us together.'

'Vanessa would be in trouble?'

'Big time. She's really sorry, but there's nothing she can do and nothing she can tell you,' said Jan.

'I know, I wouldn't want her getting into difficulties because of me. I was wondering if I could get a message to whoever it was who told her to drop the case.'

'I don't know why you think that's what happened.'

'Seriously?' said Beatrice. 'Look, she needs to let whoever it was that told her to stop know that I'm not giving up. I'm going to keep searching and I'm going to be very obvious about it. I've already sent letters to every person and organisation I can think of who would be interested. If someone doesn't respond soon, I'm going to the press. The police could do without more scandals.'

'I can tell her what you've said.'

'Do you know anything?'

Jan shook her head. 'No. I promise. We only talk about her work in a general way. We both agreed early on, there were things it was best for me not to know. I'm sorry you haven't found your mum, and I hope you do find her, but I do know if there was anything Vanessa could do to help you, she would.' She reached over and squeezed Beatrice's hand. 'You'll take care, won't you?' Jan left.

Beatrice checked her watch. There were fifteen minutes until her train back to Newark was due. She used the time to exchange texts with Charles Sharpe, and they arranged to meet at his home on Sunday afternoon.

Chapter 56

Sunday 15th July

The phone number Beatrice received the text from had been withheld. The message was simple: *Lincoln Arboretum 10.00 a.m. Be somewhere visible.* She'd immediately connected it to her conversation with Inspector Mayweather.

It was 9.55 a.m. and she was sitting on the steps to the bandstand watching every passerby, though there were few enough of them. She received the occasional odd look, but no one stopped.

The park was almost empty, when she saw a figure approaching from the direction of Lindum Terrace. He wore a long, black coat and walked in a slow, casual way, holding something out in front of him. If it hadn't been clear he was looking directly at her the whole time, she would have doubted he was there for her. Beatrice remained seated waiting for him to reach her.

He held out a coffee. 'White Americano, extra shot,' he offered, looking down at her.

'Thanks.' Beatrice took the drink, his words reminding her of where she'd seen him before. The London coffee shop, after her ill-fated meeting with Simon Atkinson. He'd been the man behind her in the queue. The same pleasant smile, reaching all the way to his eyes, he remained patient, allowing her time to think.

'Who are you?'

'Hugh.'

'Just Hugh?'

'It's all you need.' He exuded the confidence of a man comfortable in his own skin.

'It wasn't a coincidence, was it? The coffee shop.'

'I can't talk about it, right now.'

The last two words held a promise of there being a time when he could talk.

Hugh held out a hand. 'Hello, Beatrice.'

She stood and they shook hands. She was a little taller than him, but only by a couple of inches. 'Hello, Mr Hugh.'

He chuckled. 'Let's talk as we walk.'

They automatically ambled side by side, continuing around the remainder of the park.

Hugh began the conversation. 'I understand you think you can help with a certain individual.'

'We're going to talk in riddles, are we?'

'It's best if we aren't too direct. Especially here.'

'In the arboretum?'

'In Lincoln.'

He sounded like Joseph. Paranoia or a sensible precaution? 'Well, a certain someone,' she raised her eyebrows as she made brief eye contact with him, and received a knowing look in return, 'belongs in jail.'

'I'm not disagreeing. How to achieve it is the difficult part.'

'There is someone connected to this individual, who I think may be willing to give you what you need.'

'In return for...?'

'Safety.'

'That's hard to guarantee.'

'This person has seen a lot...' Beatrice stopped walking and turned to her companion. 'I can't keep talking like this. There's no one else here.' She gestured at the empty park with her hand, and stepped close to Hugh, lowering her voice. 'Astra is Malone's girlfriend. I understand he's thinking of moving on to a newer, more compliant version.'

'And he has no further use for her.' His expression was sombre. 'What does she know?'

'I'm not sure, exactly. But she's been with him for a few years. She must have seen a lot, and probably doesn't know just how much she could tell you about his operations.'

'You want her to have a new identity?'

'That would do it.'

'We can't simply give them out. I have to have something in exchange. Something I can sell to my bosses as being worth the resources.'

'But surely, under expert questioning, you'd be able to extract loads of information, like where his records are kept, the people and places he's involved with. It could lead you to concrete evidence.'

Hugh stared into the distance, as if contemplating her words.

'Please. You know what's going to happen to her otherwise. She never asked for any of this. She was a vulnerable, young woman when she fell into his hands. She deserves a chance of a different life.'

He turned back to Beatrice. 'You want to help her?'

'Yes. Don't you?'

Hugh pulled out a small card and handed it to Beatrice. The only thing printed on it was a phone number. 'Get this to Astra. If she's willing to talk, tell us everything she knows, and I'm talking about days, possibly weeks of questioning here, she should call this number. If she leaves a message, we'll find a safe way to contact her. It's a one-time thing. Once the number has been used, it'll be disconnected and she won't get another chance. She needs to understand there's nothing certain about any of it at this stage. We'll need to speak to her in person to decide how far we can take it.'

Beatrice clutched the card tightly. 'Thank you. I'll talk to her.'

'Make sure she knows not to do anything unusual until we've made contact, when she'll receive further instructions. It is vital Malone has no idea she's prepared to cooperate. Not a hint of it.'

Beatrice nodded. 'I'm sure she knows what he's like.'

'It was nice to meet you, Beatrice.'

'How do I get in touch with you? If I need to?'

Hugh looked deep into Beatrice's eyes, making her feel exposed, as if he were reading her thoughts.

'Give me your phone.' He held out his hand, not breaking eye contact.

Beatrice fumbled in her bag, without looking, and handed her mobile to him.

'I shouldn't be doing this,' he said, shaking his head.

She saw the corners of his mouth turn up in a brief smile and the expression in his eyes softened. He looked down to type in his number, and Beatrice immediately felt the absence of the intensity of his gaze. He passed the phone back.

'Thank you.' Beatrice was glad he wouldn't be disappearing. It was only a phone number, but it was a connection.

'Aren't you going to ring it? To make sure I haven't given you a duff number?'

'No.' She put the phone back in her bag. 'I trust you.' And she did. Without knowing why, there was something about him which invited her faith. Joseph had said she had good instincts, though perhaps he was only saying so to indicate she'd been on the right path about Charles Sharpe. She was going to trust her gut.

'There's one more thing, Beatrice.'

'Yes?'

'Once you've delivered the message, stay away. Seriously. I realise you like to finish what you've started, but it's not only about Astra's safety. It's about yours, too. Malone can't know you've been anywhere near this.'

'I understand.'

'Good. As extra cover you can expect a visit from the police.'

'What! Why?'

'You'll be given a final warning to stay away from Malone.

Word will get around the station.'

'And from there back to Malone?'

'Exactly.'

'So, he does have minions on the force?'

'We think so, which is why it needs to be convincing. I'm afraid your ego might have to take a bit of a knock.'

'Another one?'

Hugh looked at her, questioning.

'It doesn't matter. Besides, if it helps to keep Astra safe, it's worth it. Right?'

'Absolutely.' He stopped walking and held out his hand, as if to shake hers for a goodbye. When Beatrice placed her hand in his, he gripped it and clasped it with both of his. 'And you'll bounce back. You're resilient, Beatrice. You can cope with whatever life throws at you. I know you can.'

Why did she think he was talking about more than the dent in her reputation from a police visit?

Hugh squeezed her hand gently then let go. 'Now, you'd better get home and take your telling off from Inspector Mayweather.' He checked his watch. 'You've got half an hour.'

'She's coming to my house?'

Hugh nodded.

'But the neighbours will see.'

'It's kind of the point. To make a show of it.'

'Really?'

'The more we can do to give Malone reasons to leave you alone, the better. I'll be seeing you.' He smiled, head tilted, then turned and left.

As she watched him walk away a thought occurred to her. If Mayweather was going to be at her house in thirty minutes, it meant it was prearranged. And Hugh knew about it. Did he know what she was going to say? To ask of him? He'd had the phone number ready for Astra. Had he primed the Inspector in advance, knowing he was going to agree to her request? In which case why had he spent so long talking to her? 'I'll be seeing you,' he'd said. The thought cheered her.

Hugh was completely out of sight by the time Beatrice began to make her way home. The only other person in the park was a small, fast-moving figure. A woman. Beatrice paused. It was heading towards her, with a determined and vaguely familiar set to her shoulders. Once Beatrice recognised who it was, she walked to meet her.

'How do you know that man?' Susan demanded, as she stood in front of her friend, blocking the path.

'How do you know him?' Beatrice batted back.

Susan hesitated. 'Didn't say I did.'

'Then why are you so interested?'

Susan looked around, checking no one else was nearby. 'I don't know who he is exactly, but he's been at the station. I saw him come out of the Chief Superintendent's office late one evening, months ago. I didn't think anything of it at the time, but, the next day, Mayweather was called into a meeting with the Chief. She took the file she'd been building on Malone, and came back an hour or so later, looking very pissed off, without the file. Ever since, whenever Malone's come up in a case, we're either steered away, or Mayweather takes on the work.' Susan peered up at Beatrice. 'Were you talking to him about Malone?'

'I'm sorry, I can't tell you anything.'

Susan folded her arms and her jaw tensed.

'I'd tell you if I could. You have to keep things from me sometimes, like you did about the fires, remember? I didn't have a go at you about it though, did I?'

Susan's arms dropped to her sides. 'I suppose you're right. It's probably best I don't know.'

'I've got to get home. I'm expecting someone.'

'I'll walk back into town with you. You can walk up Steep Hill by yourself. I swear that street will be the death of me.'

Beatrice laughed lightly and they fell into step, heading towards the town centre.

'What's he like then?'

'Malone?'

'No. The secretive man. He's got a nice smile.'

'There's nothing to tell.'

'You were standing pretty close,' Susan remarked. When she received no response, she let it drop. 'Fine. How are you doing? You know.'

Beatrice did know. Susan meant James and the breakup, and she shrugged an answer. 'OK. I guess.'

'I'm sorry it didn't work out, but you weren't really sure about him, were you?'

'No. But I didn't realise he'd been thinking the same.'

'Look at it this way. He's not saying he didn't like you. It's clear he did. You're just not suited to each other and it's best to find out now, before you're committed.'

'Dented my ego though,' she said, thinking of Hugh's comments about her bouncing back. Beatrice chuckled and realised she was going to be alright, and the rawness of James' rejection would fade. She thought of Hugh and his smile. Perhaps it would be sooner than she'd expected.

Chapter 57

'You'd better come through to the lounge. Take your shoes off.' Charles Sharpe had opened the door not seeming pleased to see her, despite it being by arrangement. Beatrice placed her shoes next to a pair of shocking-pink stilettos. Perhaps they explained his irritation.

In the immaculate lounge, she found him standing by the window, a glass tumbler in his hand. He finished the contents in one gulp.

'Mr Sharpe. Thank you for meeting me.'

He turned to her. 'What have you found out?'

'May I sit down?'

Charles nodded. He didn't offer Beatrice a drink, as he poured himself another.

Beatrice lowered herself into an armchair. 'I thought I should explain things in person. So you can understand everything I've done.'

'Did you write a report?'

'Er, yes.'

'Then it will do. Just tell me what you found out. Do you know where she is?'

'Yes.'

Charles became still. 'Pardon?'

'I know where Lily is. Or was. Unfortunately, she may have already moved on.'

He placed his glass on the table and sat down. 'Have you spoken to her?'

'No.'

He appeared relieved. Had he been concerned Lily would

reveal what he'd been like?

'Why not?'

'She's too far away.'

He raised his eyebrow in a query.

'I believe she's in Spain.'

'Why?'

'I don't know why she went there?'

Charles spoke through gritted teeth. 'I meant, why do you think it's where she's gone?'

Beatrice reached into her handbag and pulled out a piece of notepaper. Jules had done an excellent job of sourcing paper which looked as though it had been at the bottom of a wardrobe for a while. She handed it to Charles. Beatrice knew what it contained. She'd told Jules, through Joseph, what it needed to say, and Jules had arranged for Lily to write it, in case Charles had it authenticated, by a handwriting expert.

Dear Andrew,

I'm sorry to have been out of touch for so long. Things have been difficult. I realise you believe Charles and I were happy together but we weren't. It's not your fault you didn't notice what he was like. I did my best to keep it from you, because I was ashamed.

I finally found a way out, for Elizabeth and me. I hope Charles won't come looking for us. He didn't really care for me, so I'm no great loss to him, but my worry is, he won't let Elizabeth disappear. I wish I'd never let him think he was her father. It seemed like a good idea at the time. I was already pregnant when I met him, and hooking up with someone so obviously wealthy, seemed like an ideal way for me to take care of my baby. My other mistake was not realising what kind of man he was.

I had to get away. Not only for my sake, but Elizabeth's too. You might wonder why I didn't tell him Elizabeth wasn't his, but you don't know him the way I do. He'd never have forgiven me for lying to him. He'd find a way to punish me. I don't think I'll ever be safe in England. We can't meet again. I know he'll use you to find me if he can, and I can't risk it. Please destroy this letter once you've read it. I'll be at this address for a few weeks, then I'll be gone. It's best you don't know where.

I'm so sorry it's come to this. You've been such a good brother, trying to look out for me, after Mum and Dad died. It's my fault, but he scares me and I can't see any alternative but to keep as far away as possible.

I need you to send me the documents I left with you, and perhaps you could include a couple of photos of when we were younger, so I remember more carefree times.

I will never forget you.

Love Lily
xxx

'The address is in Spain.' Beatrice broke the brooding silence.

'I noticed.'

'Do you want me to find you someone over there to carry on the search? It says she was going to move on, but it might be possible to find out where to.'

'Why would you want to do that?'

'I don't like failing.'

'You've done more than anyone else.' It was a begrudging compliment.

'What did she mean? Lily. About the "kind of man" you are? Why did she think you'd punish her? Why does it say she was scared of you?'

Charles glared at Beatrice. 'I told you before, she was unstable.' He stood. 'You've done your job. You can leave.' His voice was low-pitched and full of menace, and though he didn't have the same impact as Jackson, Beatrice didn't argue.

She handed him a piece of paper. 'This is my final bill. I wrote it assuming you wouldn't want me to go to Spain. I could though, if you like.'

'I'll handle this now.'

'There's an amount outstanding. I can take cash, cheque or card.'

Charles opened out the paper, glanced at it, then threw it on the coffee table. His eyes remained fixed on Beatrice as he pulled out his wallet. She was tempted to look away, but the urge to not back down was stronger.

He took out a sheaf of fifty-pound notes, and one at a time, dropped six onto the coffee table. There was a moment's pause then Beatrice bent down to retrieve her payment.

Charles remained silent; his face impassive.

'I'll see myself out.' Beatrice left the room, resisting the urge to move at a hurried pace.

Chapter 58

Tuesday 17th July

It had been exactly two weeks since Beatrice had first spoken to Astra. A lot had happened since then. Her disinclination to return to yoga hadn't changed, but she'd reluctantly decided it was her best opportunity to speak to her. She arrived early and was able to catch the other woman before the class started.

'We need to talk,' said Beatrice.

'We've talked enough. There's nothing I can say.'

'I was hoping we could help each other.'

'What?'

Beatrice lowered her voice as another woman entered the changing room. 'Jackson asked me to help you.'

'Jackson?' Astra looked up at Beatrice.

'You must realise Malone is after another woman. You need a way out.'

'How do you know?'

'Jackson.'

'You've seen him?'

'Yes, but Malone can't know.'

Astra nodded. She opened the door to the women's changing room by a small amount, and peered out. 'My driver's outside, he's got his back to us. If we're quick we can get across to the stairs. There's a café up there.'

They darted across the vestibule and out of sight of the entrance. The café was almost empty and they chose a table in the corner to take their drinks to.

'I know the situation I'm in,' said Astra. 'But I can't see a way out. I tried to leave, but I was found out.'

'Bugsy by any chance?'

Astra nodded. 'What did Jackson say?'

'That you knew things about Malone which could get him into trouble. And Malone's interested in another woman.' Beatrice was reluctant to scare Astra, but she had no choice. 'He's not going to let you leave. Jackson thinks he'll get rid of you. Permanently.'

Astra's eyes widened. 'Why?'

'It's safer for him.'

'I've kept out of his business. I never asked questions.'

'But you've seen things. You know the people he's associated with, the places he goes. If you were questioned by someone who knew what they were doing, you'd be able to reveal a lot about what he gets up to.'

'And he wouldn't want that.' Her shoulders slumped.

'No. But we do.' Beatrice placed the card Hugh had given her onto the table. She pushed it towards Astra.

'What's this?'

'A way out. If you want it.'

'I don't understand.'

'Malone belongs in prison. The person who gave me this number wants to put him there. With your help. If you agree to talk, answer all their questions honestly, they might be able to give you a new identity. At the least, they'll get you away from him.'

'Might?'

'There's no guarantee. I'd be lying to you if I said there was. But any chance is better than no chance, isn't it?'

'What do I do?'

'Ring this number and tell them you'll cooperate. They'll give you instructions. After this, I won't be involved anymore. You have to behave as normal, until they tell you what to do. It's vital. Malone can't get any idea that you're trying to get out, or willing to give information on him.'

'Why are you doing this?'

'Because you don't deserve to be in the situation you're in, and Malone should be punished for what he's done, to you and countless others over the years. He shouldn't be allowed to get away with it.'

'Thank you,' said Astra.

'Can I ask you something?'

'Sure.'

'Why is Jackson so keen on helping you? He could get into deep water with Malone because of it.'

'I guess it's because he likes me. He'd take care of me, after I'd made Victor mad somehow. I never knew what would set him off. I was always walking on eggshells.' She shook her head, as if to banish the memories. 'Once, when I was in a bad way, Jackson took me to a doctor. He even carried me in to the guy's house and stayed with me until we were done. He never said anything, well, he couldn't really, but I think he was a bit sweet on me, you know?'

Beatrice did. She bridled at the power of men like Victor Malone. How many lives had one man damaged, or ended? How could the law of a whole country be so powerless to stop or at least punish him? And if Jackson had cared for Astra, why didn't he do something more than take her to be patched up, after whatever Malone had dished out to her? Beatrice didn't want to imagine what might have happened to Astra during her time with Malone.

'Are you going to call the number?' Beatrice asked.

'I don't have much choice, do I?'

Chapter 59

Wednesday 18th July

Jackson appeared eager to see her. Beatrice sat down opposite him as he leaned forward with interest.

'Well?'

'I've done what I can.'

'Which is?'

'Astra will be considered for witness protection, if she's willing to tell what she knows. Nothing's certain, but I've put her in contact with people who might be able to help. It's up to her what happens next.'

Jackson sat back, satisfied. 'She'll talk. She's no fool. The stuff she's seen these last few years should be enough for good investigators to find what they need. They are good?'

'I don't know them. There's a guy I've been dealing with, he'll do a proper job, and try to protect Astra, but he's not in charge.'

'I'm glad you didn't come in here pretending it was all set up and guaranteed.'

'There was no point. I know you wouldn't have believed me. Besides, I prefer not lying.' Beatrice started to speak but then stopped.

'What?' asked Jackson. 'What do you want to know?'

'Aren't you afraid she'll tell on you? Astra? About all the things you've done for Malone. You could end up doing even more time.'

Jackson shrugged. 'It would only be the truth. I suspect she'll gloss over my part though. She had a soft spot for me.'

'And you for her.'

Jackson stared impassively.

'Don't you regret not doing something for her, finding a way to get her out of there sooner?'

'We'd have both ended up dead. I did what I could, when I could. It didn't amount to much, but Astra knew what the deal was.'

'It's your turn.'

'Uh?' Jackson had become lost in thought.

'Are you going to tell me how Bugsy died?'

'A deal's a deal.'

'So, what did happen?'

'Bugsy found out she was planning to leave. Of course, Malone would have blamed me, if she'd been successful. It was my job to watch out for threats.'

'But you didn't suspect?'

Jackson hesitated. 'I knew something was up. She'd changed her routine: skipped out on a few yoga sessions, but I hadn't told Victor. I should've looked into it. I thought she was trying to find a harmless bit of space for herself: a couple of hours a week when she could feel, I dunno, maybe more normal.

'Anyway, Bugsy found out. She'd tried to be careful, but there was always someone keeping an eye on her. A couple of days before she was going to do it, he cornered her. Said he knew about her plans and was going to go to Malone. Unless she had sex with him.' Jackson ran his fingers through his hair. 'Stupid really, to believe him. He was always going to tell on her, but he wanted to use her first.'

'She agreed?'

Jackson nodded. 'She arranged with him that he'd come to her bedroom the next day. Malone was due to be out overnight in London. He went to her, as planned. When it came to it, she couldn't do it. There was a struggle. He wasn't a large man and she fought him off.'

'What happened?'

'She pushed him, he tripped and fell. Hit his head on the hearth. A single blow which killed him outright. That's when she called me, knowing I'd help. I got rid of the body. I stored it in a freezer for a couple of days, then dumped it in the pub before Burgess set the fire.'

'And you're prepared to spend the next, goodness knows how many years, in prison for murder?'

Jackson shrugged. 'Better than her going to prison. There's no witnesses, the police would do her for murder. Besides, I've done plenty of things I shouldn't have. It all balances out in the end.'

'Very philosophical.'

'What are you going to do, now I've told you?'

'What can I do? Like you said, there's no evidence.'

'And I know you don't think Astra should be in jail any more than I do.'

'No. I don't. She's suffered enough. It doesn't seem right though. You being put away for something you didn't do, whilst you've got away with other stuff. It's not how it's supposed to be.'

'Lots of things aren't how they're supposed to be. You make the best of it and learn to live with it.'

Beatrice walked home thinking about her conversation with Jackson. She believed he was telling her what he thought was the truth. But, hadn't the forensics said the blow was at the front of his head? If Bugsy and Astra had been struggling, and she'd pushed him away, wouldn't he have fallen backwards? Surely the back of his head would have hit the hearth first? Was it possible he'd turned as he fell, explaining the blow to the front? Would he have had time? Would the police have charged Astra with murder, if they knew what had happened? Even manslaughter carried a sentence of years. It would be hard to prove self-defence.

She recalled the time she'd been searching for a missing teenager. She'd been found safe and well, albeit pregnant, but her boyfriend had come looking for a fight with Beatrice. She'd pushed him and he'd hit his head on the wall and fallen unconscious. What if he'd died? Would she be facing a murder or manslaughter charge? How could she have proved she'd been defending herself? It was frightening to think how easily it could have all been different.

Thoughts about how Bugsy's death had actually happened wouldn't go away, and she resolved to check the papers Michael had given her, when she got home. Perhaps there was something in them which would set her mind to rest.

The file Beatrice had in her office hadn't eased her concerns about Bugsy's death, so she arranged to meet with Susan, at the garden centre café in Scothern.

'I need to ask you something.'

Susan paused in the act of lifting cake to her mouth. 'Is this going to get me into trouble again?'

Beatrice shrugged.

'Thanks for nothing. Go on, what do you want to know?'

'The forensics report on the dead man. I spoke to Michael's solicitor about it. She said, apart from the injuries to the legs, which were post-mortem, there was a head wound. Believed to be the cause of death.'

'That's right. There were two wounds on the head. One was almost certainly post-mortem though. Quite a while after death, maybe a few days.'

'Where were they exactly?'

'The post-mortem one was on the back of the head. It fits with Jackson's confession. He said he heard it crack when he dumped the body in the cellar.'

'The other was the one which killed Bugsy?'

'Yes.'

'Was it at the front of the head?'

Susan closed her eyes, thinking. Then she raised her arm to point to where the wound had been found. The cake bounced on her head and crumbs fell onto the table. 'Bugger'.

Beatrice chuckled.

Susan put the cake down and wiped the crumbs from her hands and hair. 'It was about here.' Using her finger this time, she indicated a point in the hairline, above her left eye. 'It was a clean blow. Easy for someone like Jackson. He's much taller and powerfully built.'

'That's where I thought it was.'

'Why didn't you ask your new solicitor friend?'

'Jealous?'

'As long as you're not buying her cake, I'm not.' Susan grinned.

'I'm not popular with her at the moment. I think she was hoping I'd find a way to get Michael off the arson charges.'

'She should be happy. You prevented him being done for murder.' Susan frowned. 'Hang on, why are you asking about the head wound? We've got a full confession. It all fits with the evidence. I don't like it when you start asking questions.'

Beatrice couldn't tell Susan what she'd learnt from Jackson. It would potentially get him out of jail and Astra into a whole load of trouble. 'Do you think he could have fallen? Or maybe was pushed? Could it be how he died?'

'I don't know.'

'But you know the right people to ask, though. Don't you?'

'If this comes back on me, you and I are going to fall out.'

'Like you say, you've got a confession. It's just for my piece of mind.'

Susan sighed. 'Fine. I'll call you.'

Chapter 60

Thursday 19th July

Beatrice picked up the phone. It was the call she'd been waiting for. Since Susan had agreed to find out about the lethal blow to the head, possible scenarios had kept going through her mind. 'Hello.'

'Beatrice? It's me, Susan.'

'I know.'

'Right. I talked to the forensics guys. They reckon the head wound couldn't have been caused by a fall or push. The way his head would have landed wouldn't have caused a wound so high, almost on the top. The fracture fits with him being hit from above, by a much taller, stronger man for example.'

'Thanks, Susan. That's really useful.'

'Puts your theory about Jackson killing him by accident to bed, doesn't it?'

'I guess so.' Beatrice resisted the urge to correct her.

'We're sure it was deliberate, Beatrice. Not an accident, so stop worrying about it. Thanks to you, another pair of criminals are going to go to prison. It's a good day's work.'

'More than a day.'

'You know what I mean. Stop being pedantic.'

'You want to get together for a meal next week?'

'I'd love to, but I've got a training course. I'm away Monday to Friday. How about the week after?'

'I'll give you a call next weekend.'

'Great.'

As she'd suspected, Jackson believed what Astra had told

him, but it couldn't be true. Something else had happened. He'd confessed to murder, so he and his lawyer probably hadn't gone through the forensics in detail, and he'd no reason to question Astra's story. Would he even want to know? She did. And she knew who to ask about it.

The phone was answered on the second ring.

'Hang on,' said Hugh.

Beatrice paced in her office as she waited.

'Sorry, I was in a meeting.' Hugh sounded a little breathless. 'I'm outside now, so we can talk.'

'I'm sorry I've disturbed you.'

'No problem. How are you?'

Beatrice was surprised by the question, and the impulse to tell him about her break up with James. 'Oh. Er. OK, I guess.'

'Anything I can do to help?'

'It's about the man Jackson has confessed to killing.'

'I meant with whatever is upsetting you, but we can talk about the murder instead.'

There was a short silence, and Beatrice heard him sigh. Had something in her tone of voice given away her emotions?

'Go on then: Jackson. What about him?' asked Hugh.

'Can this stay between us for now? I don't know what to do, and I thought you'd be the best person to talk to about it.'

'I'm flattered. Yes, we can keep it between us, for now.'

'Thanks.' Beatrice smiled to herself, there was a quality to his voice she enjoyed listening to. A kind of gentleness. 'Jackson didn't kill Bugsy. Astra did.'

'I was not expecting you to say that,' said Hugh. 'What makes you think so?'

'Because he told me. He's not retracting his confession. He's accepted going to prison for murder, but he agreed if I got help for Astra, he'd tell me the truth. You've given her a possible escape from Malone, so Jackson stuck to our agreement and told me what he knows. Obviously, he'll deny it if anyone challenges him.'

'Why is he so keen for you to do something for her?'

'I think he has feelings for her.'

'OK. I get it. What does he say happened?'

'Bugsy was blackmailing Astra. She'd planned to leave Malone, to escape, but Bugsy found out. I don't know how, but it was his job to watch her and drive her places. Maybe he saw or heard something. She'd stopped going to her regular yoga class for a few weeks, and Jackson suspects she had been using the time to arrange her escape. Perhaps it's that what made Bugsy suspicious.'

'I suppose he threatened to tell Malone?'

'Unless she had sex with him.'

'Bastard.'

Beatrice nodded in agreement. 'I can't say I'm sorry he's dead.'

'But?'

'The truth matters. To me.'

'To me, too.' Hugh's sad response was spoken quietly. He coughed to clear his throat. 'So, how did he die?'

'Jackson says Astra changed her mind, at the last minute. Couldn't bring herself to have sex with him. There was a struggle, Astra pushed him away, he fell and hit his head.'

'It's possible, I suppose.'

'Maybe not.'

'Go on.'

'According to forensics, it couldn't have happened that way. The impact on the head is in the wrong place.'

'Jackson lied to you?'

'No. I'm confident he really believes that's what happened. It must be what Astra told him.' There was a pause in the conversation. 'What do you think I should do?'

'Well, as far as we currently know, there were only two people in the room when Bugsy died. Astra is the only one left. We, or rather, I, could ask her.'

'She's not likely to tell the truth though, is she. Not if it wasn't an accident.'

'You suspect she planned it?'

'Yes. She possibly lured him to her bedroom, claiming she was going to cooperate, and planned all along to kill him. But…'

'Go on.'

'The thing is he was threatening her. Malone would have killed her, if he'd known she was trying to leave. What choice did she have? I can't help wondering what I'd have done, if it were me.'

'None of us knows what we're really capable of, until we're tested. There's no point torturing yourself.'

'I guess.'

There was a moment of silence.

'I can't tell you anything at the moment,' said Hugh. 'But there may be circumstances under which Astra would be willing to talk. Can you leave it with me?'

'You will let me know what happens, won't you? You won't go off doing your secretive act?'

'I will tell you whatever I can.'

'Hardly reassuring.'

'It's the best I can do, right now.'

Chapter 61

Monday 23rd July

The text message, from a blocked number, had arrived two days ago. *Regent's Park. 11.00 a.m. Mon 23rd H*. Beatrice hadn't hesitated and bought a train ticket straightaway. She spent the intervening time trying to pretend she wasn't thinking of seeing Hugh again.

Feeling like a secret agent on a clandestine meet, Beatrice spent the time waiting for Hugh thinking about him and why he'd sent the message. Did he have news on Astra? If he'd spoken to her about the killing of Bugsy, he could easily have told her over the phone.

She recalled his smiling face, the way his hazel eyes crinkled at the corners, and in her mind, she couldn't help but compare him to James. They were two very different men. Yes, James was physically attractive, in a more obvious way, but what was it about him she liked? He was good company, easy to be with, but what did she really know about him? She was still sad about their break up, but she was already a lot better.

'Sorry, am I late?' Hugh grinned, as he sat beside her, resting his arm along the back of the bench in order to look directly at her.

'I was early.' Beatrice smiled back. She found his happiness contagious. 'So, another park?'

'What can I say. I like parks.' His laugh was warm and relaxed. 'It's good to see you again.'

'You too.' Beatrice turned away first. 'You have something to tell me?'

'Yes. Astra. She's confessed to killing Bugsy.'

Beatrice nodded in satisfaction.

'You were right. She felt cornered, with no way out. She persuaded him to sit on a stool, by the fireplace in the bedroom, and close his eyes. Let's not go into the sordid details of how. She bashed him on the head with a heavy ornament she had ready, nearby. Standing over him meant she could put a lot of force into it. Killed him with one blow. She counted on Jackson helping out afterwards and had her story prepared. It was easy for her to rearrange things to make it look like an accident, then she ripped her own blouse open and screamed. Jackson came running and saw what she wanted him to see. You know the rest.'

'How did you persuade her to tell you?'

'Part of our agreement gives her immunity for any crime committed whilst in Malone's orbit. We weren't expecting murder to be one of them, but it's watertight, and my boss doesn't want to jeopardise the chance of getting Malone.'

'It was premeditated murder then?'

'Yes. Like you said before. What would any of us have done in the same circumstances? I'm inclined to not think too harshly of her.'

'Me too,' said Beatrice. 'What happens to Jackson now?'

'He's an accessory after the fact, even if he didn't kill Bugsy. It's not likely it'll be worth taking to court, though I expect the CPS will broker an agreement. He'll be released, eventually, but not any time soon. He'll have to wait it out.'

'Has he been told?'

'No. We thought about getting a message to him, through his lawyer, but suspect it will get straight back to Malone, and we can't do anything to alert Malone to Astra helping us. He's going to be wondering where she's got to, of course, but we've left a trail, making it look like she went under her own steam. We're hoping its good enough to buy us time.'

'I guess that's that then. What a mess.'

'I'm afraid so. You've had a lovely day out in the park,

though.' Hugh's face crinkled with amusement.

They sat for a while in companionable silence, watching the birds and people enjoying the sunny day, until Hugh's watch buzzed. He glanced at it, then turned to Beatrice. 'I've got to go, but will you do me a favour?'

'What?'

'Once I've gone, wait here for another twenty minutes.'

'Is this a secret spy thing?' Beatrice laughed.

'No. I'm not a spy.'

'What are you then?'

'Just a policeman.'

'Not an ordinary one, though.'

'Will you do it, please?' He spoke earnestly, the expression on his face serious.

She couldn't understand the unspoken message, but it was important to him. 'I'll wait. Since it's you asking.'

His face lit up with a smile and his eyes crinkled at the corners in a cute way. Cute? Where had that come from?

'Thank you.' Hugh placed his hand on Beatrice's shoulder and squeezed gently. Then he stood. 'I'll be seeing you.'

Beatrice watched him retreat until he was completely out of sight. Then she closed her eyes, trying to make sense of her feelings about James, Rosie, the cat and yes, she admitted to herself, about Hugh.

She didn't know how long she'd sat there, eyes still closed, before the bench shifted under the weight of someone sitting next to her. She opened her eyes and turned to look. She froze and her heart began to race. The small woman was wrapped up inappropriately for the weather, in an oversized coat, sunglasses and a baseball hat. Despite the attempt to hide, everything about her was well-known to Beatrice.

It came to her suddenly. Why Hugh had followed her into the café that day. The day she went to London to confront Atkinson about her mother's money. Because of the solicitor, he'd know exactly where she'd be, and when. Was it why Atkinson had wanted her in London? So Hugh could follow her? What was Hugh's connection with her mother? There must be one: after all he'd urged her to remain on the bench. Beatrice was aware she'd been staring at her mum. All the imagined conversations she'd had with her since her disappearance, and now she was here no words would come at all.

'Hello Beatrice.' Helena Styles smiled at her daughter, tears in her eyes. 'I should have known you'd never let me go.'

About The Author

Denise Smith, a prolific reader and lover of books, lived in Lincolnshire for thirteen years, which is where the idea for this story was developed. Now living in Devon, she is still a frequent visitor to Lincolnshire, allowing her to keep her old home fresh in her mind as she writes the next book in the series.

For more information about Denise or her latest books go to:

www.foursirenspress.co.uk/authors/denise-smith

Acknowledgements

There have been a number of people who have been supportive in the writing of this book. There are too many to mention them all individually, but thank you all everyone who has ever been kind enough to take an interest in my writing.

Particular thanks are due to my fellow Four Sirens writers, Beverley Carter, Sharon Francis and Susan Hughes, who have given me a great deal of helpful critique and advice. Special thanks are due to my good friend Marie Lott, a fellow writer who has generously read and reread parts of this novel, providing help, advice and general motivation.

I would also like to thank my husband, Jim, who has given me the time and space to pursue my writing, even though it hasn't made us rich yet!

Printed in Great Britain
by Amazon